-Worlds Apart-
Resignation

Amanda Thome

Athena
Alley
Press

Athena Alley Press Book

Copyright ©2015 by Amanda Thome

All Rights Reserved

Cover design by Clarissa Yeo

Edited by Elaine Olson

First Edition: March 2015

ISBN: 978-0-9960608-4-4

Dedication

This book is dedicated to the two women who have taught me that
with hard work and determination you can achieve your dreams.
Thank you, Nan and Mom. I dream to follow by your examples.

Chapter 1: Nessa

"Nessa, Nessa!" Emma's voice starts softly, escalating with each call. Her words fill with a fierce urgency begging me to focus but I can't.

All I see is Garrett's face with his broken body slumped in the chair, the bag lifting to reveal his acorn-brown eyes. I take myself back to that moment. The hair on the back of my neck pricks to attention as my gut twists and spins. Just before I saw his eyes I intuitively knew something terrible was happening and my heart felt like it imploded, the same way buildings crumble and cascade inward when they are destroyed. That's exactly what I feel like, like I've imploded.

"Nessa." Papa says laying his hand on my shoulder.

I stay rooted with my knees pressing to the floor as my head spins. Garrett's eyes looked straight at me, he wasn't looking at the camera, he was looking at me. The desperation and pain was for me to see. He wasn't responsible for this, he was trying to find me. All this time he wasn't in Central, he was in the wilds searching for me.

My hands clench and my nails dig into my palms so deeply there is a steady trickle of blood falling to the floor, like the blood that dripped from Garrett's swollen face.

"Nessa stop!" Emma shouts grabbing my hands.

I look down, blood drops steadily to the floor. I hadn't realized I was squeezing my hands so hard. I turn to Emma, her face twists the way it does when she's scared. I don't like her being scared or the reason she feels that way. I've got her, papa and Ty now, I need to protect them and keep them safe.

"Jake, Kara." My voice cracks momentarily as I try swallowing through my dried throat.

The hospital speaker jolts me, cutting me off. "Doctor to room 403, doctor to room 403 stat."

Escaping inside my head I see myself hovering outside room 403 just before Kara pushed the door open. It's Ty's room, the one with the machines that are keeping him alive. I'm processing things entirely too slowly but finally it clicks that Ty is in trouble.

I push to my feet running toward his room. I watch the doctor ahead of me as he turns into Ty's room, a nurse following just behind with her ponytail bobbing as she runs.

Kara's behind me, I hear her steps and shouts but I ignore them. Maybe the doctor was wrong and Ty won't make it, or worse, maybe Ty is already gone. The hospital lights are bright and almost blinding making my eyes skip and blur.

Ty is what I need to focus on but in a dark part of my brain Garrett's swollen eyes are still staring at me. They will be there, begging me to save him until the day I do.

My legs stretch as I close in on Ty's room. I fly by 400 feeling my chest heave, then 401 as I squint nearly blinded by the overhead lights. 402, I'm almost there. I slide to a stop at 403 just as the nurse closes the door.

"Where is she? Let me go!" Ty yells.

He thrashes in bed, shaking as he tries escaping. The bed screeches and grinds across the polished floors.

"Let me talk to Nessa! What the frig is that? Wait you…" The screaming stops leaving an abrupt silence.

Kara grabs my arm, turning me to face her. I bury my head against her spiraling curls and inhale the strawberry smell of her shampoo.

"I thought maybe he was dying or dead," I say automatically.

"He's alive Nessa, it's okay." Kara says as she strokes my back.

I can't bring myself to wipe my tears away. Pulling myself together I see papa and Emma standing at the end of the long hall. Jake towers behind them like a blonde shadow. Papa is holding Emma, his green shirt is torn at the sleeve and suddenly I wonder if there was a struggle to get them to the hovercraft.

Emma stares down the hall with her gold and green eyes fixed on me.

The door opens behind me as the doctor steps out with his tablet in hand. He furiously enters whatever it is doctors enter into those things.

He looks up to Kara and me, "We had to give him a strong sedative. He was agitated."

"What upset him?" I ask, my throat nearly sticks to itself as I try forcing the words out.

"He was asking for you. Just before he became agitated he told the nurse something was wrong and that he could feel it." My face draws together, pinching at the corners as I let the pain wash over me. "Don't worry, he has been through a lot, it's expected that he will be delusional at first."

"Yes, thanks doctor." Kara says pulling me from the door.

Kara looks at me, her eyes wide. I watch her mouth part as she prepares to speak.

I cut her off, "I know Kara. I know Ty can feel what I feel. I know that is what happened."

Her shoulders relax, I suppose she's been carrying that secret with her since Ty came to her months ago. Ty should have let her know that he had told me. I'm sure she has felt awkward around me since.

"You have to control your emotions the best you can," she says. I shoot her an impatient look. "It's going to be very hard, I understand, but you need to try."

"Do you? Do you understand what it's like to almost die? To almost lose the person you love and to kill someone to save them? Now Central's got Garrett and they will kill him if they don't get me first."

I fall against the yellow wall with the handrail jabbing into my back, I push against it, using it to brace myself.

"You can't understand what I have been through and neither of us can know what I'm about to endure."

"You can't go." She says matter-of-factly, immediately annoying me.

It's like I'm a kid being punished for some silly thing, like putting papa's green socks on instead of my grey ones.

I push myself off the wall, "I have to and I *will*."

Kara shifts towards me, almost like she wants to reach out but at the last second changes her mind.

"What about your family and Ty?" She asks stepping out of reach.

"You and Jon will take care of them, you have to. I won't let Garrett die for me and I won't risk Central attacking anyone out here. They want me and I want them. There can only be one winner. I hope it is me."

I fold my arms across my waist. I'm still in my torn clothes from the mission, covered in Ty's blood and now mixed with my own.

Jake's boots land heavy on the floor. His strong body glides smoothly down the hall towards us. He's so calm and collected and I wonder if he's always this way. I suppose if flying the craft through the resistance fighters and bombs didn't shake him then nothing will.

I wish I could keep my composure like Jake does because Kara's right, I need to try controlling my emotions before I hurt Ty. I can't have him feeling what I'm feeling, he has enough to deal with without my baggage.

Jake stops nearly between us. "I'm sorry Nessa, I talked to your father and he told me who that boy was." Jake awkwardly touches my shoulder. Although he tries, he isn't comforting at all.

His hand pulls uncomfortably back and reaches for Kara. He grabs her delicate hand to focus the attention to him. I turn to look into Ty's room.

The small glass window has a crosshatching of lines that I suppose are meant to give the patient some privacy. I press my forehead against the cool glass narrowing my eyes between the black lines. I steady my stare until I see Ty. He's asleep in bed, his hand twitches intermittently as he blinks behind his heavy lids. My bloody hand touches the doorknob. I close my grasp and prepare to open the door as Jake pulls Kara away.

"You know who that was on the broadcast right?" I release the knob. There is an urgency in Jake's voice that compels me to listen.

I turn as Kara's eyes look at the polished cream-speckled floor. "I didn't believe it at first but I know who it is."

"Do you think they've got them still? You think they could be alive?" Jake's deep and commanding voice falters for a moment, lifting as if it's the first time in an eternity he's been allowed to feel any happiness.

Kara pinches her mouth together, pushing it into a tight line. Her head sways side-to-side as her curly hair bounces. Her head lifts and looks heavy as the tears ring around her eyes.

"I've prayed every day that they are alive. Maybe for once my prayers will be answered. At least they have been for Jon."

Jake stares ahead as if he's standing in a dark and empty space thousands of miles away, "I can't believe it was her," he says.

Her? What are they talking about? I step away from the door, away from Ty and toward them.

"Who are you talking about?" I wait, but neither of them say anything. "Who. Are. You. Talking about?" I say it slowly enunciating each word.

Kara and Jake look at each other, apparently deciding who will be the brave one that tells me.

"Kara, Jake!" Jon shouts from the corridor.

He flies past Emma and papa, nearly tripping over Emma as he runs. This isn't the Jon I'm used to seeing. He looks disheveled, not neat and orderly like he usually does. His suit is half-on, or half-off depending on your point of view. His hair points to the sides like he has yet to find a comb and push it through his black locks. Kara and Jake turn, their smiles growing the closer Jon gets.

What are they so happy about? Ty is nearly dead, Central is out to kill me or Garrett, actually probably both of us, *and* they've threatened biological weapons against everyone out here. It seems unlikely that my mind will ever wrap around what could be so good about this whole situation.

"Can you believe it? Did you see her?" Jon runs his hand through his messy hair.

Jake wraps Jon in a giant hug that takes us both by surprise. "We saw. I can't believe they've got her."

"Who's got who? What's going on here?" I drag out the last word as my throat clenches, protesting speech. My chest beats furiously.

Jon shakes his head once, his dark features hover in front of me before he speaks. "The woman from the broadcast…"

I cut him off, "Natalie?"

"Yes, Natalie. I've been looking for her for a long time. A very long time."

His dark eyes push past me like they are dancing somewhere in the distance, living in a memory that is buried away.

"Why do you care about her? She's the reason I'm here and Ty's in there." I jerk my hand toward his bed. "She's the reason I'm about to go to Central to rescue Garrett."

I shake my head as my mouth draws into a snarl, she's the name that's been on my lips for over a year now. The name that is the root of my revenge.

"She's my wife" Jon says pulling his eyes back to the present.

I'm not exactly sure what I'm feeling. Shock, disgust, anger and other things too, confusing things that I can't quite put my finger on.

"What? How's that possible?" I ask.

My head feels like it's banging around, like my brain is beating inside my skull. Flashes of Natalie pummel around. I see her at the gates greeting me for the leap, I see her in my home with her hands fisted on my table as she threatened Emma, and I see her wicked face stare at me as she holds Garrett's chin.

Jon grabs my shoulder and I instinctively jerk away. I feel betrayed, like he's a traitor or one of the bad guys.

"Nessa if you knew Nat like I do"

I shoot him a sickening glare. "Nat? Nice Jon. I like to think of her as the woman that destroyed my life."

"Natalie, Nat, whatever you want to call her. If you knew her like I know her, if you knew who she used to be then you'd understand." His pointed chin drops to his chest. "I can't imagine the things they've done to make her do those things. That wasn't like Nat," I stare at him, "wasn't like Natalie" he says. "This is the shell of my wife, her soul is elsewhere. I don't believe she's lost for good."

"Is that why you wanted to help my people? So you could get your twisted, sick, precious wife back? What a waste of life and resources. She isn't worth it."

I turn my back to Jon and stare at the zigzagging black lines on Ty's window.

"She is my wife, I'll remind you of that Nessa." He says sternly, almost warningly.

I spin back towards him making sure to lift my chin high, showing him I can't be pushed so easily.

"She is the woman that threatened to kill my family, the same woman that threatens to kill Garrett and initiate a war on your people." I pause, "I'll remind *you* of that Jon."

His eyes lock with mine.

"I think maybe we're all under a lot of stress." Kara tries interjecting, artfully placing herself between us. "Let's get Nessa and her family back to the loft."

"I'm not leaving Ty."

"He'll be asleep for a while Nessa. They've given him something strong, I wouldn't expect him up until tomorrow."

My hands trace along the glass window as I imagine introducing papa and Emma to Ty. That's how it was supposed to happen. Garrett wasn't supposed to be captured and I wasn't supposed to be hunted like this. Everything was supposed to be good and right.

I stay staring at Ty. Jon, Kara, and Jake's pounding steps echo down the corridor towards Emma and papa. Emma breaks free and pushes between Jon and Jake as she stretches her legs and runs towards me. I stare blankly ahead even after Emma lands next to me.

"Nessa?" She says taking my hand. She's tall now, her shoulders are just lower than mine.

"Yea little miss?"

Her eyes look through the window at Ty as he sleeps. "Who is he?" she asks.

"That's Ty, we saved each other out there." I stop to reflect before I admit my true feelings. "I love him."

I smile weakly as that dark part of my brain replays Garrett's tortured eyes staring at me. Emma's hand fills mine as she squeezes it.

"I wish I could meet him." She says leaning her head against my shoulder. "What about Garrett?" She asks hesitantly.

My shattered heart clangs inside my chest again. He will always do that to me, I know that.

"I'm going to save him. I don't have a choice."

"But they want you dead, you heard that woman. They are willing to start a war to get you, what do you think they'll do to you once they've got you?" Her head shakes against my shoulder. "I don't think you should go, I've got a bad feeling."

I stare at Ty as his hand jerks. "I can't risk anyone getting hurt or killed because of me. I'm stronger than I look Emma, plus I've got people that will stand behind me."

I wince as I say it, those people just walked down the hall and away from me.

Maybe I should have asked why they wanted to help my people sooner. I should have uncovered their motivation but I'm not sure that matters. I wonder if I still would have detonated the bombs if I knew they were using us to get to Natalie. Chances are I would have done anything to try to free my people.

"We need to leave," I say wrapping my arm around Emma's waist, guiding her down the hall towards papa.

"Are you okay?" papa asks taking me in his arms. "What can I do to help?"

I hesitate accepting my fate, "Watch over Emma while I'm gone."

Chapter 2: Garrett

I don't remember how I got here. My ears ring to the point I want to drive my fingers into them. Something pops and I pull them out to stare stupidly at my hands. My blood covered fingertips shift out of focus. That explains why I can't hear, the explosions ruptured my eardrums.

My eyes cross and uncross as they attempt to focus. I try remembering where I am, but I guess I'll never know out here. The last time I was certain of my whereabouts was by our tree, which was right after I'd seen Nessa's father.

My memory starts coming back as I remember Central with its big buildings and green walkways. They were lined with flowers Nessa would've appreciated. There was my unit in the city, a one room apartment overlooking that hideous fountain.

The water spit from the mouth of a stone fish and trickled down its scaly sides sporadically. The fountain had been a gift from somewhere I'll never see. It would have been a wasted gift if it wasn't for the freezing water that spit from the mouth. Luckily it was cold enough to soak my leg in after the cast was removed.

I'd had lots of time to reflect during those weeks before they cut the casts off. My head decided early on that I needed to get back to Nessa. My life in Central was nothing if I didn't have her. I had more time to think than most citizens, I'd been delayed getting my assignment. They were waiting for my bones to heal before testing me.

Come to think of it my wrist aches now. I twist it side to side as it screams in protest. I hope it's not broken again. I shake my head trying to recover lost time.

My head jumps back to my assignment day, it had rained the night before. I remember because I hated the rain. Ever since the regulators attacked me my bones have ached whenever it rains. It was either my aching body or my anxiety that woke me hours before my alarm went off that morning.

I laid in bed worrying about Nessa and my assignment test. Once I realized I wouldn't be able to fall back asleep I forced myself to get up.

My alarm went off as I stepped out of my unit. My white uniform was buttoned tight to my chest, they'd given me a smaller size than the time before.

I'd done everything I was supposed to do that morning. I combed my hair, pressed my clothes and stood up straight. The entire time I felt phony, I knew Central's way of life didn't fit me.

If I was honest with myself I'd admit that I prefer casual. I like the idea of loose fitted blues or greens and a tree by the river, not a pressed white uniform and an apartment by a fountain.

I was halfway to the testing center when the rain switched to mist. I never liked walking in the rain but the mist seemed different. The wetness collected slower, fooling my body.

Once I stepped out of the mist I realized how awful it was. It was still a heavy wet feeling that reminded me of how I'd felt since they took me from Nessa.

That morning I walked toward the testing center with the wet on my uniform. I thought about how clueless I was. It was how I'd felt the day of my leap test months before. I could've asked another Central citizen what to expect at the assignment and they would've told me. They don't enforce the rules like they did in the Inner. Here there is no curfew or secrets about the leap.

I passed under the cream tunnel that vibrated as the crafts flew through it. My mind was stuck on the assignment as I crossed into the park with its wooden benches. I'd seen couples sit on them before. It was like a knife twisting each time I'd see them, I knew I'd never find another girl to sit with like that.

I made it to the center with time to spare. My eyes spanned up and down the building and the two towering trees it sat between. The walls created a waterfall effect, I could have stared longer if I'd let myself.

The water came from the top straight down the marble walls. Central citizens were used to stuff like that, architecture and things that don't exist in the Inner. I wanted to touch them to see if the water felt cool but I stopped myself. I was pretty sure the citizens looked at me differently as it was. They saw me as a transfer, not a *real* citizen. I wasn't about to give them any excuses to confirm their beliefs.

In my head I knew I was smarter than the majority of them. I was definitely more capable of surviving in the wild, but that held no worth here. Wild wasn't something desirable, especially since they didn't value time outside their city. I guess there wasn't any need, anything they imagined was given to them at the Retreat.

By the time my assignment test came around I'd already figured most of the citizens out. I'd gotten good at guessing what assignments people had. Central had the self-absorbed citizens totally wrapped in their work to the point that they hardly noticed each other. Those were usually the ones that worked in the capital. They carried briefcases with documents for the government to oversee, walked around with straight backs and tight faces.

Then there were the serious ones that actively tried to be interested in someone's story even though it clearly pained them, but at least they tried.

The last group I had nailed down were the overly friendly ones. They talked to anyone about anything. Most of the time they were in charge of directing the banquets or organizing the events Central seemed obsessed in hosting. I'd heard Aria got assigned to that sort of a position. After we got here I did my best to avoid her. She reminded me of home which in turn reminded me of Nessa. I didn't need any more reminders than the ones I already suffered through.

I always knew Aria had a thing for me when we were in the Inner. Aria wasn't on my radar at all. I think Nessa was a bit jealous of her, I imagine her blood would boil thinking about us in Central together.

Aria seemed like she belonged in Central, I didn't. I blended in the best I could, staying silent when I needed to or talking when the occasion called for it. I didn't have many people to talk to in the beginning. I didn't have many people near the end either. The only friend I made in Central was Oliver.

The days I didn't hang with Oliver I'd pretend I was in the arctic water by our river. Nessa would be somewhere nearby teasing me, quizzing me, or doing any of a million things that I pictured.

I didn't want to escape in just one fantasy, I made it different every day. No matter what, Nessa consumed me. My imaginary moments reminded me of the relief the Retreat promised to the citizens of Central.

Weeks before my casts came off I'd watched hordes of citizens go in and out of the Retreat like it was a revolving door. They would walk in as a hollow body and come out a new and revived person.

I never went to the Retreat, the idea freaked me out. I'd heard two girls talking about it one day as they waited for their craft. They were the planner type citizens, the loud mouthed ones that talked too high and too fast. The first had spiked blonde hair streaked with black chunks. She was thin, too thin if you ask me. The redheaded one had soft curves and a pinched mouth that made her look serious.

The stuff they were talking about was unreal. They talked about jumping off a gorge and flying with suits that had wings. They rambled on about the smells, the wind and all the sensations like it had really happened to them.

The one turned to me, including me in the conversation like that kind of citizen always does. They were shocked when I said I'd never been to the Retreat. They couldn't wait to tell me about it even though I didn't care to hear.

"You lay in this chair and choose either a pre-programmed retreat or an open-world one."

"I do the pre-programed ones." The blonde interjected, "Why mess with perfection I say."

"Personally I like the open-world ones, gets my creative juices flowing," the redhead said with her hair lifting as a gust of wind passed. "You pick whichever you like, I suggest a pre-programmed one your first few times, just until you've mastered it." Her green eyes stared off. "Once you pick your program they inject you and off you go on your adventure!" She clapped her hands jumping me.

"Can you believe it? Anything you want is brought to you." The blonde leaned against the wall behind us, "Once I spent a whole day on a beach. Have you ever heard of one?"

She didn't give me time to say yes. If she would have I could've told her the second-hand stories Nessa had told me.

Margaret used to tell Emma and Nessa about her life in the Outer. Nessa loved Margaret and her stories. Sometimes I'd catch Nessa closing her eyes as she'd hold that sea shell to her ear.

"The water never ended." The girl continued with her story, "White rolling caps arched and crashed into blue. The water rolled up towards the sand then pulled away. Never ending white caps and rolling water. I can still smell the beach if I want to. The sounds of the ocean were amazing too. It was a steady whooshing that lulled everything around it. I left the Retreat and could feel sand and sun on me for days."

The redhead cut in, "Back before I did the open-world retreats I tried one called windsurfing. It was awesome. I was in the ocean with the beach barely in sight, the winds were crazy and I was standing on a board, teetering at first. My hands held a bar attached to a bright beautiful sail and I twisted and pushed and pulled with the wind and flew through the air and water."

She skimmed her hand in all directions like she was tracking her route.

"It was remarkable. You don't have to know what you're doing, the program adjusts for that. It tells your body what to do. Anything you want and the Retreat will make it happen."

"Anything?" I asked.

"Anything," the redhead answered nudging me. I'd seen that look before, she liked me. I bet she wouldn't have thought so highly of me if I left the apartment like I wanted to, with my hair a mess instead of combed and pushed back from my face. She didn't know me, she didn't interest me either. The only thing that interested me was hundreds of miles away on the other side of the wall.

Their craft stopped at the platform and they walked off giggling as they stepped on board. I kept walking, more like limping really. I was thinking about windsurfing or flying and how strange it was that those were the things they wanted to do.

Maybe I was the strange one since I knew I'd opt for an open-world retreat to escape back to the Inner. To the one place I'd always wanted to get away from.

But what use would that have been? It wasn't reality and when they brought me back from my Retreat I wouldn't be leaving the center smiling, I'd leave worse off than before. It would have been a tease, a taste of the life I could have had if it wasn't for Tyler.

That was the day the seed of escaping Central was planted. In the back of my mind I knew I had to escape for real, not just in some stupid simulator retreat like the rest of the citizens here did.

I was thinking of my escape the day of my assignment. I was hoping more than anything that I'd get something that would take me away from Central. Maybe a position as an educator or a regulator. That way I could spend my days in the Inner. With any luck I'd see Nessa again.

Eventually I walked past the watery walls into the testing center. I scanned my forearm and was taken into the back by one of those research type citizens, the ones that talk to you but it's obviously an inconvenience to them.

He strapped me to a chair and for a second I got nervous. He grabbed an oversized needle tapping it twice before sinking it into my arm. At first I thought I'd gone into the Retreat center like the girls had described weeks before.

I was falling into darkness but soon enough I knew it wasn't a Retreat. It wasn't a fun fall like the girls had described with their wing suits on. This was a frightening fall. My arms and legs flailed and kicked as I dropped.

I fell farther and farther into the darkness until suddenly glass shattered around me, little daggers dropped from the sky. I tucked my head covering my neck and face the best I could. There were thousands of little needles poking my body. I opened my eyes and the falling stopped. I was suspended midair, floating free. It was pitch black all around. I put my hand to my face and I couldn't see my own fingers.

All at once six beams of light blasted, six tunnels with glowing lights of different colors appeared at each end. I was in the center floating and spinning.

I heard Nessa call from the blue tunnel behind me "Garrett, it's not so bad, come try it."

I spun around and saw her standing in the blue light staring at me.

"Come this way Garrett, we've got lots we need to do." She smiled and I started pulling myself towards her. She stayed standing there in front of me, waving me to her.

I heard her voice echo from behind me. I spun and she was in a different tunnel, this time a hazy green light glowed behind her.

"Garrett help, we're not going to make it. We need to find a cure, they can't save us without it," she gasped. I pushed my way towards her.

"Garrett come this way, we've got too much to do. Seriously, stop fooling around." I turned and Nessa was standing in the blue light again.

"Garrett help me," Nessa said from the green light. "Help me…Come with me…Save me…Please…" I spun around and around from one Nessa to the other.

"Garrett!" Nessa's scream was blood curdling, shaking me to the core. I turned seeing her framed in a red light, bent over with blood spilling from her stomach.

"No, stop!" she screamed with her hand raised in defense.

I pulled my arms towards the red tunnel. The farther I went the louder the other tunnels got, each Nessa begging me to go with her, each of them sounding more desperate the farther I went. Those tunnels didn't matter to me, what mattered was protecting the Nessa that was hurt and suffering.

I got closer and closer, "Nessa!" I screamed.

She scrambled towards me trying to get out of the red light but she was jerked back like she'd hit an invisible wall. I got closer until I could see her face, her blue eyes were wet from crying. I kept pulling and kicking my legs to get to her. At last I made it and I saw the knife buried in her stomach.

"Nessa what happened?"

"Garrett watch out!"

I turned as the foreigner came at her. I put myself between them, protecting Nessa the best I could. He swung to strike but I dodged him. He had a gun, I saw it on his belt. I did what I had to do, I lunged for the weapon and pulled it free. My fingers knew what to do as Nessa laid behind me struggling to breathe.

I pulled the gun and aimed it at the foreigner. I shot him square in the chest. I didn't even bother to watch him fall, I knew I'd killed him. I turned to face Nessa but she was gone.

The red lights gleamed as the green and blue tunnels closed in. All of a sudden there was an explosion of light and the next thing I knew I was awake. The assignment test was over.

"I think it's obvious what your assignment will be," the man said. His brown hair was longer than most Central citizens, it fell past the top of his ears. "You will be a regulator" he said as he drove a metal gun to my forearm.

My arm stung and burned, "What was that for?" I asked rubbing the wound.

"Credentials, all regulators carry them implanted in their forearm. We can't risk you losing your access or having it stolen."

"What makes you so sure I'm supposed to be a regulator?" I asked still confused and shaken from my test.

"The test is a hybrid, part pre-programmed part open-world. You fill our world with what your heart most desires, the test just puts variations on that thing. Everyone chooses their own path and that path tells us what you'll do. You chose to run towards something most people would be scared of. You protected and killed for it which is why you are a regulator."

Chapter 3: Garrett

My assignment day was a long time ago. I've been out of Central for months now. I cough as another explosion detonates. This bomb was farther down the wall. Who the heck is attacking? I stumble my way towards the explosions. Crafts fly by dropping bombs from their base, targeting the Inner's walls. They aren't Central crafts, I would know.

The part of me that went through regulator training feels like I should put a stop to this but I was never really one of them. I never turned myself over to being a regulator completely. I used my assignment as a way to get myself back to Nessa, it wasn't anything more than that to me.

Even during this barrage of bombs I appreciate how lucky I was to get assigned as a regulator. Without that assignment I wouldn't have any chance of seeing Nessa again.

It seemed like everything we did in Central was appointed based on a test. Within regulator training I'd taken another test where it was a unanimous decision that I was meant to be a pilot patroller.

Every day for two months they stuck me in pods. That's what I called them. They were simulators that taught me how to fly. Arms training in the morning pods, flight training in the afternoon pods. My entire training was done inside reality simulating pods.

I surprised myself when I graduated top in my class of fifteen pilot patrollers. It was seven months of pretending to be like them before I got my chance to escape. Seven months of sim flights before my first real solo flight.

The morning of my first flight I slid my knife along the side of my black boots before leaving my apartment. I stared at my forearm guessing where my implants were. I knew I'd have to cut them out.

It was supposed to be a regular day on the job so I acted that way. I couldn't very well run around telling the world that I planned to escape into the Inner. It was hard acting like nothing out of the ordinary was going on but I managed. I checked into CC, loaded into my craft and relayed my mission before I was cleared for lift off.

I radioed to CC at my first check point. The sun was bright that day and shone through my visor. It blinded me so I veered the craft on an alternative route. I liked being a pilot, and for a second I even considered postponing my escape. There was something addicting about having the freedom and power that came with controlling an entire hovercraft. I knew that I'd never have that power again once I made my escape.

I circled around the wall and appreciated that everything was exactly how it looked in my sim training. Every rock, tree and staircase was right where the simulator had shown them to be. The longer I waited to make my break the harder it would be to let go of my power. I knew I had to do it that day.

I pulled the craft up and away from the city. I stuck it in auto-pilot and yanked out my knife. The blade was sharp and shone against my tanned skin. If there was another way I'd have taken it but this was the best plan I'd come up with.

The tip of my blade rested across my skin for a full minute before I dug it in. My arm bled bright as the knife twisted deep into my forearm. Left and right I spun it, with each turn my stomach knotted and my heart thumped. Just as I was about to pass out, metal hit metal as the implant contacted the blade. I dug the first implant out with the knife and went back for the second with my fingers. I grunted through my teeth trying not to scream as I fished around inside my arm. At last I found the implant and yanked it free. With blood covered fingers I closed the wound the best I could with supplies I'd stashed in my uniform pocket.

By the time I'd stitched myself up the auto-pilot had made the loop around Central, but I didn't turn back like I was supposed to. I was approaching the spot I'd planned my crash to happen. My heart rate rose from the adrenaline pushing through my body.

I looked at the lake below and then to the wall ahead. My eyes narrowed to the base of the wall, at the place I aimed on crashing my craft into. My hand wrapped around the accelerator as I pointed the nose of the craft for the ground. I flicked the radio on and prepared to sound distressed.

"This is RP2215 to CC, I'm in a nosedive. I repeat, craft in an uncontrolled nosedive."

The CC radioed back but I didn't listen long. I turned the transmitters off thrusting the craft towards the ground. I was gaining speed and almost at the point of no return, or PNR as they called it in training. The craft shook and the alarms wailed telling me it was time. If I waited more than three seconds to eject it would be too late.

I pressed the eject button with less than a second to spare as the craft aimed for the base of Centrals wall. This was the spot I'd scouted out every time I'd flown over it in the sim-pod.

I ejected, gripping my citizen implant which I knew had a tracker attached to it. My chute opened picking me up and thrusting me backwards. I was blasted sideways as the craft barreled full force and exploded at the base of the wall.

The flames were immediate and mushroom-like. The chute carried me over the top of the lake like I'd planned. I opened my hand dropping the citizen implant into the water. My regulator implant was still fisted in my other hand.

I came down fast with my hands pulling and steering the chute towards the edge of the lake. I got closer to the ground and freed my knife cutting the chute before it took me too far. I rolled through the brush as I landed, thorns and sticks pierced me.

That didn't stop me, not with my adrenaline pumping like it was. I ran to the wall, the part with the stairwell the patrols climbed to man the yellowing concrete. I'd landed exactly where I needed to. I ran to the top with my regulator implant fisted. By then I could hear the heavy boots of the wall-patrolling regulators approaching.

"Shit, did you see that?" The one shouted.

"Where the hell did that come from?" The other answered as he radioed into CC. "This is RP1121 I'm at the 45th parallel, we've got a Central craft down. I repeat Central craft down at the 45th parallel."

"Look at the fire. Poor bastard, I wonder if he made it out in time."

"Let's hope, he doesn't stand a chance in that."

CC radioed back, 'Copy that RP1121, we've got patrols on the way, resume your positions and await further instructions.'

"Copy that CC," the one answered.

"This is the most excitement we've had in a long time. What do you think happened?"

"I'd be speculating, but I've got a theory." The one said without missing a beat.

"What?" The other answered eager to hear what his comrade knew.

"I'd have to say a hover crashed." The regulator said, laughing as the other stalked off. He was pissed he'd believed his companion knew something.

They moved away from the staircase towards their posts. I slid along the wall inching towards the metal door carved into the yellow wall. Their boots echoed a level above me as they paced the length of the wall.

I was wearing heavy boots too, I had to go slowly and quietly. I was almost at the door to the Inner staircase when the first CC crafts arrived. They got there fast, I'd expected more time to prepare myself. The two regulators' boots thumped from above as they made their way down the stairs towards me.

They were at the junction ahead of me, seconds away from turning down my corridor. If my plan didn't work I'd be caught. I opened my palm scanning my regulator implant. There was a moment where I thought I'd failed my escape. My head rushed as the door clicked open right as the regulators rounded the corner.

I flew down the staircase and burst into the Inner. Smoke was spiraling from the crash site behind me. I stormed through the woods running as far away from the wall as possible.

That was months ago. It was before I'd found out Nessa had been taken. Back then, each day I got closer to home I felt a little more complete. I couldn't decide if I thought Central was looking for me or not. I figured they'd want to see my body as proof, but maybe they would believe I'd drown in that lake.

Just because I was inside the Inner didn't mean I was home free. It took me a month to get to our sub. I beat through trees, rivers, mud and everything in between to get there. My training from my years in the Inner helped me to forage and trap for game. It's how I managed to stay alive.

Food wasn't so much the issue, my problem was always one of water. I can't say if I hated the rain or the drought more. Each had their particular disadvantages. Each day the drought went on I was terrified I'd die of dehydration. Each disappearing stream I stumbled across became my only chance at survival. I looked at each one as a sign that I had to keep going. I told myself that if I wasn't supposed to get to her then I'd run out of streams and be left for dead.

Eventually the rains came, making my bones ache where the breaks had been. It didn't take long to appreciate that heavy rains had their own breed of danger. Creeks that were once dried raged and tried sweeping me away. After every crossing I told myself that if she wasn't meant for me then I'd have been swept away. It was my way of convincing me I was doing the right thing.

After a month of playing that mind game I crossed out of the wilds into the Inner's subs. It was strange having to hide from my own people. I couldn't show myself to the neighbors or friends that I'd known my entire life. I couldn't even risk seeing my parents.

I spent my first night by our oak tree and I remember thinking Nessa would show up. I imagined that she'd come there every night since I'd left. I imagined her sitting by the river looking at the same stars I looked at every night I was stuck in Central.

Nessa didn't come that night and when morning came I woke under the tree alone. Its winding arms covered me and for the first time in forever it felt like I was home.

I stretched my arms out to rub the sleep from my eyes. That's when I saw a green shirt draped on the branch above me. I hoisted myself up and grabbed the tattered shirt. It was part of a uniform, a green uniform that would have fit Nessa. It was old and weather worn, it must have been there a while.

My heart picked up its pace and started beating wildly. We were the only people that went there. It had to be hers but why the heck was it out there like that I wondered. My imagination got the best of me. I abandoned my plan to wait until nighttime to find her, I couldn't delay after seeing her uniform. Something told me it was out of place for a reason.

I stalked out of the woods in broad daylight, dodging the citizens as I went. I moved through the subs hiding and slinking until I made it to her house. The blue door looked just the same. I pushed it open and ran into the empty house. Hours passed as I impatiently waited for someone to come home.

Just before dusk the door pushed open and Emma and her father stopped dead in their tracks, both stared at me. Emma looked like she'd seen a ghost.

"Hi…" I said.

I was sitting in her father's clothes. My torn and filthy white uniform was a mess by that point and I needed something else to wear.

"I borrowed these, I hope you don't mind." They stood there frozen, making me feel awkward. "Can somebody say something?" I said.

"Garrett?" Her father answered.

"Yea, it's me" I said rising from the table. He turned to shut the door.

"What are you doing here?"

"I came for Nessa. I love your daughter and I couldn't be without her." I was surprised by how sure I sounded, on the inside I was terrified to admit that to him.

"Nessa's gone." Emma said.

"Where?"

"She took the scout position. They sent her away."

"What are you talking about?" I asked frantically.

Her father shifted, his face scrunched before he talked, "They told us she accepted the scout position, a new position that was offered to the second place testers. The day after the banquet she and that boy Tyler showed up on the pavilion broadcasts announcing they had accepted it."

My head jerked in confusion, "What scout position?"

"They offered it to the top testers. That's what that woman said at least." Emma answered with her eyes looking down.

"That's impossible. There wasn't a scout position."

Her father's face twisted with pain, "I was afraid of that but what was I supposed to do?" he asked desperately.

"Where did they send her?"

He stared at the ground as he pulled Emma to his side. "Who knows? She was supposed to be patrolling the perimeter of the walls."

I didn't know how I was going to find her but I knew I had to try. I hugged them both and promised I'd get her back. I swore I would or I'd die trying, and I meant it.

That night I stayed under our tree. As the sun rose the next day I left to find her. I'd spend my entire life searching if that is what it took.

Another explosion knocks me to the ground, I taste the salty, dry dirt as my blood oozes onto it. I spit the foul taste from my mouth as the bombs keep raining down.

Chapter 4: Nessa

I can't get close enough to papa and Emma. I draw them near, holding them tight. I hold them because it's what I've wanted to do for a year now, and because in a few days I'll be in Central and might never see them again.

I draw them even closer as we approach the hospital exit. Kara and Jon walk ahead of us stopping by Jon's craft. His eyes freeze to connect with mine. His eyes are cold and hostile. I hold my stare as I descend the steps with papa and Emma on each side. I clamp them to my body and tell myself that I'm protecting them but I know they are my shields. They are the ones keeping me on my feet.

I jar with each step down the stone stairs. The sliding door to the hospital pulls open whooshing the air behind me. Kara reaches for Jon's arm squeezing it until he breaks eye contact with me and turns to her.

Kara's head shakes side to side, her curls bounce as she talks. She tips her head to Jon, she's much shorter than him and actually Emma is almost her height now. Jon's dark eyes travel to the ground, they are searching eyes, ones that are looking for answers. Finally he pulls them back to Kara.

We take our last step off the stone stairs landing on the grey concrete sidewalk. I keep papa and Emma squeezed to my side as I lead them towards Jon and Kara. The closer I get the faster my heart pounds. It beats hard in my chest letting me know it's there and alive. I'm nervous, mad, scared and many other things that make my insides toss around.

What if Jon leaves us, what if he refuses to take papa and Emma? Then again, do I want them with him? It's hard to picture leaving them with a man that loves Natalie. I turn to Ty's dim window four floors up, third one over. I'm scared that I might not make it back to see him again.

"We've arranged for you to stay at my place." Jon says shaking papa's hand.

For a split second my spiraling heart stops, it holds steady and straight right where it should. It's a decision that was beyond my conscious control. My heart accepts his offer and I'm able to free myself from part of my worries at least.

"Thank you, I promise we won't be in the way." Papa says taking Jon's hand.

Papa's palms are rough and dirty compared to Jon's. I stare at papa's hands, they are aged beyond their years from moon cycle after moon cycle of factory work.

I swallow feeling another dry pit hit my throat, "Thanks Jon." I say as I hoist Emma into his hovercraft. "Buckle up," I say, fastening my own belt.

Jon takes off, flying in his usual madman ways. Emma's small hand wraps around mine. She squeezes tight so I hold her steady. Everything must be overwhelming for them.

Yesterday they were leading their lives as usual, now they're here, a world away from the Inner. Life is alien to them now. No more uniforms or curfew, no more regulators and walls. They're riding in a hovercraft through streets with towering buildings unlike anything we had in the Inner.

Their faces reflect the awe at what they are seeing. Papa stares out the window with his eyes moving rapidly from side to side and Emma can't keep her stare steady for more than a second. I've uprooted them but I have to trust it was for the better.

Time passes with me looking between Papa and Emma. Finally Jon slides the craft to a halt in front of his loft. I help Emma out of her buckle and guide her from the craft, her small feet land with a thud against the concrete. Jon leads us towards his door, swiping his card to unlock it. The chimes beep and he swings it open. I remember this place. It's confusing that something can seem so familiar and yet so distant at the same time.

In a way it feels like yesterday Ty and I were here together preparing for the mission but at the same time, it feels just shy of an eternity that I would roll over to see him in the bed across from me. I shake my head trying to clear the confusion that's settled there.

"Nessa, can I talk to you?" Jon's voice isn't as harsh as I expected it to be.

I turn to papa and Emma looking for their approval.

"We'll be fine" papa says nodding.

I follow Jon as he takes me through the narrow hall past his office. I've never gone farther than that office, I never needed to. This part of the loft is Jon's space, his private escape.

"Take a seat" he says opening the white door at the end of the hall.

I step into the grey and sage room and immediately feel relaxed, like it's a sanctuary. It's his safe place away from chaos.

"Kara and Jake are on their way." He says gesturing, reminding me to sit.

I make my way to one of the grey suede chairs and sink into the fabric. My heart pounds inside my chest, rattling around as Jon paces the room slowly and methodically. Finally Jake and Kara step in and my heart slows, and my breathing becomes regular.

Jon stops pacing and looks at me. His mouth opens and closes before he's able to find his voice.

"Six years ago a group of four researchers from our side went to meet with Central. Jake's sister and Kara's husband were two of those researchers. We'd learned years before that Central considered Prems a threat and they were trying to target and eradicate them. Our researchers were working to save innocent lives. Our team began developing a cure for the conciliate serum hoping Central would accept it."

Jon lifts a small glass figurine from the shelf in front of him, twirling it around his fingers before he places it back down.

"Natalie was the lead researcher. We'd been married just over three years when she went across the walls to Central. It feels like yesterday that I kissed her at that front door."

Jon looks across the room towards his open hall.

"You know what she said to me, she said not to worry and to have faith. She believed she could convince them to stop killing innocent people. She was brilliant and so naïve."

He starts pacing again, faster this time.

"I guess that's why I loved her though. I loved her drive and compassion and most of all I loved her for believing the best in everything and everyone, even when the signs pointed otherwise."

He stops to fold his hands across his stomach.

"She was brilliant and could've dedicated her life to anything but she chose to save people like you." He smirks, dropping his eyes to his brown leather shoes. "I knew what I was getting myself into when I fell for her but it was too damn hard not to."

He looks at me, his dark eyes collect wetness, the type we all get as we fight back tears.

"Why Prems? Why'd she care about us?" I ask.

Jon straightens his back, arching it slightly as he stands. "She didn't need a bad reaction to conciliate serum to see the future, she was born that way. She was a beautiful and talented genius that happened to be born with the ability to see bits of the future." He shakes his head. "Sometimes I thought it was a gift. Other times it was a curse."

Jon leans against his wall to brace himself.

"She was from a farming town west of here. I went to visit her hometown once, it was pitiful. She'd seen me clear as day in one of her visions and just picked up and left that town to move here and find me. Back then I thought her visions were God-sent. Anything that brought a girl like her to me had to be a gift from some divine power."

Jon jerks his head side to side, shaking it furiously.

"Now I curse it. Three years was all I got with her. Three years waking up every morning thinking I'm the luckiest man alive, and then to have that gone. To have that taken by those people!"

Jon points out his window towards the walls that lay in the distance, somewhere out of sight.

"You know what kills me the most? She had to know this could happen. She'd seen herself develop the cure and save your people. Natalie was convinced that if her team went to Central they could stop the killing and make your lives better.

The night before she left she told me she'd seen your people freed and that we would make it happen. Natalie was so damn sure of it and insistent that she go without me."

Jon turns his back to me, he never finished dressing this morning and the back end of his shirt hangs half tucked from his grey pants.

"Now I sit around asking myself if she knew this would happen. Did she know she would be taken? Did she know Central would do whatever they did to make her this way and if so, why did she go? What am I supposed to do out here?"

He whirls around to face me, this time tears are falling.

"Did she know this would happen and am I supposed to save her?"

Jon asks but I know he isn't looking for an answer. I can tell it is a question he has asked himself nightly. It's one of those questions that gets planted in your head, an ugly rotting seed of a question that with enough time consumes all the healthy and beautiful life that once surrounded it.

"Maybe" I say, looking up to him. "Maybe she knew all this would happen but maybe not. You might never get that answer. I doubt it's a coincidence that we're all connected though."

I look around to Kara and Jake and think about how their loved ones are being held by the same people that have Garrett now.

I speak again, this time looking at Jon. "It doesn't seem likely, so maybe it *was* part of a bigger plan. I do know that they've got Garrett and I have to save him before they kill him."

Kara steps from the door, her purple shirt has specks of blood dried to it still.

"We want to get him back, just like we want our families back but I'm not sure about this."

Jon shifts before he cuts Kara off, "Clint and his team are ready to help. They know everything we've got on Central. If anyone is going to find Garrett and our families it's going to be them."

Jake strides over reaching under my arm. His fingers wrap around my forearm as he lifts me from my seat and away from Jon.

I wonder how many countless days and nights Jon has stood like he does now. Stood at his oversized window and stared off into the distance as if looking far enough out might give him the answers he seeks.

"Come on Nessa, we've got work to do." Jake guides me forward through the door.

Chapter 5: Ty

The beeping alarms are gonna drive me nuts. I wonder what Nessa's doing, I felt her out there. Her heart sorta crumbled and smashed at the same time. What did they tell her to make her feel that way? Kara said they had her family here, so it's not that.

My head pounds the longer I lay, it feels like a hammer is smacking the bone poking outta the back of my skull. I should rest and try letting my body heal but I've already spent too much time in this bed.

My eyes are heavy, like rocks sinking into the ocean. If I open them maybe Nessa will be here. I try, but I can't get them to move. 'Open your eyes on the count of three and Nessa will be there.' At least that's what I tell myself. 'One, two...three!' I take a crack at pushing my eyes open but they stay shut. I try moving my fingers, toes, or anything, but I'm totally stuck. Doctors and their medications!

I coaks every fiber of myself into opening my eyes. It's a simple thing that I'm hooked on now. The alarms beep around me but I ignore them. I need to focus on opening my heavy rock-like eyes. 'One...two...three!' Nothing happens again.

The TV turns on and the annoying and high pitched voice of a reporter drowns out the beeping machines.

'Good afternoon ladies and gentleman, I'm Amy Volarn and this is Action D news.'

'Action D', what a stupid name I think.

'I'm reporting live from one of the fractures in the wall that once separated us from the citizens across the divide. In case you haven't heard, less than forty-eight hours ago unidentified crafts targeted multiple areas of the walls tearing down the towering concrete allowing for hundreds, if not thousands of citizens to flee. Those citizens now seek refuge in our cities.'

Amy Volam pauses her nasally report and I imagine the cameraman panning to the crumbled wall. Her obnoxious voice starts again making my skin crawl.

'Through all of this there's one refugee on everyone's mind. Find out who she is after the break.'

The beeping alarm rises in sync with my pounding heart. The reporters words, 'Who *she* is,' bounce in my head. As soon as that high pitched voice squeaked out the word 'she' my heart went mad. It has to have something to do with Nessa. I've learned to trust my gut and my gut is screaming Nessa right now.

The jarring theme music to Action D news blasts on again. I force myself out of the medication haze as I strain, mentally fighting to force my attention on the news.

'Amy Volam with Action D news, with the most up-to-date news of the 'downed divide' as it's being called. Just two days ago this wall behind me was literally rock solid. No crossing was permitted between the sides of these two *very* different societies. Now I stand here with more than a crack in the foundation, I stand with the crumbled remains of the wall many called an oppressive symbol of government regulations gone too far. We may never know the full details of the series of events that led to the collapse but we do know one thing, Central is working tirelessly to contain and restrain its citizens, and most importantly they are dedicated to find the woman they hold at least partially responsible, a Miss Vanessa Hollins.'

I hate when I'm right, I knew it was Nessa. The alarm is about to be one non-stop wail. My heart thuds full force, pumping the adrenaline I need to move, it gives me strength to fight. I overpower the medication and move my hand. It jerks back to my side. Restraints loop around my wrist, these nurses are killing me. I'm stuck.

'Central didn't so much urge, but instead threatened all citizens of the United Republic with chemical warfare should Miss Hollins not be returned in one week's time. According to

Central's brief message issued yesterday, they have captured a co-conspirator shown here.'

I flick my eyes open like it's on cue. The overhead lights blind me for a blink but I fight and find the screen. My stomach drops straight to my toes, it's Garrett.

Now I get it. Now I know why I felt her heart break yesterday. She saw her face on the broadcast, heard the threats and then she saw him. I don't particularly like the guy and I feel like I've been hit in the gut. His bloodied and swollen face is enough to make anyone cringe.

I can't piece together any idea of what Nessa must be feeling. She is being hunted by the most powerful individuals we've ever known and a war could start if she's not turned over. If she is, they'll kill her. Then to have Garrett hurting with no end in sight, it's a pain nobody should feel.

I wish I could take this from Nessa. I'd do anything to crawl outta this bed and pull it away from her, to carry the pain and fear as my own. I'd do it if it meant she didn't have to.

The door flings open and I think about darting my eyes to look but my reactions are slowed.

"He's tachycardic, get the doctor," the nurse says pressing a button above my bed.

'Not this again' I think as the doctor slides into the room to sink me into another oblivious state.

Chapter 6: Nessa

Jake's hand guides me from Jon's room. The hallway looks like an anomaly. Papa and Emma stand at the end seeming distant and drawn out yet the door beside them looks just out of reach.

I don't hear my steps, heartbeat, or breathing; all of which I know are pounding hard. Instead, I feel my body hum and spin as emotions collide inside me. Emotions that feel like the glue that's holding me together yet simultaneously are trying to rip me apart.

I move towards papa and Emma knowing that my reunion with them is about to end. More emotions rip and break across the jagged pieces that thrash inside me.

There's the sadness of saying good-bye too soon and it swirls with happiness that I'm even seeing them again at all. There's a gratefulness that they are here and not across the walls, not in a sterile room with Central in control.

Papa reaches his hand to mine. His rough fingers draw my attention away from the emotions tossing inside me.

"I don't want you to go." He says, squeezing my hand.

"There isn't another way." I say as we stand in the doorway.

It's the very same door Jon said good-bye to Natalie at. I suddenly imagine them standing here as two entirely different people than they are today. Two people whose lives have changed to a point that I can't imagine they will ever recover from.

"Nessa please don't go." Emma says looking straight at me.

She doesn't latch to me like she would have a year ago. She's become more independent, I guess she had to after I left.

"You heard what Natalie said, if they don't get me they'll attack. Who knows how many they'll kill and all this will have been for nothing. I can't let that happen and I won't let Garrett pay for this either."

I pull my chin up, drawing my eyes away from Emma's. I'm afraid if I look into her green and gold eyes much longer I'll break. Something inside me will shatter and I'll never be strong enough to put myself back together.

"Our people will look after you," Jake says staring at papa and Emma. "We have people that will look after Nessa too." He says, lifting the corner of his mouth a touch.

His blue eyes shine and I try to appreciate what he's feeling. I try envisioning the hope he must have now that his sister might be alive. Jake has hurt for a long time and finally a chance for relief has come.

I reach my long arms forward, bruises stand out against the paleness of my skin. I pull papa and Emma into my embrace and wish we could stay this connected forever. I hold them until our hearts beat together. Papa's arms thread around my back, pulling me closer.

With hands touching and hearts beating we stand at the door that will take me away. What should I do when I walk out that door? Who do I turn to and what happens next? I'm strong, I've had to be strong for a long time but maybe it has been too long.

Does strength keep compounding itself for infinity or is there a breaking point? I wonder. Perhaps there is a point where strength becomes a weakness and takes a person to their knees. Maybe I am one instant away from being cut to my knees for good.

I inhale knowing that no matter what, no matter if it compounds for eternity or takes me to my knees, I have no choice but to stay strong for as long as I can. I have got to keep moving forward and I have to be brave.

I step away from papa and Emma with the doorknob pressing into my back.

"I love you both and I missed you every day I was gone. I wanted things to go so differently... I'm sorry, but I have to go."

Emma cries, I hear it even though she presses her face into papa's chest. Papa looks at me sending my heart soaring. He reaches out, grasping my wrist stopping me from leaving.

"When you and Emma were born I promised myself I'd never let you girls get hurt. I failed to keep that promise but starting today, I will." Papa says as I take my wrist back.

I smile to papa because I believe he means it, but I choose my fate, not him. I turn to walk out the door with Jake behind me, his steps echo along the stairs. I'm sure Kara's inside with papa and Emma. At least they've got her.

"We've set up a meeting with Clint. He and his team are waiting for you." Jake says catching up to me.

"Waiting for me?" I ask.

"You didn't think we would send you into Central alone?" Jake says, smirking as he swings the door to his craft open.

I hoist myself inside. "At this point I don't let myself expect anything. Every time I *think* I've got something worked out life turns it upside down."

Jake closes his door powering the craft on, "Should we stop at the hospital first?" Jake asks as he throttles the craft forward.

My throat clenches as it squirms itself inward. What's left of my heart and soul wants to see Ty before I leave. It could be my last chance to see him and that knowledge tears at me.

My heart screams for me to go to Ty so I can feel love, hope, and strength by looking at him. My mind says no, it tells me he will only make this harder, it will hurt more in the end if I go.

"No, take me to Clint." I set my eyes forward as we glide through the streets towards the hole.

My mind wanders back to that night in the alley when Ty saved me. I see him punching the man, beating him to a pulp. I wrap my fingers around the locket Ty gave me that night. The closer we get to the hole, the more I think about Ty.

Jake pulls the craft to a stop in front of the broken garage doors leading to the hole and I snap back to the present. It's surreal being here again.

I hop out of the craft before Jake has powered it down. My steps land heavily as I march toward the door. I walk in front of Jake and push the heavy door open. The industrial overhead lights flicker off and on giving the room a mysterious feeling.

"Lights have been acting up since the bombs went off" Clint says, his sharp voice snaps me alert.

I watch Clint make his way across the room, as his eyes bore deeply into mine.

"I heard about Ty, sounds like he's going to make it." Clint says clasping my shoulder making me jolt.

"Yeah, it was a close call but he should pull through." I say forcing a small smile.

"What's done can't be undone, we need to focus on what comes next." Clint says looking at Jake and me.

I exhale looking to Clint, "What is next?"

His smile is frightening. It's the kind of smile he gives when chaos or the seeds of chaos and fighting are about to ensue.

"Follow me," Clint says turning towards the back of the hole.

We follow as he takes us through the busted and broke-down hall. He pauses at a grey door for just a second, in that moment my stomach flip flops wondering what lies behind it.

His strong hand drives into the door, pushing it open. I'm not sure why but seeing the people staring at me sends a wave of nausea through me. Maybe it's because they are oversized, serious, and simply frightening individuals. These are people that would take any threat or situation on without flinching.

I see Liam at the far end, his bright red hair rests above his narrowed green eyes. He's flanked by two men just as imposing as he is. There's a black-haired woman that proudly shows off her cut arms that are muscled and menacing.

"These are my graduates, The Team." Clint says gesturing to the group. "You've met Liam" he says as Liam nods, dipping his chin slightly. "That's Marcus" Clint points to the man at Liam's right.

Marcus's powerful jaw angles towards the table as his diamond shaped eyes look straight at me. His black T-shirt hugs to his body. I can't help wondering what his tattoos mean, they cover both arms extending under his shirt. Some are bright and colored and others are dark like his skin. I nod to Marcus. His grin shows his straight teeth.

"This is Gavin," Clint says pointing to the man on Liam's other side.

Even though he's sitting I can tell he's tall, probably over six and half feet. His arms are long and muscled, his brown hair's wavy.

"Ma'am" he says nodding and standing slightly. I nod back taking my eyes away and directing them to the black haired woman.

"Lastly, this is Liv."

Liv jerks her chin up, raising her eyebrows to stare at me. I can't decide what to think, she confuses me. She's attractive and actually could be beautiful if that notion of traditional beauty interested her. I can tell it doesn't though, she's too tough. I stare at her tattoos, trying to decipher the story she's had inscribed on her skin.

"Jake will be our pilot." Clint says signaling for Jake to take an open seat, "Zane will be coming on board for electronic surveillance. You and I," Clint says pointing at me, "we complete the ground team. Seven strong."

"I'm part of this group?" I ask without hesitation.

I compare myself to the others. I'm nothing like them, I'm not built of toned muscles, discipline, and fearlessness. I'm somewhere between them and a regular person.

"You are a key player in this Nessa." Clint says taking his seat at the head of the table. He points me to the last empty chair next to Jake.

My palms sweat as I lower myself into the vinyl and metal chair. Jake's steady breathing becomes my focus, I try thinking about that instead of my coursing nerves.

"I'm going to be honest; we don't have all the intel that I would have wanted for a mission of this caliber." Clint says rapping his knuckles methodically against the steel table top. "But

I'm confident the information we do have will get us into Central to secure what we'll need to execute the extractions."

"Extractions?" I ask, wondering if I misheard him. Maybe he does plan on attempting multiple rescues.

"Yes, our objective isn't solely recovering Garrett." Clint says pressing a button to the remote beside him.

A snapshot of Garrett tied to the chair flashes and my gut wads. Thankfully Clint doesn't leave it on for long.

"Brian, Kara's husband." Clint says flicking another button to reveal a brown eyed man staring at us, a mischievous smile splayed across his face.

There's a kick of pain and sympathy for Kara. How could she go so long not knowing if he was safe? It's been six years since he left and I wonder why she hasn't given up.

"Then there's Natasha," Clint nods to Jake.

I can tell immediately that they're twins, no doubt. The side by side shot of them is uncanny. Their blonde hair and blue eyes are set in the exact same places above their narrowed noses.

Clint looks to Jake before he begins again, Jake hardly notices, his eyes are locked to the screen as he stares at Natasha.

Clint hits the button again, "Dustin" he says flashing to a balding man that was probably in his mid-forties. He's got to be fifty now and I wonder if his stomach has rounded out more than it already was in this picture. Or maybe he's lost weight since being held by Central.

The slide changes and my stomach drops, it feels like it does when I dream I'm falling into nothingness. I see Natalie's face smiling sweetly as Jon stands to her side. He was crazy about her. Even in a photograph you can see the passion he had for her.

"Natalie is the only one we have confirmed is still alive. From the broadcast Central aired it seems like she's gone rogue and is acting as one of them."

"Not seems, she *is* one of them." I say with rage fracturing my voice.

"No matter," Clint says. "We will find her and the others to bring them home."

Jake nods like he's snapping out of a trance.

Clint stares straight at him, "You will be our pilot. This is a ghost mission so we will be deploying above radars." Clint directs.

Marcus fists his hand, pumping it front and back. For some reason the idea of a so called 'ghost' mission excites him.

"What's that mean? Ghost?" I ask.

Liv squirms in her chair like she wants to reach across the table and slap me for asking something so simple. I want to reach across and slap her for making me feel stupid.

"It means Central won't know we've arrived on their doorstep. To get in undetected we'll parachute in, Jake will be dropping us at 13,000 feet."

My jaw sags, "What?"

Liv smiles, rolling her tongue across her lips like a wild animal, "Not afraid of heights are you Prem?"

"The name is Nessa and it takes more than heights to scare me." I blurt the words out not knowing if I can pull that off.

"We'll see about that. I bet you'll be begging for your mom before we even step on the hover."

I shoot out of my chair ready to launch myself at her. Jake pulls me down, forcing me back into my seat.

Gavin yells breaking my rage. "Ladies, we are playing for the same team!" He leans forward looking at Liv.

"Enough!" Clint barks.

I'm the only one that reacts. I've heard his bark hundreds of times before but it still shakes me to the core.

"I don't really care if you two end up killing each other or braiding each other's hair over ice cream but you will wait and do it until after the missions completed." Liv and I both nod. "We will jump at 2000 hours, four clicks south of the AO." I stare blankly at Clint. "Area of operation, AO, Central's capital."

The screen flicks to an aerial shot of the AO, it looks like a play thing. The buildings are small like the tiny blobs of mud Garrett and I would drop along our river when we were kids.

Clint starts again, "Liam, Nessa, Marcus, and I will take lead. We'll approach from the South. We are the initial drive team."

Marcus and Liam pound their knuckles together as a sign of comradery.

"Liv and Gavin will penetrate the AO from the North with Zane."

"Great, we get to babysit Zane." Liv says staring at Gavin.

"Enough!" Clint drives his fist into the table, his chair screeches beneath him as he stands. He looks wild, his nostrils flaring.

"Yes sir!" Liv booms.

Her mouth closes as she looks at her hands. I follow her eyes and stop my gaze at her fingers. The black tattoo of a sniper rifle spans the length of her trigger finger. The tip of her finger taps the table. Her second tattoo, a bull's eye must have been painful. It fills the fleshy part of her finger pad. She wears one piece of jewelry, a gold and turquoise bullet shell bracelet that hangs loosely around her wrist.

Clint looks at Liv and Gavin, "Your focus is to protect Zane at all costs. He is our sole source of intel when we're out there. Without him we'll be sitting ducks."

"Yes Sir." Gavin says with conviction..

The photo changes as Clint pulls up the next image. "Decades before the treaty was made we obtained surveillance footage of the Capital as it was undergoing construction." He zooms in on the photo. "These bunkers were constructed with twenty-inch thick concrete walls buried underground, they are where the prison cells must be. This is likely where they are keeping Garrett and possibly the others."

Jake shifts in his seat leaning closer to the screen, like if he moves close enough maybe he'll see Natasha sitting in a cell.

"The initial drive team, excluding myself and Nessa, will pose as regulators."

"What will I be?" I ask.

"You will be yourself."

It feels like the inside of my stomach has lodged itself in my throat, "What? Won't they recognize me?"

"That's what we want." Clint says. "You will have two tracking devices implanted. Think of one as a decoy and the other as your own personal sonar. It will be linked to Zane on the outside. It emits sound waves above the frequency that humans can hear. The waves will bounce off your surroundings and send information back to Zane. He'll be able to formulate a map of the facility and your exact location."

"Who says they won't shoot me on the spot?" I ask with my hands shaking.

Time seems frozen, suspended in air as I wait for Clint's answer. "It's a possibility. Unlikely though. Chances are they will try to interrogate you before doing anything rash like an execution. Our hope is that they proceed with an interrogation. You will be the key that maps the way to the underground cells."

Marcus looks at my trembling hands. I place them in my lap. I can't have anyone thinking I'm as scared as I actually feel.

Clint stares directly at me, "Jake will take us up tomorrow to practice your jump. We can't have you making your first launch cold." Clint pulls his eyes away from mine allowing me to relax slightly. "We deploy in two days," he says staring at the group. This may be my breaking point as I stand with my knees shaking beneath me. Jake guides me away from the room, saving me from the embarrassment of having my knees give out in front of everyone.

"Sleep tight newbie." Liv's voice echoes in my ear as she walks past me laughing.

"Don't mind her." Jake says leading me down the hall. "You'll stay here," he says opening another door.

A single suspended cot hangs bare and unforgiving. I nod as he shuts the door behind him. I lower onto the hard cot and let my head spin and swim with thoughts of the mission. It spirals around into a dark abyss that I'm afraid I might never come back from.

Chapter 7: Garrett

The fiery heat from the exploding bombs scorches more than anything I've seen before. It's hotter than the summer days Nessa and I used to spend by our river. It's even hotter than the mushroom explosion my craft made after it crashed into the wall.

Oliver had told me about skin searing heat like this. He had felt it once and I believed him, he had the scars to prove it.

I met Oliver on my first day of regulator training, and if I try hard enough, I can still picture the puffy bags under my eyes. My mom used to get them whenever she couldn't sleep too.

I earned them that night, I hadn't slept at all. Eventually I gave up on sleeping and got ready for my first day of regulator training. My uniform was new and stiff, almost like it had been over starched. I laughed sliding my black boots on, one felt like a constricting vice around my muscular calf while the other sagged loosely around my atrophied leg.

I stared at the boots drawn around my calves and thought it looked both comical and appalling. It was like my body was pieced together with legs from two different men. It only took two months for half of me to waste away. I had those regulators and their beating to thank for that.

My stiff white uniform felt binding and awkward as I carried my black helmet. My boots struck the ground with a force that literally jarred the length of my body as I walked toward the CC. I'd walked there the day before to map my route. I had a feeling being late on the first day of regulator training would mean a certain brand of hell that only regulators would know how to inflict.

The citizens all stared as I made my way to the CC. I felt strange, like maybe I'd done something stupid like put my pants on inside out. I kept walking as they stared at me, the kids in awe and the men and women watching in a gripping way.

I was a block away from the CC when I crossed a massive glass building that intersected one of the parks that served as that subdivision's exercise arena. I saw myself and knew why the others were staring.

Even with half my muscles whittled away I was frightening. I looked threatening by my sheer size but pairing that with the uniform made it even more pronounced. The white and black gave me an added edge, it emphasized the threatening image even more.

I stood in front of the glass building staring at my brown and gold hair combed back from my face. My brown eyes pierced through my tan features, the white uniform hugged to my skin. And that is when I met Oliver.

"Expecting to see someone else?" he asked.

I jumped. I'd been so engrossed in evaluating myself that I completely missed him standing next to me. I smiled and turned to Oliver. He was dressed in a regulator uniform too.

"I guess I didn't expect to look like this." I said staring at the side of Oliver's face.

I remember thinking that with more bulk he could look just as intimidating as me. He was at least four inches taller than me. He kept his dark hair cut short and I wondered if I was supposed to get mine cut for regulator training.

"I'm just busting you. If I didn't have this mug I'd probably get lost staring at myself too." He said laughing.

That's when he turned to look at me, the other half of his face turning toward me. I held myself back, stopping my knee-jerk reaction, and stood looking at him calmly. I'd wanted to step back, maybe even cringe, but I held myself together.

"Name's Garrett." I said putting my hand out.

I could tell he was shocked. I imagine he'd gone through his life with people turning away from his disfigurement, or maybe others even openly joked or laughed about it. He'd probably had to field some insensitive questions over the years too. I wasn't that type of person, who was I to judge anyway?

"Oliver." he said with a smile cutting across his square-cut face. "I'll let you get back to whatever you were doing, it looked important." He said joking.

"No, I'm good." I smiled turning towards the CC with Oliver walking beside me.

Chapter 8: Nessa

"Rise and shine," Jake says shaking my shoulder.

"Time already?" I ask yawning.

I try rolling over but half of me tenses and grips. My muscles spasm and cramp as my body contorts in response to the rock-hard cot I slept on.

"Never slept on one of these?" Jake asks and I shake my head no. "It'll hurt at first." He says smiling with his blue eyes staring at me.

For a second I see Natasha. Their features are so much alike that my mind has a hard time separating them.

"I hope it gets easier." I say forcing my cramping muscles into a stretch.

"Yes and no." Jake slaps the metal rail as he turns to leave. It's him telling me to hurry.

I jump into the uniform he left at the foot of my bed. It's a strange material, thick but lightweight. I fasten the bottom around my ankles knowing that in just a few hours I'll be expected to jump from a hovercraft.

I keep repeating a circular mantra, 'I am strong enough, I can do this, I will do this, and I don't have a choice.' I chant it to remind myself that I can leave the craft kicking and screaming as Clint pushes me, or I can digest and hold the fear and jump with my dignity intact. The end result is still free falling twelve thousand feet. I may as well go on my own terms.

I pull my hair away from my face forming a ponytail that sits high on my head. I open the door as I snap the last loop of my hair band around my thick reddish-brown locks.

"Not a beauty contest Prem." Liv pushes past me.

I shoot her a cold death stare as I march behind her.

"That's right, you prefer Nessa. I forgot you cried over that last night."

My eyes narrow as I hone my stare at her. I don't think I've ever met someone that's turned me off so quickly before.

My jaw loosens as I prepare to sling another 'cry' at her. Jake rests his hand on my shoulder steering me around Liv.

"That's not a fight I would engage in, Nessa."

He leads me down the hall, keeping his hand cupped around my shoulder. I grind my nails inside my tightened fists.

We round the corner seeing Clint standing at the end of the hall. He's wearing a black version of my tan suit.

"Ready?" he says, like it's a command instead of a question.

Liv stops a few feet behind me. Her persona reaches uncomfortably to mine like her soul wants to wrap and squeeze me tightly until I'm lifeless. She reminds me of a snake with its prey.

I hold my ground doing my best to ignore her standing there. "Yes, ready." I answer.

"Ready, *sir*" Liv says, correcting me for leaving 'Sir' out of my answer.

I'm assuming she's military and that's where these rules come from. What a hypocrite she is. Just last night she was borderline disrespectful to Clint in the briefing and now she's pretending to be a well-behaved subordinate.

Clint turns towards the door leading to the hole. We follow, passing the benches Ty and I used to sit on during our breaks. I shake my thoughts clear, I can't let myself think of Ty right now.

My stomach kicks as Liv walks out behind us. We load into a small black craft parked on the side street. Jake powers it on and starts flying out of the city. Clint wastes no time as he prepares me for the jump.

"Jake is flying us to a drop zone. We'll be changing planes for the high-altitude drop."

He slaps a duffle bag that I assume contains our equipment.

"Once we reach 12,500 feet we'll jump." Clint says.

"Liv and I will jump with you. We'll communicate via radio. You'll be responsible for deploying your own chute." He says looking between Liv and me.

"No one is going to pull it for you, so don't back out." Liv says smiling across from me.

Clint shoots his piercing eyes at Liv making her back off.

"We need you to make the jump in one piece. Best way to do that is to listen to what I'm telling you. Exit the craft and do this" Clint stands getting into position, "Chin down, arms tucked in, knees bent and eyes open," he says swaying as Jake takes the craft around a tight turn.

"When you jump you'll free-fall for close to a minute at one hundred and thirty miles per hour. Your body will become a missile. If you don't deploy on time, that missile will explode."

My hands are cool as I rub the sweat across my pants.

"Normally we'd jump much lower but we've got to keep Jake above Central's radar."

I nod wondering if height even matters.

"You'll land on the balls of your feet, knees bent. You drop to your side as you go down, hitting the calf, thigh, buttock and side last," he says as he pounds each body part with his fist.

"Any questions?" He asks as Jake pulls the craft to a stop.

"We're here." Jake says leveling out the craft.

"Good then, let's jump!" Clint yells.

I did have questions, at least I think I did. I can't remember them now that they are grabbing the bags and jumping off the craft. They leave me standing alone.

The hover jolts to rest like a deer that's been hit in the kill spot. It stops suddenly and harshly. There's one duffle bag left, the black straps pull the green bag tight. I stoop over hesitating above it.

'I am strong enough, I can do this, I will do this, I don't have a choice,' I chant to myself. With exhaling breath I hoist the bag and step off the craft.

I cringe as I look at the second hover. It seems almost predatory. It's small with sleek wings, I can tell it's built for speed and maneuverability, it's a war machine.

"Load up!" Jake yells as I clench my fist around my bag.

I move onto the craft. It isn't equipped with the luxury seats designed for comfort like the other crafts I've been in. These seats are hard and sterile, a lot like the cot I slept on last night. I load last using Clint and Liv as my guides.

I unzip my bag like Clint does and pull out the harness and backpack my parachute is stuffed in. Suddenly I wonder who packed it and my heart hiccups, what if Liv packed them? My heart stutters back on course, 'I am strong enough, I can do this, I will do this, I don't have a choice,' I say hoping Jake or Clint did the packing.

Clint and Liv are already harnessed by the time I've untangled my system. Clint steps towards me as I rush to throw my leg into the giant harness loop. I push one leg and then the other through before Clint is halfway to me.

I probably look foolish but I bend down rushing the blood to my head to hoist the harness up and over my shoulders. I don't want his help yet, I need to prove myself.

Clint's normally stoic face breaks with a sort of grin that looks almost frightening. My shoulders rise and tense as he circles behind me. My body jerks backwards as he tightens the straps that squeeze down on my limbs.

He wheels around to face me, pushing a helmet onto my head.

"You'll hear my voice through here," he says into a microphone that blasts through the helmet.

"When I tell you to release, pull this," he points to the cord pressing to my chest. "Understand?"

I'm frozen, like fear has inched its way along my body and nails me to the floor. My chest collapses inward and my stomach spirals like a tornado pulling at my insides. Sticky wet sweat forms inside my palms. The ground is either inching closer or I'm sinking into it as I rack with fear.

"Nessa, do you understand?" Clint snaps.

I turn my eyes towards his as I force my stiff neck to nod.

"I can do this." I say, surprising myself.

Liv huffs in the corner. I'm sure she was expecting a big dramatic display as a sign of weakness from me. I won't give her the satisfaction of knowing what I'm feeling on the inside. I won't let either of them know that right now I feel like I'm mired in mud.

My ears pop, we're gaining altitude and we're doing it fast. The ceiling of the craft is grey and industrial looking. My eyes roll upward scanning the roof with its dozens of looped handles that hang low.

"It's time!" Jake shouts from the cockpit.

My lungs fill with air as I gasp. My stomach turns inside out.

Clint's voice blasts in my ear. "Liv's first, then you. I'll be right behind you."

"Got this?" Liv says with a taunting smirk on her face.

"Waiting for you." I say smiling, I won't let her get under my skin.

Liv stands in the doorway holding onto the side. With a maniacal smile she thrusts the latch open letting wind pull at everything inside the craft while she holds steady.

"See you at the bottom!" She shouts as she back flips out of the craft.

My eyes engorge as I watch her arch and fly through the air.

"I swear that girl is going to get it!" Clint yells to himself. "Exit the way we discussed, nothing crazy like that lunatic," he shouts staring at me.

I pull myself towards the door, my hands move from strap to strap as the wind shoves around me.

"Goggles down," Clint yells.

I lose my balance as I reach for the goggles pulling them down. The wind catches me, slamming my back to the wall.

There's a burst of light as Clint stares at me. I shake it off, reaching for the next strap hanging from the roof. I push myself towards the door.

The front of my feet land at the seam, I say it one last time, 'I am strong enough, I can do this, I will do this, and I don't have a choice.' I need to let go of my fear. This is the course my life is on and I have to accept it.

My dried throat clamps as I swallow and jump, arching my body straight into the wind like Clint told me to. Panic, sickening heart pounding panic, latches hold as my eyes dart seeing nothing but sky. Which way is up, down, forward or backwards totally escapes me. My breath quickens as I thrash my head.

"Breathe Nessa," Clint says blasting into my helmet.

I do, somehow his commanding voice is what I need in this moment of panic. It's a centering force that grounds my mind.

"Look around, find Liv and me." I tilt my head moving slowly until I see Liv spinning below me. "Now me," he says. I push my head up but I can't find Clint. "Not there," he says.

I whip my head left and right with clouds puffing around me. "Not there..."

My body turns abruptly as I clench my chest afraid I've done something wrong. Clint spins me around twice before stopping me. I laugh because his salt and peppered hair flies wildly with his mouth flapping in the wind.

"I'm going ahead, pull when I say release." He says diving his body towards the ground and closer to Liv.

I freefall for another twenty seconds or so, Clint and Liv pull their chutes below me. I wrap my hand around my cord waiting for the command. Gripping it tight I know it's the only thing that stands between me and death.

I wait for Clint's command and start thinking maybe I missed it. My mind is racing faster than I'm falling. I don't see blue skies and puffed white clouds as I drop towards the open field below. Instead my head thumps with fleeting fears that seem to pull me faster towards earth.

I'm worried about Emma, I picture her sitting alone holding my locket in her hand. I check for it around my neck but it's tucked under my jump suit. If I fail she could be alone for good, no me and maybe no locket or piece of me to hold onto.

I reach back for the cord, my hands sweat inside my gloves. The world spirals around me but my head sees papa now. He's frail and I'm scared I won't live to help him be strong again. I clench my hand tighter around the cord as I picture myself splattered across the grass below. I picture Garrett and Ty standing over my body. There's thumping inside my head again, the one that comes whenever I think of Garrett. He might never know I died in a field trying to get to him.

What about Ty? What would he do? He's given up so much for me and it would be for nothing. I can't fail this mission, I've got too much on the line. I claw into the harness and bare deep into my soul. I've got too many reasons to stay alive and I will make it through this.

Clint and Liv float below, I focus on them and let go of my fears. I trust that Clint will get me down safely, I've got no choice but to believe in him.

Finally it comes, "Release!" Clint shouts.

My fingers clench into a stiff claw, I breathe and pull the cord. The chute rips out of my bag, popping like a water pipe that's burst from too much pressure. My body jerks as the chute catches wind. I let myself relax as my flapping cheeks push a smile across my wind burnt face.

The trees get larger and the field gets closer as I glide towards the ground.

"Pull on the cords, steer yourself towards us!" Clint shouts into my helmet.

I reach for the handles that hang beside my head. I tug on the right one and shoot to the side.

"Too much!" Clint yells.

I correct myself, pulling the opposite handle. I float towards the ground veering side to side as I practice steering.

"Remember the landing, knees bent, feet first and fall to the side." Clint reminds as I approach.

The ground closes in and I hit falling to my side. The grass pushes into the side of my face as I lay there.

"What are you laughing at?" Liv asks.

"Huh?" I ask realizing I'm laughing like a fool. "I don't know. I guess I sort of liked it?"

Liv rolls her eyes reaching her hand to mine. Her bull's-eye tattoo points at me and I wrap my hand around hers as she jerks me up.

"You have potential." She says walking towards Clint.

I've got more than potential. Somewhere a thousand feet up I let go of a large part of my fear. I've grown stronger in the matter of minutes.

"Again!" Clint hollers walking towards Jake's craft.

He's not kidding, we're about to do this over and over until it becomes ingrained in my head. What he doesn't know is that I want to do it. I'm not scared anymore. Maybe I am more related to Clint and his adrenaline junky team than I'd originally thought.

"Let's go." I say climbing on board ready to jump again.

Chapter 9: Garrett

Oliver had told me that everyone in Central thought their job was the best. It seemed bizarre that they didn't have a defined set of rules or societal classes.

In the Inner everyone knew which jobs were more desirable. We knew each other's status by where we worked and what sub we lived in. In Central nobody knew where they ranked compared to their neighbors. I guess that's because there was no real ranking system.

"Regulators think their job is the most important but ask any researcher and they will argue that theirs is." Oliver was saying as he changed out of his uniform. "It's bullshit if you think about it.

We've all got important jobs. There isn't a researcher or planner out there that could handle our job and I'd rather snuff myself than have theirs. How can any of our roles be better than the other?"

"I don't know. I'm just saying that in the Inner we all knew what jobs were better than others. It was like a rule."

"Bullshit. That's all a made-up crock that you bought into. That same notion could apply here if we let it, but we don't. You know why we don't?" Oliver paused, it was a rhetorical question but I gave an answer.

"'Cuz its bullshit." I said laughing.

Oliver threw his arms over head, "About time you talked some sense." He said laughing. "It's all bullshit so we don't buy into it over here. I don't want their jobs and they don't want mine. It's not because one is better than the other. It's because different people do different things. It's human nature."

It was the end of our first week of sim-training. It didn't matter that our pod lessons were simulated, we left them exhausted as if we were trained in reality. As soon as the pod doors lifted I'd feel my body drenched in sweat.

We headed for the lockers. I stared at my locker as I thought about Oliver's theory. He dropped something, startling me. I turned to see if he was alright and that's when I saw the extent of his injuries. The skin along his ribcage was puckered and shiny.

"I was in a fire," he said catching my attention.

For a split second I wondered if I should ask any questions. Maybe it was insensitive to ask but maybe it would be more insensitive not to. Since he started the conversation I assumed he was okay to talk about it.

"When?" I asked.

"I was a kid. Sometimes I wish I was younger, then maybe I wouldn't remember every detail so vividly." He paused, "But then I think it wouldn't really matter. Some acts are so messed up that no matter the age, they stick with you."

I set my facial expression like flint, preparing myself to hear something terrible.

"My father was unhappy. When you're a kid you don't think of your parents that way. He may have been a bastard but when you're five you think of them as your hero." Oliver shook his head. "He'd come home from assignment and tell my mother to take me away so he could 'unwind.' I'd sit on the stairs and watch him stare at a blank wall for an hour. Six days a week he'd stare into empty space. Looking at it now I can say the man was totally jacked in the head. Back then I'd squint and pretend like I understood what he was looking at but I never did. I guess to understand crazy you've got to be crazy, so it's good I never figured it out."

Oliver started banging his boots together at a rate that kept time with his words.

"Thursdays he'd go to the Retreat. That was the only day he'd come home and not need his time alone. I'd walk up and hug him and he'd hug me back, sort of. One Thursday things were different, that Thursday he didn't even touch the top of my head. He just made his way for my mom."

Oliver nodded but I didn't move, I was too wrapped up in his story.

"He walked into the kitchen and grabbed my mom's wrists. She yelled and my heart jumped. Five years old and I already had protective instincts." Oliver grabbed his chest like he could still feel his heart jump.

"He smacked her. She sounded empty as she hit the floor. He pulled out a can he'd had in his jacket, it was gas. He dumped it over her and sprayed it across the kitchen. My crazy bastard father stepped back and lit a match, the room exploded like a bomb went off."

My eyes bugged out of my head. I thought of myself at five with my fox and I understood that my problems didn't compare to Oliver's.

"My mom screamed the most horrible screams you'd ever hear. My father walked out, leaving us to die. She made her way to me, I guess she heard me screaming. I wanted to stop it so I threw myself onto her," he pointed to the right half of his body, "of course the fire caught hold of me but I got it out. My mom didn't live long after that. Regulators found the man that I'd called my father. He admitted to everything."

Oliver's eyes stared off like he'd disconnected himself from his body.

"My mom's last breaths were used to apologize to me. Years later I found out he wasn't my father after all. I was the result of an affair. My bastard father had known and he'd spent years building a rage."

"Oliver," I said shaking my head.

"They investigated everything. Shit like that isn't supposed to happen here. Central is supposed to be safe and the citizens are supposed to be '*happy*'." Oliver said air quoting the word happy. "They did lots of testing on him. They even looked back to his retreats over the years. Almost every single retreat from the day I was born until that awful day was spent in an open-world killing my mother. The last retreat was the fire."

"What happened to him?"

"After they'd determined what mental ailments he had they eradicated him. He's the whole reason open sims are monitored now. For a while they shut down all sims but they reinstated them once they instituted their monitoring program."

"They monitor the Retreats?"

"All the open-world ones. They use it to screen for people like him. They have a system that sees what you're thinking." Oliver stood to hang his uniform in his locker.

That was the only time Oliver talked about that awful part of his life. I admired him for his ability to accept what he'd been handed. Every time he passed a mirror or he saw his reflection in one of the hundreds of fountains or windows scattered throughout the city, I wondered how he could keep walking and not be reminded of that day.

As the weeks went by I respected Oliver more and more. Others may have defined him by his scars but he didn't let them define his character. Everyone else lacked character like that in Central.

Since becoming an orphan he'd spent most of his time being tossed from one distant relative's home to another. Once he recited the long list of every aunt, uncle, cousin and grandparent he'd lived with. To me it sounded terrible being bounced from home to home but Oliver used it to his advantage. Along the way he'd learned things that were less than ordinary for the average Central citizen.

After I'd gained his trust Oliver let me in on some of the lessons he'd picked up. The first time he showed me the abandoned exercise arena outside the Capital was when I knew he trusted me. It had flooded years before and left the ground mushy and swamp-like. Central had built another exercise arena on the other side of town to replace it.

It's funny to think of us, two oversized men trouncing through the brush and overgrown weeds on our way to a condemned playground.

One of Oliver's uncles had been a regulator. He'd been in charge of weapons design and apparently had inspired Oliver to dabble in it. My stomach jumped the first time I saw Oliver reach behind the bushes along the falling fence line and pull out a massive homemade gun.

"Spud gun," he said.

"Excuse me?" I asked.

"Shoots potatoes." Oliver grinned. He'd made it himself from stuff he'd scavenged. It was modeled after a design he'd seen in one of his uncles books.

That black monstrosity of his would launch potatoes hundreds of miles per hour. One potato blasted a hole straight through an old door we'd found. We snort-laughed as the door splintered in two from a dinner potato.

That abandoned park was the only retreat I considered fun in Central. I'm not sure if it was the park or the arsenal of homemade weapons Oliver had but something made me forget the Inner, even if it was temporarily.

I squeeze my eyes together now and imagine seeing Oliver pointing at me. He's holding the spud gun as he fires a potato into the wall beside me. Blood ticks towards the ground as the explosion sounds. That wasn't Oliver and for sure wasn't a spud gun. I cough inhaling smoke and dirt.

I won't see Oliver again, that friendship is over. I'm in the wilds, somewhere along the walls of the Inner with bombs dropping around me. It's amazing how steady my heart beats, it doesn't even skip as the bombs drop down. My sim-training for pilot patrolling conditioned me to stay steady and calm in situations like this.

My wrist aches but I push through it and stand just in time to get blown backwards by another dropping bomb. It slammed into the wall and swelled out to me.

The noise of concrete falling is shattering. It wails like a clap of thunder does when it lands within arms reach. This time my ears hum and sing the high-pitched siren squeal that means a part of them are dying. I'll never hear the same again.

Smoke wraps around me the same way it did my craft after I slammed it nose first into the wall months ago. The thick black smoke closes in, burning my nostrils and eyes. My hands shake as I lift my shirt to shield myself.

The fabric just covers my mouth as I'm blasted from above by a cutting light. It's a hovercraft and the light beams bounce around me until I'm directly in its path. This must be how it ends I think as I drop to my knees.

"Show no resistance and you won't be harmed," a voice echoes from the craft.

I can't make out the base from where I'm kneeling. I rise to my feet to get a better view. An electric net wraps around me. It closes its grip and slams my body against the hardened ground before it scoops me towards the craft.

The electric barbs cause spasms in my muscles sending me into a state of rigidity. I'm stiffen as the coursing electricity stabs my body. 'Not be harmed' I think to myself as my skin feels the jabs. I've been caught and this is just the beginning.

Chapter 10: Nessa

The cot is cold and sterile beneath me as the bony parts of my body drive into its hard top. I run my hands across my legs, wincing as I come to the purple and green bruises. I'd gotten them during the mission, but I think today's parachute landings intensified the pain.

The room is windowless but I know it's late. The hours of night march past me as my mind twirls together in a confusing dance. I can't expect clarity in times like this. I've got too many possibilities bouncing around to hope for that.

There's the constant awareness that at this very moment Garrett is being held as a prisoner and most likely is being tortured in some sick and horrible way. The moments before now and the moments until I rescue him will be filled with his suffering. Central will take him apart bit by bit to get to me.

I pull my ponytail down. My hair rests against my cheeks as I try focusing on anything but him. With enough effort I dull the pain, but not for long. It's like having a healing wound that's constantly exposed and vulnerable to the ever-changing world around it.

I pull my hair back, piling it on my head as I think about Ty. My jaw clenches and my teeth grind back and forth. I'm mad at myself for not going to him last night when Jake offered. It wasn't right of me to leave him alone in the hospital but I couldn't risk seeing him.

He's the only person that could change my mind. I want to believe that I'm fixed on saving Garrett no matter what but I know if anyone could steer me away it would be Ty. I like thinking that no one could talk me out of saving Garrett, but that would be a lie. It's hard to admit that I'm weak, but I am. I feel like the worn out trees at the end of fall. So strong and vibrant on the outside yet swaying below the surface is weakness and dullness that's waiting to show.

If I look deep into my soul I recognize my weakness. I tell myself that saving Garrett and surrendering myself is something I *need* to do because it's right. I pretend to believe it without question. That's not the truth though, deep down in the pit of my gut I question it. I question if I'm making a mistake going after Garrett and I question if I'm strong enough to save him and myself.

I pull my hair down again letting it frame my face. Just because Ty would have tried to convince me to stay doesn't justify me leaving him like this. He would never do that to me. My stomach feels like it's a wet cloth that's being wrung dry. It twists over and over again.

The room feels a hundred degrees hotter as my stomach grinds and my head spins. It's sickening having so much responsibility and guilt. I can't determine what is right or wrong but I have to trust that the decisions I've made were the best I could make at the time.

The back of my neck starts sweating and I pull my hair up into a ponytail again. I can't get Ty, Garrett or Central out of my head. Pacing around the windowless room doesn't calm me but I find myself doing it. The duffle bag Jake put in the corner sits tilted at an angle, the green and black camouflage pattern stands out against the dark walls.

I pace the room over and over until I'm about to lose my mind. The camouflage bag calls to me and finally I give in, dragging it to the cot. My arms shake by the time I've made it across the room. I hoist the monstrous bag onto the metal bed, it slams down with an echoing strike.

The black straps cross around the bag and I take my time pulling them open. A pair of white sneakers fall out. What was wrong with the boots I wore today? I shove the shoes aside pulling out a pink shirt rolled inside a pair of white shorts. I can't help rolling my eyes, apparently this is the costume they expect me to be delivered to Central in. I might die in this hideous outfit. I reach into the bag and smile immediately. My hand wraps around the gun, I don't need to pull it out to tell it's my sidearm.

My hand dives farther into the bottom of the bag reaching a notepad and pen. Clint's already added a few pages into the book. He's included the aerial shot of Central, where we are supposed to land, and the mission details he's afraid I'll forget.

I twirl the pen around, the ink slides from tip to end. I can't bring myself to see Ty but I could always write to him. I could try telling him why I'm doing this. Maybe he'll believe me. I'm not sure if that's possible since I don't truly understand all the reasons why I'm about to risk so much to do this. I try telling myself I'd be risking more if I stay.

I clear a space on the foot of the cot. My knees nearly press to my chest as I hover over the pad of paper. I stare into space for a long time before my pen finally meets paper.

I write my thoughts and feeling, it's my stream of consciousness in words. My fears and hopes written in one place for one person to see. It makes me vulnerable but in that vulnerability I find peace. By the time I finish exhaustion has found me. It was either the passing of countless minutes or the act of bearing my soul to Ty that did it.

The paper creases as I fold it neatly, it makes me think about Garrett and the paper notes he used to fold for me. I imagine his strong hands folding them for me and I wonder if he still does it.

The cot doesn't feel as hard as it did last night, maybe I'm getting used to it or perhaps I'm just too tired to notice. My eyes close and I drop into a deep sleep that comes fast. My mind turns off, it powers down like the hovercrafts do when the engines stop.

"Nessa, Nessa," Kara's voice is soft as she shakes me side to side.

My eyes snap open, it felt like I'd fallen asleep minutes before. Maybe I had, I don't know.

"Yeah." I say pushing to my elbows.

"I wanted to talk to you before the others got here." Kara looks to the cot, her eyes fill with tears that she fights to hold onto.

"It's okay Kara, everything is going to be fine." I reach to her shoulder, my hand feels strange resting there but she needs comfort.

She reaches forward hugging me tight. Her body bounces up and down jolting me as she sobs in silence. Finally the sobbing slows and she pushes back to look at me, tears still threatening to fall.

"You don't have to do this Nessa."

"Yes I do." I say immediately.

"Brian said the same thing when he went over the walls. He said he *had* to do it. That was six years ago and I can't move on. It's like my soul is frozen in time, I can't move in any direction."

I've never seen Kara this way before, I look at her as strong and independent, nothing like she's describing.

"That's not true. You've spent six years saving people's lives, you saved mine and Ty's and countless others."

"What you see is a facade. On the inside I've been hollow for years. He was my world, my best friend…he still is."

I wrap my hand around hers.

"The first two nights I forgot he wasn't coming home, I even put two settings on the table. When a week came and went without word I knew something bad had happened. The not knowing chipped at me bit by bit. Every night for six years I've set his dinner plate out. I pretend he'll walk through the front door and I'll have my best friend back." Kara inhales, rolling her watery eyes.

"I'm so sorry Kara."

"It's not your fault." She says, spinning her wedding band around. "If you see him, tell him I love him." She hardly squeaks out the last word as her sobbing starts again.

"We'll find them. Clint and the others will bring them home." I rub her back as it quakes under my hand.

"Don't trust anyone out there, you look out for yourself." She says it fast, like the words are beyond her control.

"Excuse me?" I ask caught off guard.

"I want to believe that Jon and Clint will fight for you but I don't know for sure. The people backing this mission have been working on a way to get Brian and the others home long before you came into the picture." She pauses, wiping her nose. "I would give almost anything to see Brian again but I don't think it is right to risk an innocent life to get him. Jon and the others don't always think the same way I do. To them it is the mission at any cost and I can't be sure getting you out is part of their mission."

The cot presses into my folded legs. Of course I could be used as bait and nothing more. I'd briefly entertained that notion last night. It is one thing to think of it fleetingly, and another to hear it suggested by an outsider. It makes the notion seem all that more possible. It was an idea that bounced in my head but I snuffed the ember out before it could take hold. Having Kara say it sparks the flame into existence and it grows in my mind.

"I'll look after myself Kara. Thanks for telling me." My smile is weak but I force it anyway.

Kara stands from the cot and stares down at me with her sad and empty eyes. "I'll see you before you go, I just had to talk to you alone, and I wanted you to know the risks."

I nod, reaching into my duffle bag.

"Can you do me a favor?" I ask.

"Of course."

"It's two things actually, look after Emma and papa while I'm gone." She nods, "No matter how long I'm gone?" I ask with my voice cracking.

"No matter how long, I promise."

"And can you give this to Ty?" I ask handing her the letter. It feels heavy in my hand and I'm thankful when she reaches to take it.

"I will and we will all be here waiting for you."

Kara's curly hair bounces as she walks towards the door. I sit on the edge of the bed letting everything settle. All the particles of my life slowly drop into the dark part of my brain and I just breathe.

Chapter 11: Nessa

In less than an hour I leave for Central. I press my head against the wall willing myself to focus.

"Nessa, it's me again." Kara says knocking on the door.

"Come in." I sit straight adjusting my pink top so it sits over my stark white shorts.

Kara closes the door behind her and I find myself staring at the solid metal briefcase she's carrying.

"What's that?"

"Clint said he mentioned the sonar tracker you'd have? Did he?"

"Yeah, he did." My feet slide from the chair I'd been sitting on.

"No, you can stay sitting." Kara says stopping me from getting up.

As Kara opens the briefcase I twist my face without meaning to. I have virtually no control over my facial expressions so everyone around me knows what I'm thinking by watching my reactions.

"We have to implant two devices. The first will be deep, below the muscle." I never considered myself to have a weak stomach but my gut clenches as Kara talks. "The second one is more superficial. That's the one Central will find and remove."

"Find it how?"

"They will scan you and locate the device in your forearm. They will take it out and that should be the end of it."

"Won't they scan me again?"

"They could but Clint and the others don't think it's likely."

Apparently Kara has a hard time controlling her facial expressions too because it's clear that she's just as worried as me.

"Alright, whatever it takes." I swallow as I set my mind to it. "Where does it go?"

Kara's warm hand wraps around my wrist. My skin feels a chill from the cool table she places it on. Kara turns the briefcase towards me sending my eyes bugging. The device looks like a gun, more like a play gun that kids would use.

She sets the gun aside and opens the first container that was tucked in the case. A tiny metal capsule pings onto the white towel she laid out. I stare at it, it's about the size of the pills they used to give me when I was in the hospital for my burns.

"This is the sonar detector. It's the one that goes deep." She hovers a wand over the top of the capsule until it flashes red. "It's on and ready." She says faking a smile.

The needle she fastens to the gun looks more like a giant pointed straw. "You're going to use that?" I ask panicked.

"Yes. It's the smallest for a device this large."

It's long and wide and I hurt just looking at it. She locks the thick needle into place. Kara loads the capsule into the gun and I feel like I'm about to faint.

The room gets hot and my skin feels clammy. She wipes my arm off with an alcohol pad and stares at me for a second. Finally she aims the gun to my forearm. She presses slightly as my skin sinks in.

"I've got to place this next to the bone, it's going to hurt."

My eyes burst with light as she drives the needle down into my forearm. She pushes quick and hard breaking through my skin and crossing the under layers as she aims for the bone.

"I'm almost there." She says driving the needle deeper.

My forehead flecks with drops of sweat that form fast. I look at the thick rounded needle that is now submerged into my arm and jolt as unbelievable pain grips me.

"It's against the bone." She says.

Right as I exhale she wraps her finger around the trigger, pulling it back. The capsule shoots through the chamber and slams into my bone. For a second there's a black curtain that descends over my face, I'm about to pass out.

"Nessa! Stay with me." Kara shouts and I pull myself back.

Kara holds the gun in place as she opens the other container. "This is the second implant, the one they'll take out."

The tiny capsule flicks red as she loads it into the chamber. She lifts her hand upwards pulling the needle away from my bone and back towards the surface. She holds the tip of the needle steady inside the meaty part of my muscle.

"It's going directly into the muscle this time." She says wrapping her finger around the trigger.

I wrap the front of my feet around the legs of my chair and squeeze every muscle in my body tight.

"Do it." I nod.

Her finger pulls back against the trigger and a scream. The capsule drives into my muscle, pushing the fibers out of its way.

"All done." She says pulling the needle from my arm.

Kara wraps my arm in gauze as I try fighting back tears.

"How will they take it out?" I ask as she tapes the last bandage in place.

There are her sympathetic and apologetic eyes again. They tell me everything I need to know.

"It's okay, you don't have to tell me."

Her sheepish smile confirms that I'm about to voluntarily endure horrible things at the hands of Central.

"Knock, knock," Zane says from outside the door.

"Come in," Kara shouts as she closes her briefcase.

I recognize Zane as soon as he steps though the door. He's got the same dirty brown hair and black rimmed glasses that he wore when he changed Ty and my identities before the mission. I didn't realize how short he was before, I guess the only time we met he was sitting.

"I just need to check the sonar implant before we head out." He says opening his tablet.

"I'm going to excuse myself, I'll be right outside." Kara says nodding to me.

"Thanks Kara," I say staring down at my throbbing arm.

Zane pushes his fingertips against his tablet and the screen flashes on. He types furiously as he pulls open what he needs.

"The moment of truth." He says with his finger hovering over a red button on his screen.

He pauses building suspense before he drives his finger down against the button. It feels anticlimactic. I'm not sure what I was waiting for but I assumed there would be something to let me know the sonar implant was working.

Zane nervously smiles, "Just give it a second…"

I stare at the tablet and let the seconds pass in awkward silence. I tap my fingers and on the second tap my eyes catch hold of the screen coming to life. I do a double take wondering if my eyes are playing tricks on me.

"Wahoo!" Zane shouts banging his fist.

Little by little a digital hologram of the hole is built three dimensionally in front of me. The iridescent blue beams of light span across the room to create a blueprint of the entire building.

"Is that Kara?" I ask as the outline of a body forms in the hologram. She's pacing up and down the hall just outside the room.

"Sure is." Zane answers beaming like a kid.

There's a flashing red dot that must be me. The dot sits across from the outline of Zane. I see us both inside this room in real-time. Zane gets up and starts flailing his arms and legs. He does jumping jacks and leaps.

"What are you doing?" I ask surprised.

"Look," he says pointing to the hologram.

Sure enough the outline of Zane jumps and twists almost in time to his exact movements.

"That's amazing." I say awed.

He stops mid leap and stares, "Thanks," he says pushing his glasses back to his face. "I created it."

I can tell he's proud of his creation; he stares at the hologram like papa stared at me when I stood on stage at the leap banquet.

"This will give us a huge advantage won't it?" I ask.

"Oh yes, we'll get the layout of Central and be able to keep track of where you are and who you're with." He smiles as he stares one last time at the hologram. He powers it off just as Jake comes through the door.

"It's time to go." Jake says knocking on the doorframe with his bony knuckles.

"Thanks for doing this Zane." I say as we walk towards the door. He nods his head and leaves with his tablet tucked under his arm.

The team is outside the door waiting for us. "You need to put these on for the jump," Marcus says holding out two uniforms for Zane and me.

I reach for my uniform. Marcus is already in his suit. I can still see the tattoos that span around his forearm and wrists.

"We'll keep an eye on ya, buddy." Gavin says slapping Zane on the back. Zane staggers looking up at Gavin. I still can't get over how tall Gavin is.

"Great." Zane smiles uncomfortably. Liv rolls her eyes as she props herself against the wall behind her. Clearly she's still bitter about being paired with Zane.

"Attention team!" Clint yells walking towards us. We all stand a little taller as he makes his way forward. "What's the report on the sonar?" Clint asks Zane.

"It was amazing, I could see the room, building, and it was even..." Clint cuts him off.

"Will it work? That's all I care about."

Liv giggles and I find myself shooting her a death stare. She is so rude.

Zane scratches his head, wounded and shocked that not everybody finds his invention as amazing as him.

"Yes," he says pushing his glasses back to the bridge of his nose.

"Excellent, Gavin and Liv you will be escorting Zane. Remember his safety is your primary objective." Gavin and Liv nod. "Once we land, you three will head north. There is high ground for you to settle down in. Our team will approach from the South. Liam and Marcus will need to assume the identities of two Regulators. They will be the ones to escort Nessa in."

My brain swirls. I don't know how they plan to assume the identities of Regulators but I suppose that's their concern not mine.

"They'll take her inside the facility to hand her over. After that they will try making contact with the other objectives. As soon as you find Natasha, Dustin, or Natalie, radio back."

"Or Garrett?" I say reminding Clint.

"Of course, Garrett too."

"We will be operating offline, cutting off communication with people on this side of the wall. We can't have their incoming signals giving our position away." Clint claps his hands together making an echoing snap. "Let's go!" He yells.

As Clint talked it became more and more obvious that this plan could go very wrong. That didn't seem to matter to the rest of Clint's team, they march loyally behind him. Their oversized and powerful bodies sway as they walk. Liv's got a sniper rifle slung across her shoulders, Gavin's cargo suit is covered in explosives and knives that spill out of every pocket. Marcus keeps pace with Clint, his rifle in hand. Liam's red hair stands out as he makes his way near the back of the team. His black backpack pulls at him but he keeps moving forward.

Clint pushes the door to the hole open. I control my gut this time and try focusing on my breathing. I pass the ring Ty and I used to train in, Kara's sitting on one of the benches. She stands running over to me.

"Good luck Nessa, be safe." She says hugging me tight.

"Take care of my family Kara." I say hugging her back.

It's harder than I expected to pull away but somehow I let Kara go. I'm the last to exit the hole and the door slams closed behind me with a loud bang.

The hover is parked and I see Gavin hoist Zane inside. I set my eyes straight for the craft and try to focus on breathing.

Less than a minute and I'll be taking off towards Central. I know it's crazy but I have to try to save Garrett.

Chapter 12: Ty

"You should avoid any strenuous activities for at least four weeks. Drainage is normal but if you're changing the bandages more than twice a day you should come back."

"Yup, sounds good." I say rushing this along.

The nurse is just rambling at this point. I'm about to jump outta my head I'm so anxious to get outta this hospital and see Nessa. I can't understand why she hasn't come to see me for two days.

"Do you have any questions?" She asks.

I try not to laugh. How could I have questions, she just spent the last thirty minutes talking me through every scenario possible.

"Nope, I'm ready to go." I smile trying to gloss over my hurried tone.

"In that case we just need you to sign here," she says pointing to the bottom of her tablet.

There's a blink of hesitation as I wonder which name to use. I can sign as Eric or go back to Ty. Our cover seems blown at this point so I might as well be Ty again.

I swipe my name across the tablet and launch out of bed. I grunt as soon as my leg touches down.

"Are you alright?" The nurse asks with her voice jumping a few octaves.

"Yea, just been a while since I stood up. Fine now." I smile hoping she won't see my pain.

I didn't expect walking to feel like a knife being driven and twisted into my thigh with each step. I grab the crutches the therapist left in the room yesterday. I'd blown her off when she came with them, I guess I should have practiced after all.

I teeter my way down the hall with my crutches in tow. Part of me wants to yelp whenever my leg touches down. They did the surgery my first night here. They got the bullet out and stitched me up but it hurts as my weight pushes on it. I'm sorta surprised the bullet wound to my back doesn't hurt so much, I woulda thought it would be worse.

Jon came earlier and said he'd meet me by the nurse's station when I got out. I hobble towards the station and imagine him and Nessa waiting there. Maybe Jon and the others had rescued my family too and they'll be here waiting for me. It will be a big surprise reunion. I bet that's why Nessa hasn't visited, she's been too busy with our families.

I try tricking my brain into believing that, but I know it isn't the truth. I've felt too many of Nessa's emotions lately and there weren't many good ones mixed in there. I think about my parents and my brothers. There's a parta me that knows they won't be here. One day I'm gonna have to go find them. It has to be sooner rather than later. Central might hurt them to get to me. I couldn't live with myself if that ever happened. Once I know Nessa's safe I'll go get them.

I inhale right before I round the corner, that optimistic part of my brain hopes the room will be filled with people I love but I take my turn and see Jon sitting alone.

"Ty," he says smiling as he walks towards me.

"Hey Jon." I look around like maybe it's a joke and Nessa's around the corner.

"Listen Ty, there's something we need to talk about." Jon says as he watches my eyes dart side to side looking for Nessa.

"Where is she?" I ask.

The way Jon runs his hand through his hair tells me I'm not gonna like what he's about to say.

"She's leaving today, she's going to Central," he looks at his watch. "Actually she should be leaving any minute now."

"What, with who? Take me to her!" I shout.

"Listen Ty," Jon says as I cut him off.

"Jon, I don't care what you're about to say, take me to Nessa."

I struggle down the hall towards the exit and thump my way down the stairs with my crutches. Jon's behind me trying to reason with me.

"She knows what she's doing. Clint and his team are with her."

I wheel around to Jon, "You worried I'll talk her out of this? What's in it for you?"

"It's not like that." Jon answers.

"Bullshit, I'm not an idiot. I don't know what sorta game you're playing but I'll figure it out. Stop stalling and take me to Nessa."

Jon's pissed but I don't care about that. He climbs into his hover next to me and flings it forward. We pass the buildings and streets Nessa and I used to run along on our way to Clint's.

"They are scheduled to leave in three minutes, chances are we won't make it." Jon turns onto another street, keeping the hover under the speed limit.

"Suddenly concerned with speeding?" I say reaching across to thrust the throttle down. We lunge forward as the hover flies full speed.

"Are you crazy?" Jon screams trying to pry my hand off the accelerator.

"Desperate but not crazy."

It doesn't take him long to quit fighting, he needs both hands to steer. I've got a million thoughts pounding inside my head as Jon pulls towards the hole. I think about what I'll say to Nessa once I get there. There's gotta be a way I can convince her to stay.

I'll tell her I love her and beg her not to go. I'll offer to go instead of her, actually I'll *demand* it. Maybe then she'll stay or at least take me with her.

I'll kiss her when I see her too, 'cuz I've wanted to do that for days now. I've got no options other than to get myself to Nessa and keep her close, I don't wanna think about the alternative.

We take the last turn before Clint's place, I loosen my grip from the throttle and yank my seatbelt off. We turn and everything seems in slow motion as I see Nessa walking towards the hover up ahead.

Her auburn hair swirls in the wind. Her white sneakers push off the sidewalk and towards the hover. This might be my only chance to see her. I push the door open and jump outta Jon's hover. My body cracks as I hit the pavement. I'm pretty sure the nurse didn't say anything about jumping outta moving hovers.

Jon slams our hover to a stop and I push to my feet screaming for Nessa. One leg hangs planted on the ground, her other foot is already inside the hover. She hesitates so I scream louder.

My chest draws as she steps outta the hover and turns to me. She stares at me with her big blue eyes looking through me, cutting me deep.

"Nessa!" I scream again.

She gives the weakest smile I've ever seen, almost like it's meant to be an apology. I've seen people flash a smile like that before, usually when they pity something but don't have the desire to help it out.

"Nessa don't go! Don't do this!" I scream as she stares.

My heart feels like it's smashed to pieces. Nessa turns to the hover and hoists herself inside as it takes off. I know it might be the last time I see her.

"We'll bring her back Ty." Jon says from above me.

I'm hunched over on all fours. The cut to my thigh drips with blood but I don't care about that.

"I'm not letting her do this without me." I grunt.

"You're in no condition to travel, let alone fight." Jon snaps.

It pisses me off that he says it but what bothers me more is that I know he's right. I take the crutches from Jon and lift to my feet.

Everything I'd planned has gone up in smoke. I might not get her back again. If I'd had a chance maybe I coulda convinced her to stay.

The door to the hole opens and we both turn to see who it is.

"Ty, Jon?" Kara says.

"What are you doing here?" I ask.

"Ty, what have you done to your leg!" She rushes over, her medical training taking over.

"It's fine, don't worry about it. What are you doing here?" I ask again holding my hand up to stop her from coming closer.

"I was saying my goodbyes." Kara says staring down at the bloodied bandage that must be driving her insane.

"Did you talk to Nessa?" I choke.

"I did. She wanted me to give you this," Kara reaches into her pocket, pulling out a note.

I grab it from her hand and squeeze it tight. I pretend it brings me closer to Nessa.

I'm pretty much silent as Jon takes me back to his loft. He's back to flying at top speeds as he weaves towards his place. We ride in awkward silence. The note gradually feels heavier and heavier the longer I hold it.

"Coming inside?" Jon asks as we idle in front of the loft.

"In a minute, I need to be alone first." I answer. Jon nods before sliding outta the hover.

I move extra slow opening the note. There's something about not knowing what she wrote that makes me feel like this whole thing isn't happening.

Finally I lay it open. I feel tears burning around my eyes from just looking at her writing. These words were put there by her and I miss her already.

Ty,

There's so much for me to be sorry about lately and I feel every one of those things so deeply. I'm sorry for not telling you that I love you sooner. I have loved you for a long time, I just didn't know how to say it until it was almost too late. I'm sorry that I'm leaving you. I'm sorry that I'm not strong enough to see you before I go. I know my heart enough to know you are where it wants to be for all of time. If I saw you, my heart would win and I would stay.

I don't expect you to understand my reasons for going, I couldn't expect you to since I question them myself. Sometimes the hardest thing to do is have faith and to let that faith lead you. I keep telling myself that I have faith in us and that we are going to be together again. I don't believe it's possible for me to have found you and to lose you so quickly. I have faith that once this is done we will be together again.

You are my present and my future but I have my past. Garrett was my past and I can't forget that, or him. Central captured him, they will kill him if I'm not turned over by the end of the week. I can't risk him being killed for me.

I want you to remember that he is my past and once he is safe you are my future. I am doing this because in my head I know it is right and in my heart I have faith that we will be together again.

I am so sorry for everything you have been through. Please look after Emma and papa while I'm gone. Stay strong and safe and no matter what, don't come after me.

Love-

Nessa

I know her better than she thinks. As soon as that reporter came on the broadcast the other day showing Garrett's beat-down face I knew she'd leave. I knew she was strong enough to take the risk and fight for him.

If it wasn't for the medications they kept me pumped full of I woulda gone to her earlier. Staring at the letter makes my eyes burn. I keep them open wide and stare at her writing sprawled on the note. My finger traces the letter and lands over the word '*love*,' I know she loves me but I'm not sure that's enough to bring her back.

Kara's knocking on the window jolts me, sending me nearly outta my seat. I push the door open, "Yeah?" I say.

"Can I talk to you?" She asks coming around to the other side.

"What's going on?" I ask as she slides into the pilot's seat.

"You should know that everything I'm about to tell you Nessa knows already." I stare at Kara, I see my green eyes reflected in her pupils. I look hostile without meaning to.

"Okay." I say.

"Nessa's on her way to Central with Clint and his crew. They have Zane with them to help with the surveillance end. They are going to use Nessa as bait to get inside Central."

"They can't do that, they'll kill her."

"They are willing to take the chance. Nessa is too."

My hair swings wildly as I shake my head, "Why the hell is everyone so wrapped up in saving Garrett?"

"It's not all about Garrett. They're there to rescue others too." Kara reaches into her pocket pulling out a small stack of faded and crumpled photographs. "This is Brian, he is my husband." She flips the picture, "Then there's Dustin, another researcher that went with the group. Natasha, Jake's sister." She flips to the last picture and I feel my gut wad, "Jon's wife Natalie was the lead researcher."

I literally feel my face screw into a tight ball outta confusion. "What are you talking about?"

"They developed a cure for the side effects of the conciliate serum. They were supposed to be gone a week. That was six years ago. They went to Central to share their research and that was the last we ever heard of them."

"Central's got them?"

"We only have confirmation on Natalie. We don't know about the others but we have our theories. That's the real reason Jon and Clint are bringing Nessa over there."

I imagine my face looks strange and twisted as I stare at Kara. "What about saving Garrett and bringing Nessa back?"

Kara tucks the photos back into her pocket, "I'd like to believe they will fight for them, but I can't say for sure."

"Nessa knows all this?"

"Yes, she knows everything." Kara stops to space out. I imagine she's thinking about that guy in the photo, Brian, her husband. "I'll meet you inside." She finally says breaking the silence that was sitting heavy.

The hover door shuts and I'm left by myself again. This time I'm pissed. My fists smack against the front dash of the hover. The bones crack inside my knuckles but it's not something I really notice. I'm mad at Nessa for going, I'm mad at myself for not being with her and I'm pissed and scared outta my mind that Clint might leave her in Central.

My bloodied knuckles burn as I hobble up the steps to Jon's loft. I'm beaten worse than when I first crawled up these stairs many months ago.

I'd stood on his stoop dressed in my torn and dirty scout uniform just waiting to be shot on the spot. If I knew then what I know now, I wonder how much of it I woulda done differently.

I push the door open, my crutches echo against Jon's clean and polished floor. "Ty! Welcome home." Jon says with a forced smile.

"I'm not home yet. Home is with Nessa."

"Can I talk to you?" Jon asks leading me into the side room Nessa and I shared.

"It's your house."

Jon closes the door behind us, "I'm not sure what Kara told you," he starts.

I cut him off, "She pretty much told me everything. She told me about Natalie and the others. She told me that they are the reason Clint and Nessa are really goin' to Central. Tell me Jon, do you plan on saving Nessa?"

"Of course!" He jerks his head back like he's offended I even asked.

"If she doesn't make it back you *will* answer to me." I say stepping towards him. My face is hot, all the blood and anger rush to it.

"I wouldn't expect anything less." Jon answers. "I don't want there to be animosity between us Ty. You've known from the start that our organization had our own motives. Maybe you didn't know exactly what they were but you didn't really question them either."

He's right but I won't tell him that. I should have asked why he was willing to help me but maybe that wouldn't have mattered. Back then I woulda done anything to save Nessa.

"How about you get cleaned up and meet us in the kitchen. Nessa's father and her sister are here."

I nod and make my way to the bath. The shower blasts hot steam as I undress. My pants stick to my bloodied leg but I tug them off. I step my foot into the tub and that's when I feel her. Nessa's doing something she doesn't like. I feel the sorta fear that happens when you're on the verge of doing something deadly.

My heart pounds, drumming and vibrating my chest as her fear builds. I've never felt it this strongly before. I clutch my chest as my heart feels close to exploding. The shower steams as I crash to the floor.

Chapter 13: Garrett

I can barely open my eyes as I slip in and out of consciousness. The last thing I remember was the electric shocks running up and down my body. Every nerve was set on edge as they branched around me.

"He's waking up," a man off to my side says.

"Move over, let me see." Another answers.

I was on the edge of the Inner, somewhere near the wall when they found me. I remember the bombs, explosions and the electric net dropping around me.

I'm not sure I'll ever get out of this predicament. I'd promised Nessa's father and myself that I would save her or die trying. I suppose it's the 'die trying' part that I've gotten myself into.

"Hand me that," the one says standing above my head.

My eye bursts with light as he pries my lid open. The pen light shines bright and almost fluorescent.

"We've still got a while before he's back. Let's head in for orders."

"What should we do with him?"

"Keep him alive until we talk with the boss."

They would have known I was from Central if I'd been wearing my white uniform, I'm thankful I changed into Don's green ones before leaving.

Once they get me to Central they will figure out who I am. I wonder if they will try and extract my thoughts like they did to Oliver's father.

My jaw clenches, I wonder if Oliver will guard me in the cells. I remember our last day of basic sim-training. We'd been assigned to adjoining pods, which was fine by me. It meant that during our breaks Oliver and I got to hang out. It was time I appreciated because soon enough he'd be assigned to guard sims and I would be sent to my pilot patrol ones.

The last day of basics we came out of the pods at the exact same time, both of us winded and sweating as usual.

"Did you have that giant robot with rotating blades on its arms and legs?" Oliver asked wiping his brow.

"Yeah, I had him, he was a bastard."

"How'd you kill it?" He asked.

"You know how it windmills towards you?" Oliver nodded, "I sort of dove between the blades."

"No way, that's insane."

"He had me cornered, it was my only move. I leapt through and got behind him, I drove my knife right to the sweet spot."

"Right in the back!" He said as we punched our fists together.

"I'm glad that part of training is done." I said closing the cover to my sim pod.

"Yea, me too. Sucks we won't be in the same group anymore though."

"We'll still hang out." I answered.

"I've got a surprise," Oliver said slapping me on the back.

My crooked smile flashed. Oliver's surprises usually involved blowing something up.

"Meet me in an hour at the fence where the running track used to be?" He asked.

I rushed through my shower and I remember feeling a pang of guilt as I ran towards the park. It felt wrong being excited about something here in Central. I told myself that Central was temporary and no matter what I had to get back to Nessa.

No amount of fun out here would ever take that need away, but it still felt strange to have moments where it didn't hurt so much. I was used to having a void inside me and whenever that void felt smaller it always caught me off guard.

"Over here!" Oliver shouted waving to me as I approached the fence. The outline of the city spanned around us as I sloshed in the boggy park towards him.

"What's this surprise?" I asked staring at the mosquitoes that hovered around the marshy field.

"This way," Oliver said waving me to follow. "You can't tell anyone about this." He said marching through the field.

"I won't." I said looking over my shoulder.

The bushes and trees that probably used to be neat and perfectly shaped like the other parks had overtook the park now. We sloshed through the field and were swallowed by the green trees and bushes. It reminded me of the path that Nessa and I used to take to our secret spot by the river.

As we walked I saw flashes of Nesssa running through the trees and I imagined her doing that every day since I left for Central. I'd taken that path in my head every night since I'd come to Central. Every night I'd pretend she'd be there too and we would be together again.

"Almost there," Oliver said leading me into the brush.

"Anyone else use this?" I asked, noticing a trail had been beaten down.

"Nope, just me." He said stopping in his tracks. He pointed down to the ground, "Trip wire, step over it, and be careful." He lifted his leg up and over the virtually invisible wire.

"One of Centrals?" I asked

"One of mine. One of the ways I know nobody else has found this place."

"What happens if I hit it?"

Oliver looked back, his scarred face pulling up towards his skull, "Ka-boom!" He yelled throwing his hands in the air.

"Man you're nuts."

"I'm kidding, you'd get stuck in a snare."

"You know how to make snares?" I asked shocked. "I didn't think you had to learn those things in Central."

"I didn't learn them in education. One of my cousins I stayed with for a while was a researcher. He developed the curriculum for the Inner sectors. I used to sneak into his library at night and read his books."

Oliver had some pretty great opportunities given to him. It was wrong to think that because the circumstances around it were horrible but I still thought it.

"I'm not supposed to know half the stuff I do but I suppose when you grow up with so many people it just happens." He kept walking, winding through the brush. "We're almost there. You can't show anyone this, ever. I shouldn't even know about it."

"How do you?" I asked.

He looked back at me, for a second he was lost inside his head. "I lived with my aunt right after my mom died. Her place is a few blocks from here. She was older than my mom but they looked a lot alike. My skin was still raw and healing and I'm sure I looked horrible. She reminded me of my mom and I reminded her of the way her sister had died. She couldn't look at my face without shutting her eyes and puckering her lips. It was like it physically hurt her to look at me."

Oliver kept walking, shoving branches out of his way, "I'd disappear for hours on end, and she didn't bother to care. I suppose if I was out of sight then I was out of mind. I started coming here because it was abandoned. Every other place in Central was full. The streets, buildings, hovers and parks were full of people that stared at me. Some felt sorry and other were just disgusted by me. It didn't matter which they felt, both hurt. It hurt when they would stare and it hurt when they would turn away. This abandoned place never had eyes to stare or hurt me with." He looked down to his boots, "I used to walk around. Usually I'd kick a rock and try to forget the sounds and smells of the fire. One day I kicked it down this way and that's how I found this." He said pulling a hedge of branches away from the concrete wall.

"Does that go where I think it does?" I said automatically.

"If you mean into the Capital, then yes."

I stared at Oliver as he beamed at me. I would have looked the same I guess. This was his prized possession, his top secret.

"Can you get in?" I asked staring at the faded paint that hovered above the door. "Zone 4," I said reading the writing. "Where does that take you?"

Oliver grinned as he reached behind one of the bushes. "All it took was a bit of man power and one homemade explosive," he said lifting a rusted crowbar. "I found this door when I was a kid so you can imagine the number of days I spent staring at it. I threw rocks at it, hit it with sticks, ran at it. Naturally it wouldn't open." He slid the crowbar near one of the hinges.

"I didn't get the door open until I was a teenager. I'd moved in with my uncle, the regulator that designed weapons. That's where I learned how to make explosives. The first one was crude but it did the trick." He pulled up the sleeve of his shirt and pointed to a massive scar that traced around his elbow. "A piece of the door flew off and hit me."

"You're crazy." I smiled at Oliver.

I'd never met someone that was so clearly bold. "Weren't you scared they would find out? I mean they would have exiled you or something for trying to break into the Capital."

"I don't really worry about things like that. What will be will be." He said jamming the crowbar into the last link of the worn door. He pulled against the bar and there was a sudden metal snap as the door fell from its worn hinges.

"Come on in, welcome to my home." Oliver said stepping over the threshold into a dark hall. It smelled musty and the air was heavy with old moisture.

I followed him, trying not to cough. "Your home? That's a joke right?"

He turned to smile, "Watch out" he said pointing to another wire. "Just one of my safeguards to ensure my refuge hasn't been compromised." He said smiling as I stepped over the wire.

"So you sleep here and everything?"

"Yeah, most of the time. Sometimes I bounce to my cousins or uncle's house for a day or two. I don't do it for the human company, I do it to get more ideas. I wait until they fall asleep and then I sneak into their studies and read about weapons or traps or whatever I can get my hands on."

That was about the time I started to realize how complicated Oliver was. I'd never met someone so engrossed in survival or destruction, though I suppose it made sense. This was the mind of a kid who had watched his own mother burn to death and who had been left to die by his father. I guess it would make sense that there would be some residual effects from something like that.

"This way," Oliver said jerking his hand.

I followed his lead, stepping through scaffolding and metal beams that spanned the inside of the walls. We were in the bones of the building, the part that gave the Capital its structural stability without the aesthetic appeal. Giant cobwebs hung on either side of the path that Oliver had worn down. I still can't imagine breathing in all that dust and dirt on a daily basis.

Oliver hurdled through the maze of beams, he knew this place like the back of his hand. I followed behind with my eyes trying to adjust to the darkness around me.

"Almost there." Oliver said crouching down beside a metal duct.

He wedged his fingers into the sides of the grate and with one small jerk the entire front fell to the ground.

"I'll lead." He said belly crawling into the metal tunnel.

It was an air duct of some sort. I could tell by the path he was taking that we were making our way inside the Capital. We were moving away from the bones of the building and going deep into the actual facility.

"I've found pretty much all the rooms you could find." He said looking back over his shoulder. We came to a divide and he veered left. "I'll take you to the cells first."

My head was spinning. Was I really doing what I thought I was? We were trespassing inside the Capital and going to the cells, I thought for a second I was going to lose my breakfast.

Oliver crawled in front of me and looked like an animal, like a creature that was trained to do this. He slowed and turned to me, pressing his finger to his mouth to keep me quiet. My eyes narrowed, in front of him I could see the slits of another vent.

In the silence I heard a faint clanging like metal striking metal at a slow methodical rate. Oliver waved his hand forward and we crawled double time through the duct.

"Voila," he whispered as we came to a vent that dead ended.

"Wow," I said staring at the maze of glass cells filled with prisoners.

The clanging sound was louder than before and was enough to drive anyone insane. "The sound?" Oliver asked.

"Yea, where the heck is that coming from?" I asked leaning close so I wouldn't be heard by any regulators.

He pointed across the room. Sitting on her neatly made cot was a blonde haired woman, a tin cup in hand as she slowly beat it against the wall. Her blue eyes stared off into absentness.

"She's been like that for years." Oliver said.

I stared at the woman and felt sorry for her. I wondered if she was insane or dangerous. Maybe she had lost her mind and that's why they kept her locked up. Her hair was long and matted at her skull, her cheeks drawn-in and pinched. She was probably only in her thirties but she looked so much older than that. The empty eyes made me think about how Oliver had described his father when he'd gaze into space.

"She stops sometimes, shouts a few sentences and then cries." He said.

With the metal ticking in the background I looked around at the cells. Glass corrals with a hole in the floor, one sink and a bed. I remember feeling a wave of nausea once I realized the hole was supposed to be a bathroom. The outside of the doors had black keypads with a blue sensor. I was staring at the keypad when a humming sound whooshed from across the room. There was a flash of bright blue light passing the length of one of the corner tubes.

"What the heck is that?" I asked.

"They don't get any sunlight. They would get sick without it so they zap them with artificial rays. It cycles around, takes about an hour to make a full loop."

"They don't go outside?" I asked.

I thought getting exiled was the worst thing that could happen but suddenly I appreciated that this would be much worse.

"They only leave those tubes once every few months. I see a regulator escort them one at a time to that room," he said pointing to the center of the cells.

"What's in there?" I asked.

"Can't tell. I think it's something to do with medical. They always walk-in and end up having to be wheeled out with bandages around their heads."

The boots of a patrolling regulator sounded against the black floor below us. Oliver and I both recoiled and held our breath. The back of the regulators head turned left and right, my heart squeezed down hoping he wouldn't look up. He kept moving forward winding his way between the glass tubes. Most of the prisoners stared past him.

"I'm glad I got stationed here." Oliver said.

I was taken aback. To me it would be a nightmare to watch these people sit alone all day. "I want to know why they are here. I want to know them as people." Oliver said.

Sometimes at night I still have nightmares that I'm locked in one of those glass tubes. I wake up covered in sweat whenever I have those dreams. I guess nobody knows why any of us are the way we are, and I'll never be able to say what exactly drew Oliver to want that job.

We watched an entire artificial sun cycle digitally hum and blast the tubes before we backed out of the duct and made our way to the door bordering the park.

That next day Oliver and I began our separate training but we stayed in touch. We'd hang out between sim-pod trainings.

He took me back through the Capital two other times. Both times we'd stared at the prisoners. By then Oliver was already through most of his training and he knew some of the details about the regulators' routines. He'd point out the patterns the regulators were walking, the various security measures they took and things like that. As he got farther into his training he got more and more invested in the job. I remember being envious of him, jealous that he was so happy to be a guard.

I snap my eyes open as another bright light blasts in my face. "Who are you?" A gravelly voice barks, spit flicking onto my face.

My head feels disconnected and rolls sluggishly side to side. Ice water slaps me in the face and drenches me in bone chilling cold.

"What the hell did you do to him?" The gravelly voiced man asks.

"Nothing." I hear one of the men from earlier say. "We found him near the outer perimeter of quadrant three, just inside the Inner's walls. Nobody should be out that far. He either escaped a long time ago or he is a part of this somehow."

My head bobs and I black-out for a split second. A strong hand grabs under my chin.

"That doesn't answer my question. What the hell did you do to him?"

"He was already damaged goods. The bombs were going off and he was covered in dirt and blood. We just took him in."

"You use the net?" The man asks grabbing my limp arm and pulling my sleeve up. He drops my hand back to the side. "Apparently, look at those marks. You burned him all up."

I slowly peel my eyes open and stare down at my arm. Red welted lacerations run up and down the length of it. Marks left from the electric wires that paralyzed my body with zapping pain.

"Like I said, we didn't know who he was. He could have been dangerous. What the heck was he doing out there anyway?" The other says like people do when they try to cover their guilt.

My chapped lips stay stuck together. My jaw loosens and I try opening my mouth. My teeth separate but my dried lips stay sealed together.

"Get him some damn water!" The one shouts.

Steps ring across the room as one of them runs for water. Then cool liquid hits my lips, it separates my chapped skin and I swallow.

"That's enough." The man says and the other steps away.

"More," I say needing more water.

"Not until you tell me your name."

"Where am I?" I ask with my head rolling again.

"Bucket!" The one says. Ice water splashes across my face. It's so cold that my mind confuses it with pain. It rips across my face and burns my lacerated body.

"Argh," I scream, jolting awake.

"What's your name?" The man barks into my blooded ear.

"Garrett."

"Garrett what?"

"Blaine, Garrett Blaine." I say rolling my eyes to his.

"Shit. You two know who he is?" He says staring into my eyes. I pull my gaze around the room staring at my captors. I don't know who they are but they know me.

Chapter 14: Nessa

Liv shouts over the hum of the hover, "You did the right thing."

I watch Ty on the ground, blood drips from his leg as his green eyes stare at me. My insides squirm leaving him folded on the ground like that. I glare at Liv, shooting her the 'don't mess with me' type of look.

"No need to get pissed off. I was just saying you did the right thing. Shit." She jerks her head sideways as she exhales.

Jake pulls the hover away from the hole, pulling it high above the clouds before he levels it out. The sun's setting behind us, just under an hour until jump time.

Zane sits across from me squeezing the tablet to his chest. His head tells him it's his only protection out here. Whenever Jake hits a pocket of turbulence his thick-framed glasses slide down the bridge of his nose. Zane's shaking fingers keep reaching up, pushing them back in place.

After Jake hits the tenth pocket of turbulence Liv loses her patience, "Give me those damn things!" She yells ripping the glasses off Zane's nose.

"Liv!" Clint shouts.

"He's driving me nuts sir. I'll give them back after we jump. He's going to break the damn things if he keeps 'em on anyways."

Clint stares at Liv who's already tucked Zane's glasses into her jacket. Zane looks at the ground as he trembles. He doesn't belong on a mission like this.

I reach my hand forward taking Zane's. "We will be alright. They'll look after you, they'll get you home, I promise." I say as he squeezes my hand. His small mouth forces the weakest smile I've ever seen.

"You ready for this Mino?" Liv says as she and Gavin pound their knuckles together.

"Mino?" I ask staring at Gavin.

He sits half a foot taller than anyone on the hover, his rolling brown hair is hidden somewhere under his helmet.

"It's my nickname. Liv came up with it." Gavin says in his slow drawling speech.

"Get it? Because he's small, like a minnow." Liv says waving her hand up and down the length of Gavin's giant frame. "We've all got nicknames. They call me Bull's eye."

"For the tattoo?" I ask staring at her trigger finger.

Liv grins and Marcus answers, "Because she's a beast with a sniper rifle."

"Sixty-two clean kills." Liv says pointing her index finger at me, she pulls an imaginary trigger. "Boom, bull's eye!" She laughs as my face drains of color.

Sixty-two people dead because of her. Jake was right, she isn't someone I should mess with.

"They call me Ink and yes it's because of my tattoos." Marcus says.

"Not very original but it suits him." Liam says from the corner.

"What about you?" I ask.

"They think my name is pretty funny." Liam says rolling his eyes as the rest of the team laughs.

"Ruse!" Liv shouts slapping her leg. "Like the children's book, get it?" She yells between her uncontrollable giggles.

The others laugh, grinning at each other before Clint cuts in, "They don't have children's books in the divide you idiots." He looks back at me. "It was a book about a red rooster named Ruse, he thought he was a chicken or some shit like that."

I look at Liam, he's shaking his head side to side. His cheeks flush red like his hair. The others are on the verge of hysterics.

Everything inside of me wants to hold myself together but I burst out laughing instead.

"Even Prem thinks it's funny!" Liv yells stomping her feet.

"Really funny guys. Just because I have red hair doesn't mean I've read that book, liked it, or am anything like that stupid chicken."

"It's a rooster, not a chicken!" Liv snorts, "You are exactly like it." She laughs rolling her head backwards.

I bite my lip trying not to laugh. Liv turns to Zane, "I'll call you Frames," she says pushing an imaginary pair of glasses to the bridge of her nose.

Zane nods his head. I bet he regrets accepting this mission.

Liv stares at me, "You know your name?"

I nod my head, with this team I'm Prem and I'm okay with that now.

A loud buzz blasts startling Zane and me. The inside of the craft flashes red and I see Zane doing his best to hide his turning stomach.

Clint looks at his watch then back to us, "Suit-up!" His deep voice directs.

We hoist up, steadying ourselves with the straps that sway above our heads. The pulsing red alarm continuously wails around us.

"Gavin, buddy-up with Zane, you will be jumping tandem. Liv you exit first, eyes on them and remember your objective." Clint shouts over the buzz.

Zane looks like a ragdoll as Gavin positions his limbs into the harness. Zane's sheet-white skin is accentuated by the blinking red lights. He's trembling and almost pitiful looking.

"Nessa, suit up!" Clint shouts snapping me alert.

I fumble with my harness as I jump into the black straps. Marcus tugs the loose ends securing me.

"Thanks," I say craning my head up to his.

As he secures the last strap the flashing red lights switch to a continuous yellow glow and the buzzing stops.

"Hold on Prem!" Liv shouts looking to the strap swinging above my head.

I'd forgotten I was supposed to hold onto it. Just as my hand wraps around the leather the back of the craft opens wide. It's hard to believe, but Liv just saved my life.

The darkness of night eclipses everything and for a second my eyes begin to water. What am I thinking? I ask myself. For a second I think about sitting down and rooting myself to the chair.

The yellow flashes to a steady green, "See you down there Frames," Liv says as Gavin jumps from the craft with Zane attached to his front.

Liv's smile cracks her face wide open as she runs towards the opening. She throws herself out of the craft with her rifle secured to her front.

"We're up!" Clint shouts.

Liam jumps first and then its Marcus's turn. They both look so tall flying out of the hatch into the night.

"You're next!" Clint's eyes bore into mine.

I move towards the opening. My stomach grips itself tight. I imagine looking sheet-white like Zane did. My feet carry me to the edge. This is my last moment of safety. As soon as my feet leave this craft I'm in Central.

"Jump!" Clint screams into my headset.

My chest squeezes down and I throw myself from the craft. I freefall towards the people that want me dead. I break through the clouds and make out the enormous buildings that blast bright with lights. Tall and powerful buildings unlike anything we had in the Inner. I picture Garrett trapped in one of them suffering. My eyes keep searching as I wrap my hand around the release cord. I fall like a missile aiming for the ground.

I wait and wait for Clint's command, finally his voice blasts.

"Release!" He shouts through my helmet.

My hand jerks sideways as I pull the cord. The parachute fires open lurching my body to the side.

"Steer yourself towards the dark patch." Clint screams.

My eyes frantically search for the dark area he's talking about. Buildings and lights are all I see. My eyes keep sweeping across the lights and skyscrapers until I finally see it, darkness in the middle of life.

Now that I've found it I panic. I don't remember how to steer towards it. I grab the two handles dangling above me and start pulling on them wildly. My left hand pulls down and I veer away from the landing zone. I switch and tug on the right handle as it spins me to the side.

I pull and release on the straps as I glide towards the ground. My arms tremble as sweat breaks across my brow. I glide closer and closer, adjusting until I'm almost there. One last adjustment is all I need to make. I pull my right arm to my side but it's too much. I spiral towards the trees that boarder the field.

"Oh shit!" I scream as I fly for the green tops.

The sound of bones breaking is almost as bad as it feels. The cracking and crunching of my bones echoes in my head. The left side of my body screams in pain as I slam into the trees. My ribs crack as I dangle from the branches.

"Ruse to Prem, do you copy!" My helmet rings as Liam shouts.

My breath wheezes, my broken ribs must have punctured a lung or something. My throat whistles as I inhale and exhale. "Copy that, I'm in a tree." I say bracing my ribs.

My feet dangle ten feet off the ground. My legs look limp and loose as I hang.

"Activate your external beacon." Clint says.

Using every ounce of energy I've got I crane my body towards my ankle. I twist and reach down and my ribs scream in pain. I make myself do it. I bite down on my lip and finally reach the beacon. My fingers dance around until I find the switch, I flick it letting out a scream.

"We've got you in sight." Clint says.

My head rolls side to side as I listen to the conversations between the teams. Apparently Liv, Zane and Gavin made it without event. They are already making their way to their objective.

"Inside your second pocket is a knife." Clint says as he, Liam and Marcus march towards me. "Pull it out and start cutting yourself free."

"I'll fall." I say as I find the knife.

"We'll be there. Just do it."

This is crazy I think as I begin sawing through the parachute cords. I cut through the front right one first and move towards the back left. My ribs scream and my hollowed breath whistles.

Two left to cut. I twist behind me and saw through the second back cord. It breaks free and I dangle from the last cord. I swing like a pendulum. I draw my blade to the cord and saw through the fibers.

The last cord breaks and I shout as I drop towards the ground. My body can't take another fall.

"Gotcha!" Marcus says catching me in his arms.

"I thought I was going to fall."

"Have a little faith." He says smiling, lowering me to the ground.

Clint and Liam break through the trees. "What's the damage?" Clint asks.

"I think I broke some ribs on the left side."

"You'll live." Clint says turning his back to me.

Marcus smiles and Liam rolls his eyes as he turns joining Clint. I know I'll live but a little sympathy would have been nice.

"Status?" Liv says blasting through the helmet.

"All accounted for. Nessa came in hard, probably broke some ribs but she will be fine."

"Permission to secure the Northern point?" Liv asks.

"Permission granted." Clint says switching his radio off. He wheels around to face us, catching me bracing my ribs with my palms. "Our team will approach from the South. Nessa and I will get into secure positions. Liam and Marcus you two will be making initial contact."

They nod in unison, Clint turns to walk forward, leading us away from the cover of the park. I follow Clint, he crouches cat-like dancing from building to building. Liam takes the back and Marcus guides the middle. His strong hand closes around my arm as he pulls me between the shadows.

Adrenaline pulses through my body as we slink deeper and deeper into Central. I hear Liam breathing behind me and watch Clint run across an open street. He pulls to a stop behind an enormous pillar.

Marcus makes eye contact with Clint and holds steady. Clint waves us forward and my arm jerks as Marcus pulls me towards the open road. We run through the shadow of the towering building behind us, the streetlights don't hit this stretch. We approach the open road where we'll be exposed.

My heart beats stronger as we get closer. I stretch my legs trying to keep pace with Marcus's long strides. My legs spring as I leap to cross onto the road. As I do Clint throws his hand straight up. Something has gone wrong. Marcus follows Clint's signals, it's an unspoken language they share.

The sound of an approaching hover drums down the street behind Clint. I watch Clint twist himself around the pillar trying to stay hidden. Marcus pulls me down a darkened side street.

My chest pounds as I listen to the craft humming behind us. I hope with everything that it turns left or keeps going straight. Just as long as it doesn't turn right. My sneakers sound weak compared to Marcus's boots.

"It's a patrol and they're coming your way." Clint whispers into the head set.

"Copy that." Marcus answers into his.

"We've got to make it to that building, it's our only shot." Marcus says pointing down the block at a grey stone building. "Take the stairs and hide behind those bins."

"Okay." I manage to whisper.

My ribs blast with pain but I straighten out and run as fast as I can. The hum of the hover gets louder as it takes a right turn. The fluorescent lights dance along the ground as it searches the darkness for people like us. I imagine the pilot having a picture of me posted in his cockpit, I bet there's a reward for capturing me, dead or alive.

"You've got to go faster Prem." Marcus barks as he pulls my arm forward.

I reach my feet out as my head spins. The lights skim left and right closing-in on us.

"We're almost there." Marcus says pushing me to keep moving.

My side splits and my chest squeezes, the lights sweep close behind us. We keep running and are almost at the stairs. I hit the first step with a thump. Marcus pulls me up, taking them two at a time. My foot catches and I know I'm about to fall. I can sense my body losing its center. I plow forward reaching my hand to break the impact.

"Like hell you are!" Marcus shouts reaching under my legs, pulling me into his arms like a child.

It all happens so fast that I can't process everything. My head bounces as he scales the stairs with me cradled in his arms. The lights close in. The craft rockets forward toward our position and the lights dance less than an inch from the back of his boots.

I open my mouth to scream, just as I do Marcus throws us sideways. He dives on top of me with his chest beating against my back. My ribs scream as he bears down over me.

"All clear." Clint says as the craft veers down another side-street.

"Sorry about that. I didn't want to throw you but desperate times call for desperate measures." Marcus says standing up from behind the giant bins.

I don't know what to say. I suppose I don't need to say anything, that's the beauty of this team. You can say as little or as much as you want, it makes no difference to them.

"Thanks," I say brushing my legs off.

Marcus flips his radio on, "We're on our way."

"Copy that. Liam's got eyes on two targets." Clint's voice pierces even though he whispers.

Marcus squeezes down on my arm as we run towards Clint. My breath squeals when I inhale, it must have something to do with my broken ribs.

"Glad you made it," Clint slaps my back as we stop beside the pillar. He stares at Marcus, "Liam's secured one target, and he's working on the second."

"Target?" I ask.

"A regulator, actually two." Marcus says staring at his watch.

"Secured," Liam blasts through Clint's headset.

"On our way." Clint flicks a button patching over to Liv. "We've got our targets secured." There's a long pause, I lock eyes with Marcus. "Liv do you copy?" Clint barks.

Liv breathes heavily into the radio. "Copy sir. We hit a bit of a snag..."

"Clarify." Clint asks staring coldly ahead.

"We stumbled onto a patrol. The package compromised our position."

I hear the frustration in Liv's voice. There's an immediate pang in my gut as I wonder if Zane made it, no doubt he's the package. If he survived the patrols Liv might kill him just because.

Before Clint has a chance to respond, Liv's back, "We eliminated all possible threats."

I break into a cold sweat as I picture her and Gavin killing the regulators. It's strange but for a minute I feel sorry for them. They were living, breathing beings doing their job and all of a sudden they are gone, dead.

"We're almost in position. Package is safe." She pauses, "For now." She sounds menacing and I picture Zane trembling as Liv talks.

"Get into position and prepare for data extraction." Clint says flicking the radio off. "Follow me," he says waving his hand forward.

Marcus and I follow behind Clint as we make our way through the giant maze of a city. If I'd never escaped to the foreigners I'd be shocked right now. I try to imagine how Garrett must have felt coming here, he must be blown away everyday by how massive this place is.

We weave behind Clint, making our way to Liam. We creep through the shadows and sprint in the light. Clint takes a turn and standing in front of us is a massive dome topped building that I immediately recognize from the briefing. It's the Capital. It looms tall and ominous against the black night. Marcus pulls my arm, dragging me behind Clint.

Clint's strong voice breaks through the head sets, "I've got you in sight Liam. We're approaching from the east."

"Copy that." Liam answers back.

My eyes squeeze together looking for Liam, we keep moving forward until I see him at last. He's crouched over two lifeless bodies. My stomach knots around itself.

"Sorry I wasn't here to help," Marcus says stooping next to Liam.

"You always pull your weight Ink, you had other things to deal with."

Liam and Marcus begin stripping the white uniforms off the regulators. Their bodies thump and roll as they push and pull at them. I turn to Clint but he's already stalking around the perimeter.

"Are they dead?" I ask with my voice cracking.

Liam grins staring at me, "The rules of engagement don't allow us to use deadly force unless fired upon first."

I stare, he didn't answer my question. "So are they dead?"

"Nope. They didn't even know I was there. I tranquilized them. They should wake tomorrow without any major side effects."

"A killer headache and maybe wounded pride." Marcus says as he pries a boot off the dark haired regulator.

"What are you doing?" I ask as they finish tugging the last regulators uniform from his limp body.

Liam looks at me then turns to Clint, "Ready for extraction sir." He says.

Clint wheels around, drawing a knife from his jacket. "Hold them just in case." He says as Marcus and Liam pin the first one down.

Clint reaches in his pocket and pulls out a black box. He sweeps it up and down the regulators body. It passes the left side without alarm. He runs the box over the man's right arm and the box beeps wildly.

"Got it." Clint says driving his knife into the man's forearm.

I cringe looking away but I can't stop hearing his knife twist inside the man's arm. Just as I'm about to faint there's a tiny metallic ping.

"Bingo." Liam says grabbing the device.

It looks like the tracker Zane implanted in my arm earlier. Clint moves to the next regulator and digs into his arm, extracting the second tracker.

"Load it up," Clint barks at Liam.

Liam pulls out a small tablet from inside his jacket and slides the two devices into a compartment.

"Clint to Liv, do you copy?"

The radio echoes momentarily, "This is Liv."

"Extraction ready for upload."

There's a pause on the other end before Liv answers back, "All clear." She finally answers.

Liam punches his code into the tablet and without hesitation hits the enter key.

"What's this all about?" I ask looking at the three of them.

Clint answers, "Liam's sending Zane their credentials now. Zane will extract the encoded data, tell us the names and identities of these two men. Liam and Marcus will assume their identities."

I screw my face in disbelief only to see Liam and Marcus already slipping into the regulators' uniforms.

"Zane will replace the regulators' finger prints with Liam's and Marcus's and we'll inject the trackers into them."

"So they will be impersonating these two?"

Clint nods.

"Why?" I ask.

"They will be the ones that surrender you. Hopefully they can get stationed inside the Capital for an easier extraction."

"So after this I get surrendered?" I ask with my hands shaking.

"That's the idea Nessa." Clint answers, spinning on his heels away from me.

The radio cracks as Liv comes back on, "Transfer complete. Liam is attached to this device," she says as one of the trackers blinks blue. "Marcus takes this one," the other device blinks.

As soon as she's assigned them Marcus is already loading his tracker into the gun. The gun pops twice as they inject the devices into their forearms.

"Marcus you are now Devon Faubion, Liam you are Seth Zion."

"Copy that." Liam answers.

"So that's the plan?" I ask frantic. "You're going to march me into the Capital and hope they believe you?"

"We will make them believe us." Marcus answers guiding me by the arm.

"We'll be looking out for you Nessa." Clint says sensing the absolute fear coursing through my veins.

"Take the jump suit off." Liam says. I step out of the suit and stand in my ugly pink shirt and white shorts. Liam reaches down to the dirt that surrounds the bushes the regulators are lying in. He smears it across my shirt and legs.

"Got to make it believable." Marcus says taking me towards the Capital.

Clint stays behind to guard the two regulators lifeless bodies. The chatter between him and Liv's team is constant.

"What's your status?" Clint asks.

"We're in position. The package is ready for intel collection."

"Copy that," Liam says walking beside me.

He looks down at me as I push myself forward. Perhaps this is where the weight cuts me to my knees and I can't press on. The fear and anxiety grow and engulf me like the fire that took my hillside months ago.

"We'll do the best we can to protect you Nessa but you've got to remember we can't blow our cover." Marcus says looking down at me.

He hasn't lowered the visor to his helmet yet. Once he does he'll be hidden.

"I know." I say swallowing.

Together we round a corner and without warning the Capital shoots into the night ahead of us.

"Sorry Nessa," Liam manages to say as he clasps cold metal handcuffs around my wrists. "Got to keep appearances up."

I twist my wrists around and grind into the metal. The pain is my only distraction from the fear that fills my stomach.

"Bull's eye to Ruse." Liv says through the headset.

"This is Ruse." Liam answers

"You're about to have company. Frame's sensors are picking up four bodies approaching the doors. They know you're coming, put her in the dark."

"Copy that." Liam says reaching to my earpiece. It snags on my hair as he pulls it out. "We don't want them picking up our chatter." Liam says squashing the device beneath his boots.

I hear Liv through Marcus's ear piece, "Tell her to stay strong and remember pain is temporary."

Just as she finishes a blinding light blasts from the entranceway. We're framed in the beam, blinded and exposed. Liam and Marcus lower their helmet visors and march forward tugging me harder than before.

I nervously count twenty steps before the gates swing open to let three regulators greet us.

"We've got Hollins." Liam says confidently.

"No shit!" The first regulator shouts staring at me.

"She's here to surrender." Marcus interjects.

"Did you call it in?" The second regulator asks.

All of them stare at me like I'm an endangered species. I suppose I am. If things go as Central plans I'll be extinct before the day's out.

"Not yet, our radios have been acting up. You mind putting the call in?" Liam answers.

The regulator reaches for his radio then stops, "Who are you two? I don't recognize your voices?"

"Devon and Seth." Liam says nodding beneath his helmet. "She put up a decent fight; hit us both in the throats."

"Hit you even though she came to surrender?" The regulator cocks his head sideways.

We need a distraction before he figures us out. I open my mouth and talk before I realize I'm doing it.

"I'd hurry and call. I imagine they'll be pretty anxious to see me. Unless you want more bombs to go off within the next hour." I stare into the glassy visors of each regulators helmets.

"You're a cocky little bitch aren't you?" The one in the back says. "You killed quite a few of our comrades. You know that, right?"

I smile because I think it will keep them distracted.

"Smile now little girl. It won't be long until you're begging for the pain to stop." He snarls spinning his baton in his hand.

"He's right. One of my buddies was killed the other day because of you." The middle one says stepping towards me. "I don't think it's right that they get to have all the fun inside." He says jerking his head to the Capital. "I deserve some fun. We all do after what you've put us through."

He steps forward blocking the bright light that's been blasting my eyes. I cower as his boots land near me. Liam and Marcus tighten their grip. They will do something right? The man steps towards me pulling out a long dark prod.

He points it up and pulls the trigger. The electric blue bolts dance at the tip. He lowers the prod to me and steps closer. The bolts dance at the tip and crack like a whip.

I try backing up but Liam and Marcus hold me steady. My eyes widen as the regulator drives the electric tip to my ribs. I roar in pain. The sparks course through my body. I can't control myself, my teeth chatter against each other as I buck and flail. Electric torture sears into my bones.

"Woo! Now that was fun!" He hollers stepping back. "Didn't bring anyone back from the dead but it sure felt good to watch you hurt."

I pant wildly, slumped in Liam and Marcus's arms. I'm pissed. I'm pissed at Liam and Marcus for standing there and I'm pissed that there's nothing I can do about it. Just as my rage peaks I think of Liv, 'pain is temporary.'

She was right, this is temporary. This can't be permanent. Pain is what they want, they get pleasure out of it. I don't want to give them that satisfaction. Not yet at least.

"Anyone else?" I ask smiling.

The first one steps forward winding his fist back. I've taken hits before but this one nearly spins my head off. My cheek bones crack as blood sprays across the ground. Even if I wanted to I couldn't smile now. Not with my face broken the way it is.

"We done yet?" Marcus asks. There's a subtle urgency in his voice. This situation is hard for him, I'm afraid the regulators will hear his concern and suspect something.

I act, not because I want the pain but because I think it's the only way to make the regulators believe Marcus is one of them. I line-up my knee and drive it into Marcus's gut. I hit him hard. He's got no choice but to retaliate.

I imagine behind that visor his dark eyes are staring at me like I'm a wounded animal. On the outside he's got to prove himself. He pulls out his baton and cracks me against my leg. It's hard and the small bone beside the shin cracks in two.

I scream once and drop to the ground. This is just the beginning.

"Get her inside." The first regulator says as Liam and Marcus drag me towards the doors. Pain feels more than temporary now.

Chapter 15: Garrett

The ice water they threw drips from my face hitting the floor. The leader left a few minutes ago, he was dragging one of my captors by the neck. My eyes twitch as I try figuring out where I am.

"What's your problem?" The remaining guard asks.

I watch him from across the room. Even if I was in my peak condition I doubt I'd be able to overpower him. He's tall, much taller than me. He's more than a tall body though, he's muscled and conditioned for work like this. His searching eyes constantly assess and reassess for possible threats. He holds his gun like it's an extension of himself. He is no amateur.

"You're not wearing white." I say out loud. It was meant to be a thought, not a statement.

"Neither are you." He says staring dead on.

"Where's your uniform?" I ask as it starts connecting that he's not dressed like I'd expect a regulator to be.

He raises his gun to me, "Why so many questions?" He asks with the barrel pointing at my chest.

"Point taken." I answer staring into his eyes.

He lowers the gun to his side as the others step back in. "You get his story yet?" The leader asks the man.

"No sir. Didn't bother to interrogate without you."

"Doubt there will be any need to interrogate this one."

"Sir?" The guard asks disappointed.

"He doesn't know what's happening yet. He'll talk soon enough." The leader walks towards me.

His dark hair has flecks of white giving him a salt and peppered look.

"Do you know where you are?" He asks cupping my chin.

I shake my head no, "Not yet." I answer.

There's a knock on the door. The second guard walks over pulling it open.

"You called?" The man says.

His pinched face hides behind his dark framed glasses. He's a small man in stature and presence.

"We need to have him scanned." The leader says.

The skinny man enters setting his briefcase on the only table in the room. I watch his trembling hands pop the case open and remove a small box.

"He dangerous?" His voice cracks as he asks.

"We'll find out." The tattooed man the leader had dragged by the neck answers.

Shakily the man approaches with a black box in hand. "Don't do anything crazy, alright?" He says. I nod because I feel sorry for him.

The box flashes a steady red light as he scans it around my body. He traces a full circle and stops in his tracks. "He's clear...you found him inside the walls?"

"Yeah, wearing a green uniform."

The leader squeezes my chin, "Where's your tracker?"

"Huh?" I ask.

My head spins as he drives two punches into the side of my face.

"Don't play dumb. Where's your tracker?" He barks.

"I cut them out. Both of them." I spit the salty blood from my mouth.

"Why?"

I hesitate just long enough to earn another punch to the back of the head.

"Why!" he yells.

"I had to get away." I manage to say as I try to stay conscious.

The small pinched-faced man rolls my finger over another one of his boxes. He drops my hand as soon as the box beeps.

"I think I've got a match." He says staring at the others.

"So." The leader asks.

"He didn't lie, his name is Garrett Blaine. Says he was born in the Inner Sector but made the leap into Central." The man looks up from his tablet with his glasses slipping down his face. He clears his throat, "He became a pilot, his craft crashed on the perimeter of Central's wall months ago. His body was never recovered. It looks like they did locate his citizen tracker in a lake but that was it."

The leader shifts towards me again, "So whose side are you on?" He asks.

I don't know how to answer that. "I don't have a side, I'm on my own."

"Why'd you fake your own death?"

"It was the only way I could get back to the Inner." I pinch my eyes appreciating the pain that radiates through me. "I was trying to get back to Nessa."

The tablet falls to the floor as the skinny man drops his hands to his side. "Nessa, as in Nessa Hol…" he starts but the leader cuts him off.

"That's enough Zane." He says staring at him coldly.

"You know who he's talking about right?" Zane answers back.

They must know Nessa. My heart jars in my chest. How do they know her?

"Who are you? Where am I?" I ask frantically.

"Clint you need to tell him!" Zane shouts as two guards pull him kicking from the room. "You are on the other side of the wall, with the foreigners!" The small man shouts as the guards throw him from the room.

"What about Nessa?" My voice cracks.

"She's none of your concern right now." The salt and peppered haired man answers.

"She's my only concern! What have you done with her? Is she alive?" I thrash in my chair.

"Today she is. I can't say what tomorrow will bring." He turns towards the door.

I scream for him and Nessa. I twist and pull until the chair crashes to the ground. My face presses against the cool floor but I don't stop shouting for her.

Maybe Central exiled Nessa outside the walls after the leap. That would explain how they know her. I hope they didn't tie her to a chair and beat her the way they've done to me. For a second I picture her head pushed against the floor like mine is now and I'm hit with a wave of sickness.

What did they mean that she was alive today but maybe not tomorrow? I try tipping my chair upright. Each unsuccessful attempt results in me slamming my head against the hard ground, finally I stop. They left the door to the room cracked. If I lay perfectly still I can hear them talking.

"What's the plan Clint?"

"We've got to keep him a secret until we're in route. If she finds out he's alive she may not go through with it."

"So we're just going to keep him locked up? What about Zane, he'll tell her for sure."

"We can't transport him, Nessa could see. This is the only room out of sight and earshot from her. We'll use our leverage over Zane. He keeps this secret, completes the mission and then he's free." Clint answers.

"Did you hear Zane say Garrett was a pilot in Central? He might know something about the cells. Don't you think we should find out, get as much information as possible before we go in."

There's a pause before Clint answers, "That's a good idea Marcus."

Their boots march down the hall towards me, I start thrashing again. I need to get out of here to find Nessa. I'm not sure where we'll go, nowhere is safe now.

"Lift him up." Clint demands.

My arms burn as the two grab at me and hoist the chair upright.

"What's going on?" I ask with blood dripping into my eyes.

"Tell us about the Capitol."

"I don't know anything about it." I lie. I don't trust them. Who knows what their plans are.

Clint stoops to look at me, "We don't want to hurt you. Just give us the answers and you will be fine."

"I don't know anything." I lie again. The tattooed man drives his fist against my face.

"Marcus, remember who we're dealing with." Clint snaps. "There are other ways. Gavin, go get the serum."

Marcus steps back towards Clint as Gavin leaves the room. Nobody says a word the entire time Gavin's gone. I don't care what they do to me, I'm not going to talk. I won't put Oliver or Central's citizens at risk.

"Got it sir." Gavin says with a syringe in hand.

"Go ahead," Clint nods. "We've only got thirty minutes before our next briefing, make it quick."

"What is that?" I shout at Gavin.

"Truth serum. You have no choice but to tell us everything."

I panic, they are going to find out about the cells, and Oliver's hide out. They'll kill him without hesitating. I do the only thing I can think of, I teeter on the tips of my toes and push my chair backwards. They can't interrogate someone that's unconscious.

The chair tips and my head explodes against the wall behind me, lights blast and then there's darkness.

Chapter 16: Ty

There's a crunching feeling sitting inside my chest. My insides rip as Nessa's pain pushes through me. I gasp for air because the pain's too deep to breathe through. I only feel a bit of what Nessa feels. My throat clamps down thinking about how much misery she's in.

I finally relax as her hurt stops. I know it won't break for long, there's bound to be more suffering ahead.

"Jon!" I scream, wrapping a towel around my waist. "Jon! Get in here." I yell again as his steps thud down the hall towards the bathroom.

"What's going on?" He says pushing the door open. "Ty, are you alright?" He grabs under my arm lifting me up.

I look at his fogged mirror, my pale and ragged face shakes me. There's no color to it as I stare ahead.

"What happened?" Jon asks again.

"I felt her, she's in trouble. I don't know what happened but she was scared and then she was hurting, serious pain." I shake my head.

Jon rests his hand on my back, my bandaged shoulder drips with blood. "There's nothing we can do. Clint radioed a few minutes ago." I jerk my eyes to Jon's, "He said they were going dark." I stare confused. "We won't have any contact with them from here on out."

"What else did he say? When was that?" I ask.

"Not more than five minutes ago. They were about to parachute into Central and after that they would be offline."

"That's it?" I ask hoping he'd said something about Nessa.

"He talked to Kara briefly but that's it."

"Where's Kara? I want to talk to her." My eyes look wild.

"Kara left, she said Clint needed her to do something. She'll be back."

"There's gotta be a way to talk to them." I beg. I need to know Nessa's okay.

"They cut off all contact. They are communicating with each other now, not us. We won't know anything until the mission is over." Jon pats my back turning to leave.

I lift my eyes to the mirror again. I look sorta sunken and weak but I gotta try and pull myself together. I hop one legged as I pull my pants over the bandages. My shirt scrapes the gunshot wound on my back but I keep dressing. I limp my way into the kitchen.

Nessa's father stands, his wrinkled face draws together, "Jon's told me all about you." He stops in front of me, hesitating for a blink before he pulls me into his arms. "I heard what you did for Nessa. I'll never be able to thank you enough."

He takes me by surprise. I suppose I didn't anticipate a welcoming hug so quickly.

"Thanks Mr. Hollins, I'd do anything for her, plus she saved me a time or two." I lift my eyebrows pointing to my shot leg. "You raised a pretty amazing girl."

"Please, call me Don." He pats my back, turning to face Nessa's sister.

"I'm Emma." She walks up to me, Emma's exactly like Nessa described.

"Emma, nice to finally meet you." I push my crutch to the side and shake her small hand.

She's delicate like Nessa said but she's more than that. Behind her gold and green eyes I see a fierceness, it's something they've both got.

"She told me she loved you." Emma says lifting her chin the exact same way Nessa does when she states a fact.

"I hope so, I love her too."

"Dinner." Jon interrupts from behind us.

We turn to sit at his oversized table. Food isn't appealing to me, my stomach's still reeling from feeling Nessa's pain earlier.

"Looks good but I'm not hungry, I think I'll go to bed, I'm dead tired."

Jon nods and my chair squeals as I push outta it. I barely get ahold of my first crutch before I fall to the floor screaming.

"No!" I shout as another wave of Nessa's pain tunnels through me.

"Ty are you alright?" Emma flies to my side like a rocket.

Pain and terror drives through me. "I can't stay here." I stare into Jon's dark eyes. "She's hurt. I've got to go find her."

"Who's hurt? What are you talking about?" Nessa's father asks frantically.

"Nessa. I can feel what she's feeling." I rock on my hands and knees as my gut grips and spins. "We're different, we can predict the future. We're connected in a unique way, I can feel what she's feeling."

Emma scrunches her small face, "Huh?" She says shocked.

"What do you mean she's hurt? What do you feel?" Her father asks desperately for answers as he pulls at my shirt. He accepts what I'm saying too fast, Jon must have prepared him already.

"I can feel her fear and pain. It's been coming and going since I got here. She's in trouble now."

Her father pushes to his feet. "I promised her I'd protect her." He locks eyes with Jon, "You've got to get me into Central." He sounds more convincing than I'd expected him to.

"Impossible." Jon answers immediately.

"Don't tell me about impossible. Impossible was bombing the walls and rescuing Emma and me, but you made that happen." His eyes cut into Jon's. "All I'm asking for is a chance to get inside the walls. I don't need a team with me, I'll risk my life alone."

"Mr. Hollins it isn't a matter of having or not having a team to send with you. The fact is we can't jeopardize the mission Nessa and the others are on. They *need* Nessa if they want any hope of rescuing Garrett. Sending you over would be reckless."

"She's my daughter. I failed her once, I won't do it again!"

"Give them time. She knew it wasn't going to be easy and there would be pain but she went anyways. She went for Garrett and she went to save us. She appreciates that the larger the objective the bigger the sacrifice."

My gut coils again, "Argh!" I scream as another wave of her pain hits me.

Emma points at me, "It's happening again! They're hurting her, make them stop!" She screams with tears rolling down her face.

"We can't make it stop. We need to carry out the mission as planned. I'm sorry everyone, I am." Jon answers.

He flops back in his chair. He's hardly touched his dinner but I suppose none of us have an appetite now.

My gut relaxes, "She's just scared now, no pain." I say staring at Emma.

I'm gonna have to control myself. It's not fair to let them see what I'm feeling. From here on out I'll suck it up and suffer in silence.

"I'm gonna go lie down," I say. My crutch trembles as I drive it to the floor. Emma's the first to help me up.

I get two steps towards the room before there's a pounding on the front door. We all whip around sensing the urgency in the bang.

"Jon open up, it's Kara!" She screams beating the door.

I don't know that I've ever seen Jon move so fast. He sprints towards the door and rips it open. All of us make our way towards the front.

"Kara, what the hell is going on?" He's shocked, there's no other words to describe it. "Who is that?" He asks helping Kara hold the lifeless body upright.

"Get him inside, take him to the back. He needs treatment." Kara directs.

Emma's father pushes forward relieving Kara of the burden. Kara's eyes look wild as she sprints towards the back. She's taking him into the treatment room they used for Nessa and me. I shudder thinking about being submerged in the whirlpools with our burnt skin exposed.

"Who is he?" Nessa's father sounds panicked as he asks. "Was he on the mission, has something gone wrong?"

Kara shakes her head and Nessa's father relaxes a touch. The man's head rolls loose as his chin sways across his chest. His arms flop and twist as they drape across Jon and Don's shoulders. They drag him across the loft, he looks dead.

Right when I figure him for dead he lets out a gasp then sucks in a mouthful of air. His clothes are filthy, they are caked in blood and dirt. His skin looks a lot like mine did after the fire, except there's something different about his burns. They aren't patchy like mine were, his has a neat pattern. Almost like the marks were made by ropes.

The bones in his face are broken. I've seen breaks like that, I'd even given them before. Someone's beat this guy pretty hard. His legs start reaching for the floor, it's his way of trying to walk but Jon and Don keep carrying him towards the back.

They move around the kitchen and come towards me. I wish I could help but I'm useless with this bum leg.

"Ty, get Emma out of here." Jon says hoisting the beaten man up.

Something Jon said must've struck a chord 'cuz all of a sudden the man pulls his head up. His eyes shoot open and I'm immediately kicked in the gut with shock.

"Garrett?" His name feels strange coming out of my mouth.

"Papa, it's him!" Emma cries moving out of the way.

Jon and Don stop in their tracks. We all freeze trying to put it together.

"Bring him in here before he dies!" Kara shouts from the back room.

I wish I knew Jon better, if I did maybe I'd understand the look on his face. He drags Garrett towards the back looking confused, anxious and angry all at the same time.

"Stay out here Emma, Kara will take care of him now." I say stopping Emma in her tracks. "She's a great doctor, she saved me and Nessa more than once." Slowly Emma steps back towards me.

Without thinking I lower myself into a chair. I need to sit before the shock knocks me out. How can Garrett be here? I saw the report of him locked in Central. That was only a few days ago. He couldn't be free yet, could he?

I shake as another wave of Nessa's pain hits. I imagine myself turning green as my stomach twists. I can feel what she's feeling and it isn't good.

"You alright?" Emma asks. I was trying my best to hide it but I suppose that's impossible.

"Yeah, just confused is all." That's partially the truth. I am confused by why Nessa's going through the hurt and the pain if Garrett is already safe. He was the primary reason she went over there.

My mind tries all sorts of scenarios as to how this could be happening. None of them make sense. Jon's got a small gold clock that sits in the middle of his mantle. I watch the minute-hand tick by slowly. With each tick there's another question that pops into my head.

"He was supposed to be in Central." I finally say out loud.

"What's this mean for Nessa?" Emma asks shifting on the couch.

"I don't know and I don't feel good about it" I say.

Another minute passes on the gold clock and finally I hear them leaving the back room. Emma stares at me trying to read my face. I'm doing my best to hide the feelings I'm getting from Nessa.

I shove down Nessa's emotions and face Jon.

"What is going on?" I glare without meaning to.

Kara wipes Garrett's blood from her hands. The towel she's holding is covered in it too.

"I got a call from Clint right before they turned their radios off." Kara answers dropping the towel to her knees. "He told me to go to the hole. He said he'd been keeping someone there and that he was hurt and needed help. He wouldn't answer my questions, I begged him to tell me more but he wouldn't."

"Clint had him?" I spit my question out. This whole thing sits badly with me.

"Did you know about this?" I scream at Jon. I'll kill him if he did.

"Sit down Ty, I didn't know about this." Jon stares, "I promise." His arm directs me to sit back down.

"Doesn't Clint answer to you?" I ask.

"I finance him. That's basically where my role starts and ends with Clint. I have my theories as to why he did this."

Emma's father looks pale, "What are those theories?" He finally asks.

"I imagine he was thinking about my wife and the others that have been held in Central for the past six years. They went over for research and were supposed to be gone a week. We haven't had communication with them since." Jon rubs the back of his neck, "My wife was Natalie, Jake's sister Natasha went, Kara's husband Brian and one other researcher was in the group. It was Clint's plan to use Nessa as a means to get inside the Capitol. She was more than willing since Garrett was being held there. I suppose Clint thought if Nessa knew Garrett was with us she'd stay. He knows how much we want our families back and that we'll pay to get them."

"So he'll risk my daughter's life for money?" Don snaps.

"They will look after Nessa. I've made sure she's got a price on her too, if nothing else; they have financial reasons to bring her back."

"Money isn't everything, don't you people get that? I'd rather not leave it on good faith that this maniac will put enough stock in the value of my daughter's life because to me, she's priceless." Nessa's father bangs his fist on the coffee table.

"There's nothing I can do now. They've gone dark, there's no communicating with them at this point." Jon answers.

I speak up, "Send us over there. Put us inside the walls with her. Nobody wants to get Nessa back as much as us." I stare at her father.

"We can't do that Ty. I told you to wait until the missions completed. I'm sorry but we have to be patient." Jon answers back.

Kara gets up shaking her head, "I've got to check on Garrett." She starts towards the back then stops, "After this mission, I'm out. Even if they don't rescue Brian I'm done. This isn't the way we were supposed to run things. I don't agree with it." She stalks off towards the treatment room.

There's a small part of me that hopes Clint and his team will rescue Nessa but I'm smarter than that. I know if there's any trouble they'll leave her behind to save themselves. My gut clenches as another wave of Nessa's pain hits me. This is going to be a long night.

Chapter 17: Nessa

It would help if I could keep my eyes open. That last punch nearly knocked me out. The rubber soles on the toe of my sneakers drag across the floor as Marcus and Liam drag me. Again I try to open my eyes but only manage to crack them.

"This way," One of the regulators waves to Liam and Marcus.

They follow behind him, their breathing increases the farther we go. I must be getting my senses back because my survival instincts start kicking in. I force my eyes open only to be blinded by the bright white halls that make up the Capitol. The flecks of my blood that drop to the floor look unnatural. I like that I'm ruining their unspoiled white floors.

At last the lead Regulator comes to an elevator shaft. He jabs his gloved hand to the button.

"We'll radio it in once we're downstairs." He says to Liam and Marcus, they both nod in unison.

My toes scrape against the seam to the elevator. It rides slowly, sinking farther and farther into the ground. I picture the cells Clint showed us in the photograph. I imagine travelling down into the bottom of the Capitol. It's the place where dark things must happen.

The elevator pings and the white lights from the levels above are replaced with industrial yellow lighting that casts everything into a dull and grimy shadow.

The lead Regulator flicks his radio on, "RP0232 to CC, I've got Hollins inside base level one. I repeat, Hollins inside base one."

"This is CC, copy that RP0232. Remain with Hollins. Backup is on the way."

Liam and Marcus lower me slightly so my feet can lay flat on the floor. It sounds like an army of soldiers moving through the halls on either side of us. Their steps echo as they close in surrounding us.

"Who found her?"

I know that voice, it's too familiar. My eyes roll and make contact with hers. Even knowing what she means to Jon I still want her dead.

"I surrendered myself." I answer so Liam and Marcus won't have to. "You've got me so let Garrett go."

Natalie grins her wicked smile as she rolls her tongue across her teeth. "Patience Miss Hollins, all in good time." She waves her hand and looks to the pack of Regulators that brought me down, "You follow my team, they have some questions for you." She's talking to Liam and Marcus directly.

They squeeze my arms one last time. I suppose it's their way of wishing me luck. Without their support I crumble to the floor. My leg must have broken when Marcus hit me with his baton.

"If she wants Garrett to leave here alive she'll walk." Natalie says to one of the Regulator's that had come to help me up.

Natalie marches forward with a pack of Regulators on her heels. I bite hard on my lip until I taste salty blood. I've got to bite down or else I'll scream. Each step is agony, every time I strike down I want to cry.

I push myself forward, bracing myself against the wall as I go. I move as fast as I can but I'm losing ground.

Natalie turns around, "Keep up Miss Hollins, and no more wall." She signals to the Regulator behind me. He's obedient and quickly shoves my hand off the support.

With each step I grunt in pain but I keep pushing forward for Garrett. Natalie comes to a fork and turns right. Her dark hair whips around as she stops, "Take her to the cells, straight into the box."

The Regulators nod as they pass her. She stays rooted to her spot. I think about lunging and choking her to death as I pass but that wouldn't solve anything. I let my eyes stare at her neck as I envision wrapping my hands around her soft skin. I picture squeezing down until she's lifeless. I'm so fixated on my fantasy that I nearly miss the circular scar at the base of her skull. I can see it peeking just below her hairline.

She notices my eyes because for the first time ever she looks caught off guard. She slings her head around whipping her braid over the scar.

My shoulders jerk forward as one of the Regulators shove me past Natalie. There was a moment of vulnerability, for a fraction of a second her tough outer shell cracked.

"Keep moving." One of the Regulators barks from behind me.

I do what I'm told. I keep telling myself that the farther they take me the better it is for the team. Somewhere on the other side of these walls Liv is probably harassing Zane to get the intel on the layout of the building. I picture myself as a little red dot on his virtual blue print.

I wonder if they can see me limping and surrounded on both sides by Regulators. I hope Zane's idea works, my only chance of getting out of here depends on his design.

The group of Regulators marching in front come to a halt and part ways, splitting in two lines leaving the middle open. I stop mostly because it looks so strange and organized.

"Move forward Hollins." This Regulator's voice isn't smooth like the last one, this voice is harsh and jagged.

I step towards the latched door. It's a thick and strong door, like one you would find on a vault of some sorts. This must be the way into the cells. I hope Zane is getting a picture of this because they are going to need a lot of explosives if they intend on getting into that.

The Regulator closest to the door punches in some sort of code. The alarm rings from inside the other room but I still hear it from where I'm slumped.

A Regulator from behind the monstrous door steps into view. He stares at me for a second before he pushes the door open. The Regulators file inside, my stomach twists as I step toward the cells.

I follow behind the group and hardly manage to step over the threshold without screaming in pain. My broken leg catches on the step and sends me to my knees. I crash down landing inside the cells. My knees ache from the fall but I'm too stunned to pay attention to that now. Endless glass tubes span around the room. I stare from tube to tube at the prisoners inside. Some look back at me, others don't give me a second thought.

I hurry to my feet, if I don't, one of these bastards will kick me until I'm up. I hope Zane's system is working now, I'm exactly where they need me to be. It's hard hiding my motives but I do my best to discretely search the tubes we pass. I think about the pictures Clint had shown us. I look for Natasha, Brian, or Dustin but it's too hard to tell with regulators around me.

We move forward toward the center of the cells, to the big boxed room. It looks out of place in the middle of all these tubes.

I stare at the walled box listening to a steady banging noise that must drive everyone crazy. I'm not as discrete this time as I crane my head around trying to find the source. The banging echoes around the room. I limp closer to the room and that's when I see the girl with her cup in hand. She bangs it against the wall with her blue eyes staring off somewhere far away. I gasp without meaning to, for a moment she broke her trance and stared at me. It was like looking into Jake's eyes, they were just the same.

Natasha is still alive, though I don't know if you can call that being alive. She looked closer to death than life. Either way it gives me some hope that what I'm about to endure inside this room will be worth it. If they save Natasha and Garrett then that's two lives for the price of one.

I don't think it's natural for a human to accept their death, but I'm coming as close to that as possible. It's like I'm balancing on a thin line, putting one foot in front of the other and teetering between two worlds. The world where you fight for your existence and the one where you give yourself over and accept the end.

The door buzzes in front of me, half the Regulators step into the room, the other half wait behind me. My neck snaps forward as one of them pushes me from behind. I catapult into the room wincing as I catch my balance with my broken leg.

I brace myself against a giant reclining chair. It looks more frightening than the chair from my leap, though it's similar. They both have the same cuffs that will lock my hands, legs and head in place. Both look sterile and cold.

I rub the base of my skull and picture Natalie's scar. My eyes stay fixed to the chair, to the cold metal ring that will sit just above my neck. The way the sharp and jagged edges of the ring catch the fluorescent lights makes my stomach curl around itself. It won't be long until they drive that thing into my head.

It can't kill me, otherwise Natalie wouldn't be here. What scares me is not knowing what exactly it does. Maybe after it's done I'll come out as evil and brainwashed as her. My stomach knots again thinking about turning into a Natalie.

"Sit," Natalie directs as she steps into the room.

I shoot my eyes to hers. For the first time ever I'm not filled with hate, instead my eyes are soft and pitiful. I suppose my heart hoped she would see my face and she would stop this. She would somehow remember back to the first time they had done this to her. Maybe Jon was right and she was a shell of her former self. Inside I hoped that if she saw that same fear she'd had she would snap out of this and save me.

"Now Miss Hollins," she says coolly, her wicked grin pulling across her face.

The Natalie Jon talked about can't be in there still, she's been replaced by something evil. Now I know she won't break for me, I've got no choice but to do as she says.

My skin pricks to attention as I lay across the cold seat. Specks of my red blood splash across my white shorts, somehow I feel like it's an improvement. My throat clenches as Natalie locks the first cuff around my wrist. I don't try moving this time, it isn't worth the fight.

Natalie directs two regulators to fall into place locking my legs and opposite arm down. Each cuff that tightens closes my throat a fraction more.

"You will remember this Miss Hollins." She says smiling as she wraps the halo around my head.

"Who says I don't remember the first time you locked me in one of these." My throat wasn't sealed as tight as I'd thought.

Her pupils flick, constricting into pin points. She looks frightening as she stares dead and cold at me. Her eyes blink, blasting her pupils back open. What I said struck some sort of cord with her.

"Natalie?" One of the Regulators asks attempting to bring her back to the present.

Her head snaps up, "You're dismissed." She directs excusing the man.

The way he storms out of the room confirms that he's mad about something. Natalie rolls her neck to the side, cracking the bones inside as she stretches.

"The scanner," she says looking to the closest Regulator.

My heart picks up again, this is not going to be pleasant. I hope with everything that somewhere out there Clint and his team are close to making the rescue.

Natalie grabs the black box from the Regulator's hand and slowly hovers it above my skin. She waves it up and down, sweeping my body.

One side is clear, her hollow steps walk around to my other half. The scanner slides up my leg and torso and I know it will be beeping soon. Clint and the team were right, they are searching for a tracker. Tiny beads of sweat peak and roll as she slides it closer to my arm. Her hand hovers for just a second before the black box wails an alarm. She's found the tracker.

"Clever girl." She says reaching for the knife laying on the sterile table next to her.

I try jerking my head down to see what she's doing but the halo stops me. It's the most sickening feeling to be trapped. I'm literally bound to the chair without a way to escape. She can inflict as much pain as her sick head can create. I know that I'm about to be tortured and there's nothing I can do.

Air draws into my lungs as I inhale and gasp. Natalie drives the blade into my arm. "May take me a minute," she says sweetly as she twists the sharp edge inside my arm. "Best to go in with my hands." She draws the knife out sending blood shooting across me.

"No, please don't." I scream.

I never wanted to beg but I can't control myself. Not with her fingers buried into my muscle. She digs and grabs and finally takes hold of the tracker.

"Not clever enough." Her voice is sweet and singsong as she hands it to the guard. "Go ahead and bring this to the chamber. Let her team of village idiots track her there." My chest pushes as I gasp for air. "It's okay Miss Hollins, they will die quickly which is more than I can say for you."

I'm panting because of the pain, but more than anything I'm terrified that she'll go back for the second tracker. Maybe she'll find the second one sitting next to my bone. I imagine her finding it, scraping it out and destroying it. If that happens I'm as good as dead.

I can't see her hands, the halo holds my head in place. I can hear her though. She wipes my blood from her fingers and drapes the bloody rag across my face.

The box ticks as she picks it back up. I try holding myself together. I know she'll find it if she sweeps the box one more time. The overhead lights blast through the blood stained rag. Her manicured nails tick at the side of the box, beating fast like my heart.

"Let's get down to business." She says, laying the box against the sterile table.

I control myself, afraid she'll sense my relief and pick the box up again. My throat rasps as I speak, "My only business is getting Garrett out alive."

"Patience Miss Hollins. There's far too much road ahead of us for that." She pulls the rag off my face, her head hovers inches from mine.

She smiles reaching for my forehead. My skull drives into the chair but I can't retreat.

"Now, now Miss Hollins, this is for your own good." Her thumb sweeps across my forehead. She's sick and twisted.

"Don't touch me." The words creep between my clenched jaw.

"Did you forget that I'm in control?" She moves fast wrapping her hand around my broken leg. Her bony fingers bare down around the fractured bone and twist.

My scream sounds terrible even to me. She's going to kill me. "What do you want? You got me, I came! Just finish this." I pant.

"I don't *want*, I need. I need to know everything Miss Hollins. I need to know who you are, what you think, have thought before or will think in the future. You are a threat and that isn't something we take lightly in Central."

"Kill me and get it over with."

"It doesn't work like that Miss Hollins. We need to make sure that once you're gone we won't have any surprises to deal with." She walks around the chair, her finger drags across my body as she paces. "For example we know you've been working with the foreigners."

"Is that what you call them?" My eyes lock with hers, "I just assumed you'd have some sort of pet name for your husband. Foreigner just doesn't have a warm fuzzy ring to it."

Her hand squeezes down on my bleeding arm. "Excuse us." She commands her Regulator's to clear the room.

The door closes behind the last one and her hand releases slightly.

"That part of me is gone, but I do appreciate your efforts." Her finger sinks into my wound making me scream in agony.

"Jon's not over you." I wince. "I told him you were a lost cause but he still believes his wife is in there."

"What about you Miss Hollins?" She sinks deeper into my wound. "Do you think I'm in there now?"

"No!" I scream terrified that if she sinks farther into my arm she'll find the second tracker.

"Good," her hand withdraws from my throbbing arm. "Tell me, how did you escape from the Inner?"

The halo blocks most of my vision but I can see her hovering over another table off to the side.

"I don't know." My back arches as my breathing takes control of my body.

Natalie whips around, her hands clench an electric prod. It snaps and zaps as she comes at me with it. "Don't lie to me!"

My body bucks as the electricity jolts throughout me.

"Stop!" I scream desperately.

"Don't lie Miss Hollins. I know Jon and the others had something to do with it. I've got endless time and tortures I can inflict."

There's only so much physical pain a person can take. I'm nearing my limit, my closing eyes tell me that soon I'll be passed out. It's my body's only way of protecting me from feeling such utter agony.

"We have video Miss Hollins. You can't protect that other boy either. What was his name?" She pauses twirling the prod in her hand. "Oh that's right…Tyler." She drags the tip of the prod along the length of my leg.

She knows about Ty and Jon. "Why are you asking if you already know?"

"Extraction is a process Miss Hollins. I wouldn't expect you to understand it yet."

"Extraction?" I yelp as she electrocutes my thigh.

"Now, now Miss Hollins, let's not get ahead of ourselves." Her hands land on either side of my head, her face hovers directly above mine. "What are you doing here?" She asks as she whisks a rogue hair from my face.

"Don't touch me." I snap.

Natalie pushes away laughing, "I'll do whatever I want Miss Hollins. That's the beauty of being in control."

"Control like Central has, you mean? Drug the citizens to keep them pacified, that way you can live your perfect life over here in a totally oblivious state? How did you leave the foreigners to come to this?"

The prod clangs to the table as Natalie reaches for another tool. "I ask the questions, not you!" She jabs my skin with a sharpened blade.

It's no larger than a pin but the pain seizes my entire leg. Natalie holds the blade in the air, rolling it between her fingers.

"Poison." She says staring at me. "Right about now your leg should be burning. Judging by the look of your skin you know what being burnt alive feels like."

"Make it stop!" I scream.

The poison travels, burning from my toes to my hip. It's like hot coals are being driven deep into my muscles, setting them on fire.

"What are you doing here?" She asks hovering another pin above my chest."

This is one answer I can't give. I can't tell her I'm with a team that plans on rescuing her and her former researchers.

"To save Garrett!" I scream hoping she'll believe me.

"You risked your life for him? You'd sacrifice yourself for a boy?" She guides the pin closer to my sternum. She's waiting for me to break down, she wants me to tell her everything.

"Yes! That's the only reason, please stop!" The cuffs clatter as I shake and twist but she keeps spiraling the pin closer.

"I don't believe you." Her hand flies as she drives it into my breastbone.

"Please stop!" I scream as the fiery heat takes hold.

It sears along my ribs and burns along my spine. I can't get away from the heat, it radiates around my torso squeezing me tight.

"Why are you here?" She screams, her face inches above mine.

I can't tell her our mission, there are too many lives at stake. "For Garrett, that's it. Please, I'm telling the truth." The fire extends down my groin colliding with the searing burn that's filled my leg.

"We'll see about that." She turns setting the pin down.

I exhale, knowing one more prick might have sent me over the edge. I try picturing Clint and his team on the other side of the facility preparing to breakdown the doors and save me. With hope all things are possible.

Natalie flicks her radio on, "We can start the extraction now."

The man on the other end answers, telling her he's on his way.

"Extraction?" I ask again, my body burns like it's being roasted in flames.

"Not to worry Miss Hollins, by the time we're done you won't remember much."

Her grin is evil and pulls at her mouth. The Regulator she'd radioed enters, his visor is drawn down over his face. I suppose he doesn't want me looking at him while they do this.

"Ready?" He asks Natalie.

She nods as her fingers furiously type into her tablet. The halo around my head presses down against my forehead as the back of my neck feels a rush of cool wetness.

The regulator does something to the back of my chair and I know what's going to happen next. I can imagine the sharp round blade that shone through the space at the base of the chair's neck. I think about Natalie's scar and I know at some point years ago they strapped her to this very same chair and drove that jagged circle into the base of her skull.

"I'll tell you what you want to know!" I beg as the blade rotates just below my skin. It sounds like a grinding drill as it spirals closer and closer to my head. I can't move, the halo squeezes my head too tight.

"We need more than that Miss Hollins. We need to know everything, even the things you didn't realize you knew." She nods to the regulator, "It's the only way we can protect the citizens."

My jaw clenches as the blades screech. I scream out of shock and raw pain as the tip of the first blade presses into my head. Flashes of Ty and Garrett draw in my mind before everything becomes black.

Chapter 18: Ty

It only took a couple blasts of Nessa's pain before I was ready to kill Jon for his involvement in this whole mess. The pain's getting worse by the minute.

Kara dabs another wet cloth across my forehead.

"Enough!" I shove the towel aside. "Zane can't be the only hack you know." I pant staring at Jon.

"I told you there's nothing we can do." Jon rubs his bloodshot eyes.

For a blink I'm able to shutdown Nessa's pain. I drive it away long enough to stumble into the kitchen. I'm pretty sure threatening to kill someone isn't the best way to solve your issues but I'm sorta outta options.

I wrap my hand around one of Jon's sharpened kitchen knives. My crutch drives against the ground as I hobble back with the knife tucked behind my pants.

"We won't know what they're doing until after the mission. Even if we could hack into Clint's radios, we'd risk Central detecting us." Jon leans into his leather chair.

"He's still sleeping." Kara whispers coming from the hall. She must've checked on Garrett while I was in the kitchen.

Kara's the last person on this side of the wall that I'd want to hurt but I don't have leverage. Another wave of Nessa's hurt smacks me, knocking me off my feet.

Kara's quick, nearly catching me before I hit the ground. There's a blink where our eyes meet and I feel sorry for what I'm about to do.

I push to my hobbled leg and wrap one arm around Kara's head. My free hand jerks the knife from behind me and I press it against her throat. Emma screams moving to her father's arms. Kara digs into my forearm but I hold steady.

"What the hell Ty?" Jon shouts flying to his feet.

"Get another hack here and have them break into Clint's radios. I need to talk to Nessa or I'll kill Kara."

"No you won't." Jon barks as Kara clenches down, her sobs shake both of us.

I press the blade into her throat, just enough to draw blood. My eyes lock with Jon's, "Do it or I will kill her and then I'm comin' for you."

Nessa's father stands slowly, holding Emma away from me as he places her behind him.

"Ty what are you doing?" Don's voice rattles inside his throat.

I keep my stare locked with Jon's, "Whatever it takes to get Nessa." I cut a touch deeper into Kara's throat.

"Alright Ty, relax." Jon demands, his fingers wring through his hair. "This could compromise the entire mission!" He shouts exasperated.

"Nessa needs to know Garrett's here. If I find out that you knew about Garrett this whole time… I won't stop till I've hurt everyone you've ever cared about."

It's awkward and uncomfortable staring so hatefully into Jon's eyes, but I do it. This isn't how I figured it would be. Jon was supposed to be on our side.

Finally his dark shark-like eyes look away and I discover that we aren't so different, him and me. He'd kill for Natalie just like I'd kill for Nessa.

Kara shakes in my arms and I hope Jon doesn't call my bluff. It's true that I'd kill to get Nessa back, but I wouldn't take an innocent life like Kara's. If it came down to it I'd turn this knife on myself before I hurt Kara. I can't let Jon see that though, not if I want a shot at talking to Nessa.

"I'll call Victor." Jon nods to Kara. Her chest stops thudding as her nails release from around my forearm.

"Who's that?" I ask loosening my hold.

"Zane's brother, he's the only one I'd trust to access the team without compromising the mission." Jon shakes his head as he reaches for his phone.

Jon's leather shoes shuffle towards his study. It's awkwardly quiet in the room now. I fidget with my hand just to make noise.

Emma stares at me. She's too young to understand what love will do to a person. Everybody should experience this bitch called love so they can truly appreciate the limits of their humanity.

Loving Nessa has pushed me to the edge of mine. For Nessa I'd cut down enemies or anyone that stood in my way. It's scary having feelings so strong but I accept it as truth.

"Sit over there." I release Kara and point to the chair in the corner.

I feel awkward wielding a knife. I must be convincing 'cuz she cowers towards her seat.

"He's on his way," Jon snaps as he walks back into the room. "Should be here in fifteen minutes. Why don't you take a seat Ty, you're making everyone nervous." He slides into his cream chair. "I'm glad you've let Kara go."

I step closer to Kara proving that I'm still marking her as a hostage. "It shouldn't have come to this Jon. It's not right."

"I agree, holding a person at knife point when she's only protected you and Nessa *isn't* fair." His dark eyes narrow.

"You know what I'm talking about. I get why you used us to get into Central. I'm pissed, but I understand. What I don't get is how you could send Nessa over there. Garrett or not, she shouldn't have been allowed to leave. They want her dead and they will do it."

"It's a risk we had to take and one that Nessa agreed to. Remember there was more than Garrett and our families on the line here. Central threatened war against us. Who knows if it's a bluff or not. It wouldn't be the first time those weak bastards played a card like that, but Nessa didn't want to take that chance."

"She shouldn't have been given the opportunity to leave. I shoulda gone in with Clint and got your people, then blown the whole shitty government up without her."

"It doesn't work that way Ty, don't pretend to be so naïve."

His eyes soften as he stares across the room at Kara. Time ticks away on his gold clock. Emma holds her knees to her chest, she looks like a small package ready to spring open. Her head tucks as her fingers tap against her legs. At least her awkwardness is a distraction from the mounting tension.

Finally the door knocks. We all spring up and I immediately direct Kara back down. She sinks into the chair before Jon's opened the door.

"Hey Jon, what's this all about?" Victor steps into the loft and I'm surprised, he's identical to Zane. Everything except the voice. Victor has a fuller tone that's not as nerve grinding as Zane's.

"Come in," Jon directs as Victor tugs a suitcase across the threshold.

"Kara," Victor nods before doing a double take.

Her bloodied neck paired with the knife in my hand would be jolting for someone like him.

"Jon what the hell's going on here?" Victor stumbles backwards over his luggage as he heads for the door.

"It's okay Victor, we've got the situation under control." Jon answers calmly.

I don't hide the knife and Kara doesn't cover her neck, "You sure about that?" Victor already knows the answer but he asks anyway.

"Listen, Zane's on a mission with Clint and his crew." Jon's struck a chord, Victor's attention pulls away from Kara.

"Are you serious?" Victor spits his question. "I thought he'd paid his debts to Clint? He doesn't owe him anything."

"This isn't the time or place to talk about it. Suffice it to say he hired Clint to clean up one of his last jobs and now he's returning the favor."

Emma's face scrunches as they talk. I can almost see the wheels spinning in her head, she's just like Nessa, constantly thinking and assessing.

"I'm going to kill Zane when he gets back." The chair sinks as Victor slams into it. "This will square them I assume?" He asks.

"Yes, he's square now." Jon nods.

"What do you need from me?" Victor shimmies back, pulling his suitcase near him.

"The team is in Central, they've gone ghost."

Victor's eyes swell behind his glasses. I imagine his chest exploding through his checkered shirt and I think if he breathes any harder his tie is gonna bust.

"Central? Please tell me I heard you wrong. Zane's got no business being there!" Victor doesn't hide the fact he's pissed.

"He's there, whether you think he belongs there or not." Jon looks back at me, "He's running intel for Clint's crew. They are attempting the extraction of Natalie, Dustin, Brian, Natasha and one other."

"Shit." Victor rubs the back of his neck, his face gets redder with each second. "Who's the other?"

"Vanessa Hollins." Jon puffs his chest as he says it.

"As in *Vanessa Hollins* from the broadcast? The one Central was requesting we turn over or die?" Victor asks.

"She's my daughter." Nessa's father turns towards Victor. "She turned herself in to save your people and in hopes of rescuing that boy from the video. Garrett was her friend, he had nothing to do with the bombings." Don says.

"So what's Garrett's story? We aren't rescuing him now?" Victor asks.

Jon relaxes his puffed chest, "No need, he's already here. Clint and his team had him this whole time. They didn't tell Nessa, I guess he thought she'd back out if she knew Garrett was safe. Clint didn't want to risk the opportunity to recover Natalie and the others."

Victor pans his eyes to Nessa's father, "I'm sorry. I'd be beyond pissed if someone messed with my daughter's life like that." Victor looks back to Jon, "What do you need from me?"

"Ty over here," Jon nods to me, "he wants us to hack into the team's communication systems and turn the ghost settings off. He wants the chance to tell Nessa that Garrett's here before it's too late."

For a blink I can only see the whites of Victor's rolling eyes, "Hacking into the system could alert Central to what we're doing. It might trigger them to search for threats and discover Clint and the others, my brother included."

"I've made that clear, but as you can see," Jon's eyes point to my knife before darting to Kara's neck, "the boy's insistent."

Victor's dark hair sways atop his small frame, "I suppose I don't have any choice?"

Kara's voice cracks, "Please Victor, try."

He sighs tipping his suitcase to its wheels. "Where can I set up shop?"

"Here." I blurt. "I need to watch what you're doing and keep an eye on her." I jerk my head to Kara.

"Perfect." Victor snaps with attitude.

In a blink Victor hauls out tablets and cords. Little boxes with blinking lights get synched into Jon's home system as he directs Jon in how to help. I imagine Victor and Zane growing up together, spending their days doing exactly this.

"This isn't going to be an easy hack." Victor reminds me.

"Didn't think it would be." My hand digs into the butt of the knife. "Let's see what you've got."

Victor cracks his knuckles, then he's off. His fingers ping across the keyboards, rapid fire ticking like monsoon rain striking an empty pail. If the situation was different I probably woulda found it comical seeing someone's hands and eyes move so fast.

"Shit." He groans for the third time.

"What?" I ask from behind him.

"Zane's got another wall. That's four levels of security, I knew he was paranoid but this is extreme."

"Can you break it?" I ask frantically.

I've insulted him, I can tell by the look he gives me.

"I can hack anything." He gives another head shake before he's back at it.

Victor switches from the tablet to the computer, his fingers grind the keyboard. Occasionally he mumbles something under his breath. I imagine hacking into Zane's system might be easier since they're brothers. Growing up with someone must give you an advantage into their tricks.

"Holy shit…" Victor falls back into his chair. "Zane did it."

"What?" I lean forward.

"He finished the sonar matrix." Victor jerks his head, "Unbelievable."

"What the heck are you talking about?" I move towards Victor pulling Kara with me.

"See for yourselves." Victor jams a button on his tablet.

Within seconds blue and red lights grow from the tablet expanding around the room. Blocks of blue beams morph into walls and people.

"What the hell is this Victor?" Jon asks shooting his eyes around the room.

"It's the Capitol. We're inside the virtual Capital. Zane's been working on this system for years." Victor runs his hand through his hair, "You implant a sonar tracker into a person. In this case Nessa," He points to the red outline of Nessa's body that lays strapped to a chair. "The sonar bounces signals off solid particles and transmits a three dimensional map of the facility and anything inside or around it."

"That's insane." Kara says from behind me.

"It's in real time. Look, you see that group of regulators patrolling that wing? And those cells, that's where the prisoners are held." Victor points out.

"That's Natalie." Jon says leaning over the miniature hologram of Natalie as she paces around Nessa's chair.

About as soon as he says it I'm on the ground in pain. Emma screams and I look to the hologram of Nessa strapped to the chair. Now I can feel *and* see her pain. I can see Natalie driving a prod into Nessa's arm.

"That's your wife?" Nessa's father asks with his face white and drawn together.

Jon's silent for a minute before he finally talks, "Yes, that's my wife but she's not the same woman I used to know."

"Emma why don't you go to another room, you shouldn't see this." Don pushes Emma from the couch.

For a blink it looks like she's going to protest but she knows she shouldn't be here.

I catch my breath as Natalie pulls the prod from Nessa's arm. I look to Victor, "Where's Clint's team? How do I talk to Nessa?" I ask lifting myself back up.

Victor punches into the tablet until a second virtual world comes into view. "That's Zane," Victor says pointing to the red hologram in the middle of the tree cover.

He's got two of Clint's graduates nearby, both surrounded in foliage.

"Those two with him are wearing the V-glasses. Zane transmits the virtual Capital into their glasses so they can see everything that's going on."

"So they know Nessa's in there being tortured right now?" I spit.

"Yes. I assume they are planning on rescuing her, they need intel first I'm sure."

"Can't they see Nessa and the cells? What else do they need?" I ask.

Jon interrupts, "They can see that *and* those regulators too." He says pointing to the corridor leading into the cells. "Clint's team is probably hatching out the details as we speak."

"I want to talk to Nessa." I demand.

"Can't do that Ty." Victor answers. "She's already been separated from the others. There's no getting to her now."

"You've gotta be kidding me! I want to talk to Clint then."

"That's going to take time." Victor answers as he plugs away at his tablet. "I might be able to get access to their personal communications. Let's start there."

I get sick watching the hologram of Nessa laying helpless in the chair. I lean over bringing my head just above hers as my face falls through the hologram. Man I'd kill to be there to save her now.

"I've got access." Victor says at last.

That's when we hear the first radio communications come through Jon's surround sound.

Clint's voice echoes through the room, "Do we have confirmation on the objectives?" He asks.

"Natalie only sir, we're still in location B awaiting questioning."

I stare at Victor as he points to the holograms in the corner of the Capital. One man's pacing the room while the other sits like a statue.

"Liam and Marcus, two of Clint's men." Jon says.

Clint comes back across the radio, "Copy that. We've got eyes on your position. If anything goes south we've got Bull's eye on it."

A raspy voice breaks, "That's affirmative. I've got your asses covered."

Victor points to the camouflaged hologram. I can see the outline of a woman laying prone, her sniper rifle holds steady to her shoulder.

"Another one of Clint's, probably his deadliest." Jon says. "Her name's Liv but they call her Bull's eye."

I recognize Zane's voice, "You've got company approaching B." He says.

Liam had been pacing but stops and steps towards the door, Marcus stays sitting.

"How many?" Marcus asks.

"Two." Zane stutters, "Make that three."

"Showtime boys." Liv answers from her hilltop position.

The first regulator enters their room. "Tell me again how you found Miss Hollins?" He asks without introduction.

"We found her near our patrol point. She surrendered at first but she changed her mind as we got closer. We contained her and brought her straight here."

"Lift your visors." The regulator directs to Liam and Marcus.

Clint comes across the radio, "Bull's eye get ready."

"Copy that." She answers, her finger switching the safety off the gun.

Liam lifts his visor slowly, Marcus follows his lead.

"Come in!" The regulator shouts to the two regulators that had been standing in the hall.

"Ruse you take chunky, Ink take limp. Bring them to the back and do it fast. I'll take this bastard." Liv says across the radio.

I have enough time to register she's talking about the heavyset regulator and the one with the limping gait.

I turn to Jon, "What are they gonna do?"

The two regulators march into the room. Liam and Marcus stare straight ahead.

"That's not Devon!" The one screams.

The other barks, "Not Seth either!"

There's a blink where nobody moves and then mayhem breaks. The heavier regulator reaches for his gun but Liam attacks. He wraps around the gun barrel and jerks it to the ceiling as he simultaneously drives his hand into the man's forearm. Liam flies around the man and pushes him towards the back of the room. His arms lock him in a choke hold.

Marcus doesn't give the other regulator the chance to draw his weapon. In a blink Marcus flies behind shoving him to the back. The regulator stumbles and Marcus lunges, wrapping the regulator's head between his hands. It's a quick jerk but it's a fatal one as Marcus snaps the man's neck.

The first regulator reaches for his radio, if he makes contact with others Marcus and Liam will be caught. The mission will be over. Liv marked that one for herself.

I look across the room at the hologram of Liv. She's up in the bushes at least a full mile from the Capital. Her eyes stare down the scope as her gun kicks once before she fires a second round. There's a pause as the bullet flies through the mile of land. It bashes through the wall, the explosion is enough to open a space for her second shot. The second bullet follows behind landing at the base of the regulators skull.

"Holy shit!" I stare at Jon. "How'd she do that?"

"She's the best." Jon says wiping sweat from his brow. "The first round was a piercing bullet, cuts through concrete and steel, nothing civilians would know about. It's like a grenade pressed into a bullet. Second shot was made for the kill." Jon says staring at the bodies of the three regulators.

Liv breaks the radio silence, "I'd high tail it boys. Won't be long before someone comes to check on those poor bastards."

"Copy that, thanks for the help Bull's eye." Marcus says as he and Liam step over the bodies and make their way back towards the cells.

Jon's living room is covered floor to ceiling in blue holograms that Clint's team is emitting.

"They each have their own sonar?" I ask Victor.

"It gives them full coverage of their surroundings. It's genius." Victor stares at the hologram of Zane tucked behind a giant log with his tablet in hand.

I collapse to the floor again, the back of my skull shoots with pain. "What's happening?" I shriek.

Victor jumps from his chair pushing Nessa's father out of the way. He squats down beneath the hologram of Nessa. "Oh no!" he says pushing back to his feet.

"What are they doing to her?" My hands fist the base of my skull. I can feel Nessa's fear and pain like it's a sharp pick digging into me.

Victor looks to Jon, "Evanescent," he says with dark eyes.

"Natalie was right." Jon mutters.

My head bursts with light and then the pain's gone. The pain stopped so fast, maybe Nessa's dead. I belly crawl across the room towards her hologram. Her hands twitch as her head tremors inside the halo.

"Evanescent?" I ask relieved that she isn't dead.

"Natalie had warned me about this. She'd had a vision that Central devised a barbaric device called evanescent. She saw Central bore it into the base of Prems' skulls. They use it to extract their entire memory bank. Past, present and future visions." Jon answers.

"Is that possible?" I ask staring at Victor.

Don interrupts, "You lost me at Prem. What are you talking about?"

I spare Jon the hassle of explaining it to a newbie again. "Jon told ya how Nessa and I can see the future?" I stare at Don and he nods. "We got that way when Central inoculated us as children. The serum was supposed to control our mind and behavior." Don looks like he's about to interrupt so I push on, "It's rare but in some people; Nessa and I included, it doesn't work. It gives us visions of the future. Out here they call us Prems."

Don slumps onto the couch, he sorta melts into it. I imagine this is information overload.

"If she can see the future, than why is she there and Garrett's here?" Don asks.

"We can't control what we see. It just happens."

"That's convenient." Don shakes his head like a mad dog.

Victor interrupts, "Not with evanescent." He locks eyes with me. "Zane and I have done some research. It's high-level intel that's hard to hack but we've been able to access some files. Prems have different levels of conciseness. There are doors to each level that usually stay shut. Every once and a while one of those doors opens, that's when you get your vision. That doesn't mean that those few visions are your brains only accounts of the future, it's just that one happened to slip through the door. Central believes there are thousands of visions buried inside each Prem's mind. Evanescent opens the doors and extracts all of those visons."

"So that's what they're doing to her?" My finger shakes as it points at Nessa's hologram.

"I think so, it's the only thing that makes sense." Victor looks empty as he stares ahead

"How much time do we have?" Don interrupts.

"Zane and I never broke into the system far enough to get specifics. I'm guessing a day, two at most."

It's driving me mad looking at Nessa strapped to the chair knowing that their taking her brains secrets. Secrets she's never known herself.

"You think they did that to Natalie?" I ask Jon.

He hesitates trying to absorb everything.

"It's the only thing that makes sense. I don't see any other way that they could've made her like she is today. Somehow they must have changed the way she thinks." He points to Natalie's hologram, "That isn't the woman I married."

We all sit for a minute, each of us watching the different holograms moving around the digital map. Liv packed up her gear and is getting into another position. Zane's still hidden, frantically typing as he tries hacking into Central's systems. Marcus and Liam are on the run as they make their way towards the cells. Clint and Gavin are on opposite ends of Central's perimeter pacing back and forth.

We spot a group of regulators moving towards location B. Zane breaks the radio silence, "We've got a problem, regulators are on their way to location B."

"I'm on it." Liv answers outta breath.

All our eyes fly to her hologram. She throws her pack down and loads another bullet into her rifle. She doesn't have time to set up a tripod, she rests it against a tree as she slows her breathing. Even as a hologram I'm scared shitless by her. She's a killer, that's for sure.

The glasses she's wearing lets her see the same holograms we are, she knows just where the regulators are. As soon as the first regulator turns into location B she squeezes the trigger and lands another perfect shot.

The poor bastards don't have time to realize what's going on before their comrade drops and an explosion follows. Their bodies toss as they slam into the walls, all of them dead.

"What was that?" Don asks awestruck.

"It's a bullet Liv designed. Uses it when there aren't any friendlies around. After it hits the first human target it explodes sending hundreds of tiny supercharged shards. She could clear a room of twenty with a single shot."

"You guys are sick." Don says staring at the hologram of location B.

"Don't look to me, it's Clint's team." Jon reminds him.

Liv starts talking as she packs her equipment. "I've got to get out of here guys. They're going to pick up on the attack and come looking for the shooter. I can't hold this location anymore." Liv grabs her pack and runs towards Gavin and Zane.

"Copy that. Thanks Bull's eye."

"Let's hope it's enough time for Frames to get his shit together." She barks.

Victor shakes his head, "She must be talking about Zane. Poor guy, he's in over his head." Victor says.

Victor is probably right, Zane's fisting his hair as Liv speaks.

"What's your status Zane?" Clint growls across the radio.

"Getting close. I just have a few more walls to get through and I should be there."

"We need you to work faster. Don't make me remind you what's at stake." Clint snaps.

"I know, please give me more time. Don't hurt her." Zane begs.

Victor jerks his head to Jon, his short stature grows tenfold as he stalks towards him. Victor pushes Jon against the wall.

"Where is she?" He screams.

"I don't know what you're talking about!" Jon yells turning his head to the side.

"My niece you ass! Who else would Zane do this for?"

"I don't know, this is Clint's doing not mine."

"Bastard!" Victor lowers Jon back to the floor. "As if holding Zane's debts or whatever he had as leverage wasn't enough. He had to use Myra as an insurance policy too."

"We don't know that." Jon protests with his hands held up.

"I do know that. Clint will pay for this. He better hope he doesn't make it back alive."

"Guy's, look." I say pushing them apart, pointing to Liam and Marcus.

They're standing back to back down a narrow hall as regulators close-in from each side. There's no place for them to go.

"Ink and Ruse, you've got company coming." Gavin whispers into his radio.

"Copy that, we see 'em in the goggles." Liam says reaching for his knife.

Both of them have their side arms drawn as they separate for the ends of the halls. They're going to have to take on three regulators each. Those odds aren't very good.

"Man-up boys." Liv says, "I'll see you on the other side."

The regulators converge on Liam and Marcus. The regulators are unsuspecting of the threat they'll face when they round the next corners.

The first regulator takes the turn and Liam's ready as he drives his knife into the man. It's so fast, the regulator's down in no time. The remaining two sprint around the turn but Liam's prepared. He ricochets himself off the wall as he spins around the second regulator. His feet run along the wall landing behind the man. The last regulator doesn't have time to correct himself. He draws his gun and shoots, aiming for Liam but it's too late. Liam uses the regulator's comrade as a shield. He takes the bullet to the chest and drops to the floor. The last regulator is an easy target now. His shock doesn't last long before Liam's putting him down.

Marcus isn't as sneaky as Liam. No fancy wall climbing for him, he's pure brute force. His arms twist and turn as his legs kick and sweep. He takes the regulators down one by one with force and speed. By the time the third one's down Liam's at his side ready to help.

"Looks like you two got lucky." Liv laughs across the radio.

Liam's breathless as he answers. "Thanks for the vote of confidence."

"Any time." Liv laughs.

"Enough chatter." Clint barks. "You two get into position for entry, Zane's almost ready."

"Yes Sir!" Marcus chimes as they haul towards the cells.

"They're going to try and save her right?" I ask staring at Nessa pinned to the chair.

Jon answers with his eyes, telling me he doesn't know the answer.

"I'm in!" Zane squeaks across the radio.

"They're moving into position. Jake, be ready for extraction." Clint barks over the radio.

"Copy that, ready for pick up on command." Jake answers.

Zane comes back, "Codes have been uploaded to your new implants, and they will open the room."

"Nice job Frames." Liam says as their holograms approach the entrance to the prison.

My heart beats straight outta my chest. They're just a few hundred feet from the room Nessa's in. I need them to keep their word and get her out.

Marcus and Liam stand just outside the room. "Three, two, one." Marcus mouths as he and Liam push through the door together.

They're hit head on by a regulator with his gun shouldered, ready to fire. Marcus dives in time to miss the bullet but Liam wasn't so lucky.

"Shit!" He screams grabbing his arm.

Natalie's head shoots up, she knows something's gone wrong. The Borg posted outside the room pushes through the door with his gun held ready to protect her.

We can't hear into Natalie's room but she and the regulator look like they're yelling at each other.

"We need backup ASAP!" Liam hollers as he and Marcus take fire.

"Clear the room, I'm coming in from the back." Gavin answers. His hologram runs for the entrance to the Capitol.

"Frames you've got to get me access now!" Gavin barks as he makes his way towards the fighting.

Gavin runs straight for the enemy without any access to unlock the doors. If Zane can't get them unlocked he'll be killed in an instant.

Zane's hologram crouches behind a tree typing frantically.

"Permission to abort mission!" Liv shouts to Clint.

"Denied. Stay with Zane, we need him." Clint answers back.

She's ruthless, she was gonna leave Zane there to die alone. He wouldn't last ten seconds under attack.

"I'm joining Gavin, patch me in Zane." Clint orders as he takes off too.

"I've almost got it." Zane's voice tremors.

Gavin's close to the entrance, if Zane doesn't patch the codes to his tracker he'll be a sitting duck ready for extermination.

"One hundred feet Frames, get me in!" Gavin yells.

"I'm trying!" Zane screams back.

Gavin pulls out his gun running straight for the door. Clint's just behind him.

"Fifty feet Frames, don't let me die in this place!" Gavin's almost pleading with Zane.

"Got it!" Zane yelps, "Upload complete, you're both in!"

Everyone but me drops to a seat like a ton of falling bricks. I stay standing to watch Clint and Gavin climb the stairs to the

Capitol. As they bound up the stairs Marcus and Liam are on the inside killing the Borgs guarding the cells.

They trade blast for blast as they alternate taking shots and taking cover. Liam and Marcus tuck behind one of the cylindrical cells, the prisoner inside lays belly down as bullets ricochet off their walls.

"Marcus and Liam, what's your status?" Clint barks.

"Taking heat, but I can get us out of this." Marcus growls. "Cover me?" Marcus asks looking at Liam's wounded arm.

There's a blink as Liam hesitates but ultimately he nods. Even in a hologram you understand the history between 'em. Two men made brothers through their line of dangerous work. Both willing to die for the other.

Marcus lunges from behind the cell, zigzagging like a jackrabbit. Shoot and recoil, shoot and recoil, all repeated in a rapid succession as Liam covers him.

There's another change of direction as Marcus barrels sideways and hurls a grenade towards the last two regulators. They aren't prepared to accept death without a fight though. The tiny bomb drops to their feet, they've got time to fire one last round.

With guns already raised they hone in on Marcus as he dives for cover. It's too late. The regulator's recoiling gun and Marcus's exploding grenade sound simultaneously.

The Borg never got the satisfaction of knowing he'd hit Marcus just above his vest. The smallest fraction of a second could have saved him, but life comes and goes in fractions of seconds.

Clint's screaming drowns out the background noise. "Liam, what's the status?"

"Threat neutralized but Marcus has been hit." Liam stutters. We watch his hologram sprint towards Marcus.

Marcus hasn't moved since the Borg shot him mid dive.

"Ink, Ink?" Liam says rolling Marcus to his back.

You can tell when someone's gone without needing to hear anything. The way Marcus's head flops to the side tells us he's dead without doubt.

"Ink?" Liv groans across the radio.

She's seeing the same thing we are so I'm surprised she asked, she's got to know he's gone.

Liam stares at his downed comrade. Liam's hand holds against Marcus's throat checking for any signs of life. It hovers above his body for a blink like there was something he'd wanted to do but forgot.

Finally he stands, "Ink's gone."

Silence falls on both ends. The sorta silence that fills you up and makes your head and heart feel jam packed with an emptiness that's somehow heavy.

"I'm going to kill every last one of those bastards." The radio whistles as Liv slams it down.

"We're on our way." Clint radios to Liam. "Look for the objectives." A blink passes, "Liam that's an order!" Clint yells.

The way Liam jolts stirs some sort of pity in me. Here's a guy who's always tough and ruthless, but now in front of us he becomes just a guy who lost his friend.

Clint doesn't let him have that human moment for long, "Now!" He screams at Liam.

"Copy that sir." Liam echoes over the radio.

Clint and Gavin march their way toward the cells. Both of them picking their routes to avoid detection. Pounding step by pounding step they make their way to Liam. Zane's somewhere off in the bushes, I imagine he looks more pitiful than before now that Marcus is gone.

In a way everyone is depending on Zane to keep 'em safe. It's a frightening thought that the weight of this mission comes down to a guy that's probably scared of his own shadow.

My mind is void of signs from Nessa. I wish I could say I felt good about that but I don't. I'd rather feel her pain than nothing at all. At least the pain told me she was still alive. I can't help wondering if that metal rod poking into the back of her head is taking the girl I love away forever.

The hologram of Natalie shows her pushing her shoulders against the wall inside the room. Her gun points to the ceiling, I know she'll use it if needed. The Borg bounces around inside the cell, weaving around Nessa's table as he shoves cabinets and medical equipment in front of the door.

Jon stares at Natalie as she barks directions to the Borg, no doubt she's making him barricade the room. She won't let Nessa go easily.

"Liam what's your status?" Clint radios as he and Gavin turn the last corner before the cells.

"Holy shit." Liam stops in his tracks staring at one of the long cylindrical cells he'd been weaving between. "I found Natasha." He bangs his fist against the cell, pressing his face to the glass.

When Nessa and I got out here to the barrens I'd seen a kid do that one afternoon. He pressed his face to the store front window all fish-eyed as he stared at the latest toy on display. Liam looks like a fish-eyed kid staring at a toy right now.

Clint doesn't answer, he doesn't need to, he'll see for himself soon enough. His hologram darts into the prisons as he and Gavin hurdle through the doorway. They race around, jumping over the bodies that litter the floor.

I turn to Victor, "Where are the other Borgs? I mean regulators." I say catching my slang.

"The alarms must be disabled, I'd bet anything that's what Zane's working on now. I doubt he'll be able to keep them off for long, soon enough all those explosions and bullets will catch up with them."

I probably looked rude since I didn't turn my eyes to Victor during his winded explanation but I doubt anyone else noticed. I'm pretty sure everyone was looking at the same thing I am now.

Natasha's got herself squeezed into a tight little ball at the foot of her tiny cot. Every time Clint or the others try coming at her she swings her fists wildly like an animal on the defensive.

"We're from the United Republic, we're with Jake. You remember your brother right?" Clint coos as he tiptoes towards her. He hunches, turning to Gavin and Liam, "Go find the others." Even in a whisper it's obvious he's giving an order. Crouching lower he turns back to Natasha, "We've got to get you home."

There's a swing of an arm and then a wailing cry as Clint catches her in his hand. She thrashes like a suffocating fish outta water but Clint holds tight. He wraps her wrists behind her back, securing them together with zip ties.

"I'm bringing Natasha out, keep me updated on the others." Clint radios to Liam and Gavin. "Liv, how are things at your position?" Clint asks.

Liv's been thrust into overdrive since finding out about Marcus. She's close to Zane, apparently realizing she could lose her team if he goes down.

"We're in the clear out here, Frames is still beating down that tablet." She says side glancing towards Zane.

She pulls her rifle back to her shoulder as she stares down the scope. She's out for another kill, that's clear.

"Don't do anything rash Bull's eye, that's an order." Clint barks as Liv's finger prepared to squeeze down on her trigger. "I can see you." He reminds tapping his goggles.

Her finger releases and I wonder if that Borg will ever know how close he came to dying. It won't bring Marcus back but I suppose it would have eased her hurt some.

"I'll be on my best behavior." She answers lowering the gun.

"Sir, I've got Dustin here." Gavin stands outside the cell at the far end of the room. "I need access Frames."

"I'm on it," Zane answers switching tablets. His fingers flick as Liv stares over his shoulder. "You're in," Zane squeaks as the cell door swings open.

"I'm with the Republic, we're here to rescue you and the others. It's time to go home."

It's safe to say that Dustin and Natasha's rescues couldn't be more different. Dustin wraps Gavin in his arms, practically pulling him to the floor outta excitement.

"Sir, don't do that. Let's get you out of here." Gavin pries Dustin from around his neck.

"Get him to the front with Natasha." Clint orders just before Liam interrupts.

"It's Brian!" Liam shouts pounding against a cylindrical cell.

Kara looks like she's spring loaded as she flies from her seat. I raise my knife as I remember she's supposed to be my hostage. Kara swats me away like I'm a gnat.

She crashes to her knees, falling like a tree cut at the roots. Her fingers break through the holograms beams as she tries reaching to touch Brian.

I've never seen something so pathetic before. The way she reaches and keeps her hands there makes me uncomfortable. It feels like I'm intruding on someone's private moment.

"It's him." She says at last, still holding her hand to his hologram. "You've found him." She says to Jon. She doesn't take her eyes off Brian's blue image.

"We're with the Republic, we've come to take you home. Kara's waiting for you." Liam announces as Zane opens the lock to Brian's cell.

I thought Kara coulda won an award for the most devastatingly shocked look ever, but Brian's a close second. He stumbles and stays on his feet only because Liam catches him.

"I'm going to see Kara again?" His voice cracks. His hologram shakes as he breaks down, sobbing.

"I'm here." Kara answers, her hands covering her face and tears. "I'm right here."

"You've got company." Liv announces snapping us from this one-sided reunion.

"Liam and Gavin, get the objectives to the rendezvous, I'm going after the N's." Clint orders.

The 'N's', he must be talking about Nessa and Natalie. It's pretty hard to believe he's gonna be able to get to them now that Natalie's barricaded herself deep inside the room.

"Liam, set as many remotes as possible and leave the manual with me." Clint snaps, referring to the pack Liam's got swung over his shoulder.

"Copy that, Sir." Liam answers as he hauls off with Brian tucked under his bleeding arm.

"They're closing in fast, they know we're here." Liv loses her voice as she shouts into the radio.

She's right, the Borgs know what's going on now. A bomb or bullet musta triggered them, or maybe Zane lost control of the alarms finally. There's three groups of twenty or so Borgs converging on our team.

Clint rips through the bag Liam left. He tears out pieces of an explosive. Liam and Gavin sprint down the hall, dropping their own explosives along the way.

"Zane you're going to have to detonate these. Do it as the regulators approach." Liam commands as he runs ahead setting a trap for one of the packs of Borgs.

"We'll hang back until you've taken them down."

Liv's hologram stares at Zane's, she can tell he's not strong enough for war.

"Frames! You'll do it or die." Liv whips out her sidearm, the barrel presses into his temple.

"I'll do it." Zane answers trembling.

Liv keeps her gun pressed to his head.

Liam drops three explosives along the wall the regulators are marching towards. He sprints back to Gavin and the others.

"Take cover!" Liam shouts.

His goggles show him that any second now Zane will detonate the charges, blowing up the Borgs in pursuit.

His glasses even show Zane hesitating too long. There's a bang like thunder as Liv fires her gun. Victor turns white as we all look to Zane.

Liv's warning shot was enough to convince Zane to act. He punches his code to detonate the bombs. Rolling clouds of fire and smoke barrel down the corridor.

Liam tucks around the corner, landing flat on Natasha as the ball of hot firey smoke flies past him.

"You've got one wounded." Liv stares like a cold dead fish at Zane.

They should all be dead but his hesitation left the Borg in the front alive.

"We're on it." Gavin answers scooping up Brian and Dustin.

Liam's stuck dragging Natasha along, she looks like she's gone catatonic.

Clint's got his grenade launcher pieced together. Apparently he's going to blast through the door. Nessa's still laid out lifeless on the table, Natalie and her Borg stand like statues with weapons drawn.

Zane detonates another one of Liam's dropped bombs. He's not cut out for this, the way he vomits after each detonation tells me so.

"Sir, you've got a group approaching, anticipate them coming in hot, less than two minutes." Liv radios to Clint.

"Copy that." Clint answers as he ejects a grenade from the launcher.

The blast sends him backward, but not nearly as bad as it did to Natalie and the Borg. The debris sent them both flying like limp rags. Natalie stays slumped, rubbing her head as blood drips outta it.

I imagine Clint looking like a superhero as he strides into the room, smoke settling around him with his gun drawn and ready. He'll get no resistance from the Borg, he's pinned beneath one of the cabinets.

"Natalie, I'm with the Republic, you and Nessa are coming with me."

Head injury or not Natalie's got some fight to her. She leans for the gun that's just outta reach but Clint's too fast. He kicks the gun farther away, lifting Natalie to her feet.

"Get her off this machine." He barks into Natalie's ear, pointing to Nessa.

"No." She answers squaring her shoulders.

Clint cocks his weapon and points it to her forehead. "Take her off."

Natalie doesn't cower or crack. She steps towards Clint, pushing the barrel hard against her forehead.

"Do it. Shoot me because I'm not taking her off."

I'm pretty sure none of us breathe as we wait for Clint's next move.

"I'll kill her then." He drops his gun and points it straight for Nessa.

"Stop!" Natalie shouts realizing he means what he says. "Shit!" She screams racing over to her tablet.

"Sir they're closing in, I'm sending Jake. Be ready for a 'hi from the sky.'" Liv radios to Clint.

Clint steps closer, pushing his gun to Nessa's head. I feel myself grow hot. My body tingles and pricks with a burning desire to kill Clint. The fact he's even considering doing this is enough to make me snap. Don's white, not red like me, he's pale and fragile. We both shake though, he shakes from fear and I shake from rage.

"I'm doing it!" Natalie screams trying to hold Clint off.

"They're coming Sir, get them ready for extraction." Liv hovers over Zane's shoulders reading the map he's got on his tablet.

Clint and Natalie both hear the Borgs at the same time. There's a blink when they both freeze as the group of Borgs cross into the cells.

I suppose Clint makes up his mind that if he can't get Nessa out, it's better to kill her than leave her here alive. It's sorta slow motion as his finger starts drawing back on the trigger. My heart slips into overdrive, beating against my sternum and vibrating down my ribs. I shouldn't watch this, I'll never get it outta my head if I watch her die.

I close my eyes 'cuz that's what my head and heart tell me to do. All at once every glance, laugh, touch and kiss we've shared combines into a million snapshots of Nessa. My heart and head are tangled up with each other. My head sees her and my heart crumbles as it knows she's about to be gone.

Two shots blast back to back and I jump with each one. I can't feel Nessa, and I never will again. The snapshots of Nessa crumble away, dissolving like ash in fire.

I open my eyes, she's lifeless on the table.

Clint's forearm is bleeding but it's not a fatal wound. If I had watched maybe I woulda understood what happened. I scan the hologram trying to see who shot him.

I squint and see the pinned Borg lifeless now. I shouldn't have counted him down and out. Even with the cabinet crushing his body he must have got his gun and shot Clint. The Borg's dead now, Clint landed a kill shot to finish him.

Two shots, one that landed in Clint and the second that hit the Borg. I'd thank that Borg if I could. He just saved Nessa's life. Course he wasn't trying to save Nessa, he was trying to protect whatever it is they're pulling outta her head.

He did manage to buy enough time for the other Borgs to get there. They surround the door, all guns point at Clint. They won't shoot, not with Clint holding Natalie as a shield, his gun presses to her head.

"Jake's coming." Liv interrupts, staring off in the distance at the Capital.

Right on cue there's an explosive boom followed by crumbling debris. Jake took the roof clear off the Capital. The few Borgs that are still alive are too disoriented to stop Clint from dragging Natalie and himself onto the basket Jake's lowered.

By the time they're up and away from the Capital the first Borg is finally on his feet putting together what just happened.

"Holy shit he did it!" Jon's bouncing on the balls of his feet. "He's got Natalie." He spins as he flops down in his chair.

I imagine my look says enough but I can't stop myself from talking.

"You kiddin' me? Nessa's still in there and you really want to celebrate? Your bitch wife wants nothing to do with you. She only cares about killing us."

"Mino, Ruse, get out now!" Liv screams taking our attention back to the holograms.

Jake must have picked up Zane and Liv during our exchange but he still hasn't recovered the others. Liam takes the lead as he carries Natasha across his shoulders. Dustin and Brian follow with Gavin in the rear.

"We're almost there!" Liam shouts as he breaks outta Central's front doors.

Even with Jake firing all weapons there're too many Borgs to get 'em all at once.

"Cover us!" Gavin yells as he directs the others into the craft.

Liam throws Natasha and himself onboard. He and Liv jerk Dustin into the craft. Brian and Gavin are the last ones left. Gavin fires his last shot, Liv and Liam grab Brian's hands. Kara can hardly watch, I imagine her chest beating the way mine was earlier.

Brian's feet pull off the ground as they try lifting him into the hover. He's about on board as another blast of bullets fly towards him. Brian's body blows sideways, he goes limp fast. There were too many bullets to avoid, it was a matter of time before someone got hit.

"No!" Kara shouts collapsing to the floor.

I've got a pit in my gut now. Her scream will stay with me forever. I think it's 'cuz it sounded exactly how I felt when I watched Clint leave Nessa behind.

Brian was so close to coming back. They'd just dodged close to a hundred bullets and then to go down so close to the end, it's sickening. Any one of a million things could have gone down differently and the results would have been changed. But, that was not to be.

They pull Brian's crumbled body into the craft as Gavin hangs onto the doorframe. Jake lifts up with guns still firing. Kara's scream makes me want to jump outta my skin. She stops just as the hologram cuts out and we're left in darkness.

Chapter 19: Garrett

My head whirls as the overhead light fixture looks like it's spinning circles above me. I know it can't actually be spinning, and it's something to do with my head instead. I imagine any number of things could be blamed for my vertigo. Maybe one of the hits I took in the recent past caused it, or the fact that I haven't eaten a meal in days could be the culprit.

My lips stick together and I manage to pull my eyes away from the spinning light. There's no water that I can see, unless you count the bag of fluid that's dripping into my IV. My eyes pinch together as I try to make the spinning stop. The dizziness reminds me of how I felt when I came off the merry go round that one afternoon with Oliver.

That was fun, even now I smile thinking about it. He'd laid targets around the perimeter of the abandoned merry go round. He always wanted to do this but he'd never had anyone crazy enough to join him.

"You ready?" He asked eyeing the sidearm tucked in my holster.

"What is this?" I asked staring at the pile of rust and rods.

We didn't have playgrounds in the Inner, I always felt foolish when Oliver had to explain these things to me.

"Sit." He pointed to the rusted disc.

I sat, reaching for the gritty handle. It was rough and red from years of neglect and exposure. I wondered how long it had been since someone had played on it.

"Hold on." Oliver said digging his feet into the soft ground.

The faster we went the more I appreciated that kids in the Inner are robbed of so many things. We didn't have playgrounds to retreat to, we didn't have any organized fun to release from the pressures of the leap. This was the kind of thing I should have been doing instead of spending my life studying for the one test that took me from Nessa.

Oliver hopped on and we spun around on the spool. I followed his lead and let go of the rusted handles and stood on shaking legs. It was liberating and fun, I hadn't felt that way in a long time.

The top slowed to a stop and it occurred to me what Oliver's plan was. This childhood pastime was about to get a grown-up adaptation.

I let him shoot first since this was his idea and he'd waited years to try it. Oliver hopped onto the metal disk, handles bracing him as he stood in the center. He flashed a smile that I rarely saw from him. Oliver raised his gun, the one we'd just been issued as our regulator sidearm. I stood behind, grabbing the cold metal rail. I heaved and pushed hard into the ground. Oliver made it seem so easy earlier but I appreciated that years of corrosion had made it difficult to get started.

Finally I began picking up speed and Oliver howled as he held his gun. The shots rang out across the abandoned park as he fired at the targets that went whirling by.

A jug of purple paint exploded as his bullet struck it, we both howled as the paint flew through the air. I kept spinning until I heard more shots fire and glass breaking, he'd hit another target.

Oliver emptied his clip leaving a total of four targets untouched. Pretty impressive since he'd been spinning fast and had never tried something like this before.

His breathing huffed fast as he hopped off the merry go round. We both laughed as he stumbled with his equilibrium all out of whack.

"You're up!" His hand slapped my shoulder once he got his footing back.

I braced myself against the polls and drew my weapon. I nodded to Oliver and off he went. The spool spun as I wheeled around and around picking up speed with each turn. I aimed my gun, appreciating that this was a lot harder than it looked. I fired and missed the first two targets. I wasn't about to embarrass myself so I honed my senses and aimed again.

After that I hit the jug of orange paint and felt my heart skip. This was fun, there was no way around it. I timed my shots and hit two more in a row before I missed the last target twice. I narrowed my eyes and fired one last round into the brown glass bottle.

"Woo!" I yelled as I holstered my weapon.

"Nice work." Oliver reached his hand out helping me off the merry go round. "What a mess," he laughed looking at the glass and paint that had landed on the dying bushes around the park.

"I don't think anyone will notice." I joked knowing that nobody came to this part of the city.

I tried standing to see the damage that Oliver and I had inflicted. My legs were wobbly and my balance was nonexistent. Glass shards and paint splatter wound circles around me. My head spun like it does now, here in this sterile room. Instead of paint covered trees spinning I see a dripping IV bag spiraling in a dizzying circle.

As the last drop of fluid squeezes out of the bag my vertigo calms and I appreciate that I don't know where I am. It's some sort of medical room, maybe a hospital or a clinic. But that can't be right, I remember being carried through a kitchen and sitting room.

As I remember seeing Tyler there's a shriek that sounds from the sitting room I'd come through. It's a woman's scream that makes my blood run cold and sends goose bumps across my arms.

Concern drives me from my bed. My wrist aches as I realize it's been splinted. My memory comes in flashes as I see glimpses of a curly haired woman that had helped me. I think she had splinted my arm but I can't say for sure. I brace myself on the giant stainless steel tub that sits next to my bed.

My legs buckle but I hold myself between two fixtures, furniture-walking my way toward the door. The woman in the other room lets out another scream as I reach the knob. I open the door and turn left, the room ahead is covered in bright blue light beams that give me an immediate headache. Even after closing my eyes I can still see the blue beams, it's like they've been imprinted to the back of my eyelids.

My shoulder braces against the wall as I rub my eyes. I cautiously open them again but this time the room is completely black. There's not a single light on and the only sound is the woman sobbing.

My shoulder scrapes the wall as I lean into it for support. As I step I remember seeing Don and Emma, I pick up my pace trying to get to them. They will know what's happening and maybe where Nessa is.

"You all right?" I ask staring at the curly haired woman that I'm now positive was the one that fixed my arm.

I suppose they were expecting some sort of warning before I marched myself out of the room because each of them snaps their heads to me, their jaws hang slack.

"Garrett!" Don shouts rushing to me as another man flicks the lights on.

The curly haired woman is on her hands and knees, coughing as she tries pushing herself upright.

"Kara, let me help you." Tyler says reaching for the woman.

Her open hand sounds like a pile of books dropping as she slaps Tyler hard across the face. I don't know what's happening out here, by the looks everyone in the room is just as surprised as me.

"Don't you dare touch me!" She scolds pushing Tyler by the shoulders. "You think you can threaten my life and get away with that? Or how about making us watch that, what good did it do? You didn't get to talk to Nessa and all that happened was we watched people get slaughtered. I saw my husband gunned down in front of me!" She shoves Tyler backwards but he rebounds forward.

"I'm sorry Kara, we don't know about Brian yet. They got him to the hover, maybe they can patch him up."

The dark haired man steps forward, "Ty's right, Gavin used to be a medic, I'm sure he's doing everything he can for Brian."

Kara pounds Tyler's chest but he stands there taking her beating. Exhausted her legs buckle beneath her, and Tyler's there to catch her. He surrounds her small frame as she sobs.

"I'm sorry Kara but I had to try and save Nessa. It was the only way, I'm sorry."

The one thing that sticks with me is his use of the word tried. If he tried that means he failed and something bad has happened to Nessa.

Don hoists me up over his shoulder, honestly I didn't notice him there. I'm too engrossed in figuring out where Nessa is.

"What happened to Nessa?" I ask with Don helping me across the room.

"She's in Central." The man I remember Kara called Jon answers.

"I want to hear it from him." I direct my eyes straight to Tyler. "From the one that started this whole thing."

It's funny because Jon and Kara both share awkward exchanges, the same ones you'd have if you stumbled into a screaming match between your parents.

"How do you know each other?" Jon asks.

"And how do you know Nessa?" Kara adds. Both of them needing answers.

"Nessa and I grew up together." I answer because it's obvious Tyler won't. "We've been together since we were six. We started off as friends but just before the leap we admitted we were more than that. We love each other. We'd planned to go to Central together, that's until he came along." I stare at Tyler.

"Listen I didn't know about you two." Tyler answers.

"Nessa and Tyler got offered the leap, I was second in line. She refused so that she could stay with me. He refused too and that's how I ended up in Central." My fists clench tight. "And how he ended up with her I guess." I'm not stupid, I can tell he's got feelings for her.

"Listen Garrett," Tyler starts.

"No!" I yell cutting him off. "You listen to me, I don't know what you think you've got with Nessa but it's not real."

"Yes it is." Tyler answers defiantly.

"She's mine, not yours." I stare at him.

"As pleasant as this exchange is," Don interrupts, "I'd like to think my daughter will choose for herself. She doesn't need you two out here fighting over her. How about you fight *for* her instead." Don's eyes sink to the floor.

"Fight for her?" I ask realizing I'm not up to speed.

"Like Jon said, she's in Central." Tyler answers, lifting his chest like an animal ready to fight.

"What are you talking about?" I ask trying to hide my shock.

"You have the recording?" Tyler asks Jon.

"Yeah, I've got it." Jon shakes his head, "You two have some demons you'll need to work out before you get to Nessa." Jon marches towards a poorly lit hallway in the back.

"So how'd you get to her? How'd you convince her to forget me?" I ask Tyler but I don't really want an answer.

"I don't think we should talk about it." Tyler answers, his hands wringing as he shoves them in his pockets.

"No, I'd like to know." I lie, stepping towards him. He stays rooted.

"We are meant to be together. I've known it for years now, I just had to show Nessa the truth."

"Are you crazy?" He must be. "You've been around for barely a year, or did your delusional mind forget that?" I've got a snarky tone that I can't control.

"I meant it when I said *years*. I can see the future and I saw us together *years* ago. I saw her and knew we'd be in love one day."

"Did she tell you that?" I step closer to Tyler, my chin lifts reaching just below his jawline.

"Not now Garrett." Tyler steps back but I'm unleashed.

"Did she tell you she loved you?" I spit in his face.

"I'm not about to answer that." Tyler stares like a statue.

"Did she?" I scream as my palms push against his chest. "Did she say it?"

Tyler stumbles backwards but I stay on top of him.

"Tell me!" I yell pushing him backwards again.

"Yes!" Tyler screams in my face, "She told me she loved me." His dead eyes stare through me.

If I had control of my anger maybe I wouldn't hit him but I don't have control right now. My arm winds up as I drive my fist hard across Tyler's face.

"Stop it you two!" Kara shouts from the corner.

Blood drips from the side of his mouth, "I deserve that." Tyler says wiping the blood away. "Don't go thinking about doing that again. You got your one shot, now it's done."

"It's not done." I throw another punch and see blackness as Tyler lays me on my back.

"We're in no shape to fight and we don't have time to waste." Tyler yells pressing my splinted wrist into the floor. Hot pain drives through my arm but I don't let him see it.

"What the hell!" Jon steps back into the room, running to pry Tyler off of me.

"Just workin' out those demons." Tyler answers tugging his shirt down.

"You finished?" Jon stares back and forth between us.

"I'm good." Tyler raises his arms in surrender, one crutch tucked beneath his armpit.

"You?" Jon narrows his dark eyes to mine.

"For now." I answer cradling my arm.

"Play the video." Tyler directs pointing his eyes to the disc in Jon's hand.

Tyler and I sit on opposite ends of the room. I'm sure it lets everyone breathe a bit easier knowing we're not within reach of each other.

"Nessa went to Central to get you." Jon says pressing play on his monitor.

I'm about to ask but the video starts and in a seconds time I can't find the words I was about to say. Not after I hear Natalie's familiar voice and her threats. She mentions Nessa, blames her for the attacks and I cringe, unable to believe Nessa would ever do such a thing.

Natalie's braid sways as she makes her way across the screen towards the man sitting limply in the metal chair. My chest clenches as she pulls the bag off his head and I'm left staring at myself.

"What the heck's going on here?" I finally ask with the disc frozen on the final shot of Natalie cradling my chin.

"You tell us." Tyler answers pointing to the projection.

"That wasn't me. I swear!" My hands raise in defense as Jon and Tyler both stare.

"It couldn't be him." Don interjects, putting the focus on him.

"Why's that?" Tyler asks with obvious attitude tinged in his voice.

"He was in the Inner looking for Nessa. He'd escaped Central and came to find her weeks before the attacks. He wouldn't go back to Central without her." Don pays no attention to Tyler and Jon, his eyes are soft as he looks at me.

"He's telling the truth." I say sounding more desperate than I feel. "I escaped Central and was trying to find Nessa when the explosions went off. Don had told me she was supposed to be patrolling the wall so that's where I went. I got there as those pilots were dropping the first bombs."

"How'd Central get the video?" Tyler asks, unfazed by my truth.

"Beats me. I don't think it would be a technological feat to fabricate it. They have some pretty incredible technology over there. My regulator training was done in simulator-pods for goodness sake."

"You are a Borg?" Tyler snaps with the slits of his green eyes pinching through.

"If you mean a regulator then yes, I was. Everyone gets a job and it happened to be the one they assigned to me. It's not like I was begging for it. Plus I literally bailed the first chance I got. I crashed one of their crafts in order to escape."

Jon touches Tyler's shoulder, "Give him credit, he did betray Central to find her. If I recall you weren't totally honest yourself. I remember your account of your relationship with Nessa being much different than the version Garrett just had."

The way Tyler looks at Jon tells me he's got some sort of guilt tied to Jon's last statement.

"They had holograms and simulators all over the place. They had images of my hologram stored from the sim-pods. I'm sure they had plenty of bruised and bloodied ones to pick from. They must have just superimposed them into that room and had Natalie play along." I answer pointing out a logical explanation.

Tyler looks at Jon, "The more we hear about Natalie the less likely it's going to turn out bright for you two." He says shaking his head.

"This wasn't the Natalie I knew. She would never do those things, never play along to something like that." Jon defends her.

"He could be right." I speak before thinking. "They can extract people's thoughts and memories." I answer.

"Yup, just found that out." Tyler chides.

"They can replace them too. It's not so much replacing them, it's more like hiding them with their own programmed memories."

"Borg training teach you that?" Tyler snaps.

"No, my friend Oliver did."

Oliver knew what Central could do to the mind. Even before training he knew a lot thanks to his father's experiences and years of spying through the vents. Still, it wasn't until being assigned to the cells that he fully understood the extent of what Central was capable of.

They had him sign a contract, he couldn't tell another soul what he knew or else he'd face consequences. The main consequence was his memories would be extracted, and each person he'd told would have the same fate. Extraction after extraction until Central's secrets were once again secured. I think Central would have wiped out every citizen's memory if that's what it took to keep their secrets safe.

Oliver had told me about the contract and what would happen if they found out he'd told me. He gave me the option to hear, which was right of him since *my* brain was on the line too. I couldn't turn him down, curiosity is part of human nature and with something so enticing, how could I say no?

He'd told me Central's secret one afternoon as we sat cross legged under the lattice of Oliver's refuge.

"You're sure you want to know?" He asked for a second time.

"Oliver man you're killing me, tell me already." If he was holding off to build suspense it was working.

"You can't ever tell another soul. Remember, they will find out and turn our brains to mush."

"I'm still waiting for the con?" I joked but he didn't laugh.

"Seriously." He said, even in the dark room I could see his eyes staring sternly.

"Seriously, I won't tell a soul."

"Inside that room, you know the cube in the middle of the cells." I nodded in anticipation. "They do some nasty stuff in there Garrett. I know those prisoners are supposed to be serious offenders, the scum of scum but I still don't know how I feel about it."

"What?"

"They can do more than just see what people are doing in open-sims. They can get inside their heads. They drill a hole in the back of their skull and make a connection there. Everything is fair game. Your first breath in life, your first kiss, love, hate or whatever is inside can be unlocked. They can pull it all out."

"Oliver, you've got to be kidding."

He shook his head, "They do Garrett, and I've seen it. Everything loads into tablets. There's an algorithm that filters all the mundane shit the brain stores and focuses on the stuff Central's flagged as important."

I whispered under my breath, "Holy shit."

Oliver didn't need to hear what I said, he nodded knowing I was having trouble accepting this.

"They said some people have foresight, they call them Prems. They told us they are the worst of the worst offenders and their punishment is brutal." Oliver rubbed the back of his neck, for the first time ever he looked fragile to me. "Once they filter out all their memories they either wipe them clean or upload new identities."

"No way."

"Yes, I'm telling you. They turn them into different people, mold them however they see fit. Sometimes they leave them in a mental tailspin, I think that's what happened to that girl we saw banging the cup."

My mind switched back to the woman's matted blonde hair as she beat her cup methodically against the cell wall.

"That's wrong." I say as I think about her.

"I thought so too but I tell myself those people were like my father, they did something bad to get there."

"I suppose." I stared off wondering what type of a person I'd be without my memories.

If I didn't have the thought of Nessa to hold onto I imagine I'd be a totally different person.

Tyler's voice echoes, "Hey, ya in there? Garrett!" He shouts and I pull myself back to the here and now.

"Yeah, I'm here."

"Don's right, we'll let Nessa choose between us once we rescue her. Are you in or out?" Tyler's eyes bounce from me to Don.

"Nessa?" I ask confused again. My minds still hazy.

"Yea, Nessa. She's in Central and they are probably erasing her memories right now!" Tyler's face is turning red as his frustration rises. "She went there to save you. You just saw that video. She thought you were there and she could make a trade to keep you alive…remember?"

"But…" I start.

Tyler cuts me off, "No but's, she's there right now. She's strapped to a chair with some rod sticking into her brain. Does that sound familiar enough to ya? Shit we just went over this!"

"Yes." I swallow, it's just like Oliver had said. "They can't do that to her." I answer and even as I'm saying it I know Central will.

"Nessa and I are what they call Prems, we can see the future. I saw us together and I'm sorry to be the one to separate you but if I didn't, she'd be dead. I saw her burn to death in a fire three years before I ever leapt to the Inner. The only reason

I stayed was to save her. Hate me if you must but I'm tellin' you the truth. I stayed because she needed me."

As if my head wasn't already spinning, now it feels like a tornado's picked me up and is tossing me around. Is it even possible that Tyler's telling the truth? Wouldn't Nessa have told me something like that?

Tyler had called them Prems, those are the people Oliver had said Central considered the most dangerous offenders of all. They were the ones Central made suffer the most.

"We used to tell each other everything. She never mentioned anything about seeing the future." I answer not believing she'd keep something like that from me.

"You better accept that she didn't tell you everything." Tyler rolls his eyes making me want to punch him again. "She told me about seeing her mother die and about seeing the attack on the Inner before it happened."

"Did you know about this?" I ask Don who looks just as shocked as me.

"I just found out myself but I didn't know she'd seen Emelia die."

"She was just a kid and didn't know what it meant." Tyler answers trying to defend Nessa. "She was probably confused or scared, who knows why any of us keep the secrets we do. She only told me after I said I could see the future." Tyler steps closer to me, "I can feel her emotions too. I've attached myself to her and I know when she's in trouble. I felt her nerves, fear and pain today. I felt her body and soul hurt as *his* wife," Tyler points to Jon, "as she tortured Nessa. She tied her to a chair and drove a metal probe into her brain."

"It's not Natalie's fault, they've brainwashed her," Jon tries interrupting but Tyler doesn't listen.

"Nessa's gotta be there for a reason. She didn't just go to save you or these foreigners out here. She's there because Central needed her to be. I'd bet somewhere inside Natalie's brain Central saw this whole thing play out. Jon even told me Natalie could see the future too. They pulled memories from her and I believe somewhere inside them Central saw the threat Nesssa could be. They knew she could take 'em down and that's why they did this. That's why they changed Natalie, maybe even why I was offered the leap two times. Who knows what information they've pulled from Natalie that could hurt us all."

"What will they do to her?" I ask picturing Nessa tied to the chair inside the cubed room like Oliver had described.

"Whatever it takes to keep control. Maybe they know Nessa's got something inside her head that could take Central down. Maybe they need to drag it outta her brain and force something else into it. Either way they won't stop till they get what they want."

Victor interrupts, "They're back online and crossing into our territory now." He says referring to Clint and his team.

"I'm going to the hospital, Brian needs me." Kara jumps to her feet running for the door.

"Kara wait!" Jon snaps but she's on a mission.

"Shit, come on everyone, we've got to follow her. Tyler, Don, Garrett; come with us. Maybe Clint and his team can give us information that'll help get Nessa back."

Don nods, "What about Emma?" He asks Jon.

"She'll be safe here, the loft is secure."

Tyler clears his throat, "We *will* get Nessa. I'll listen to what Clint say's but after that I'm leaving for Central."

Tyler hobbles behind Jon as we leave the loft tailing Kara as she lifts off in Victor's hovercraft.

"That's my hover!" Victor yells running out the door.

"Looks like you're riding with us." Jon answers as we pile into the craft and pull towards the hospital.

Chapter 20: Ty

Sitting next to Garrett is awkward at best. My face throbs where he landed his punch. I'd given him a free shot, it was the least I could do considering everything he'd just found out.

Victor's got his tablet sitting across his lap, I can see the little green ping that's supposed to be Jake's hover, it's almost at the hospital. If Kara keeps cutting off hovers and taking corners at seventy she's not gonna make it to the hospital alive to see Brian.

"They're landing." Victor announces looking out the front window.

His head lowers, peaking through the skyscrapers 'til he catches a glimpse of the hospital.

"We're here," Jon says throwing the hover in park.

I let Don help me outta the hover, I didn't have time to grab my second crutch. I hobble along, leaning as much weight as possible onto the crutch I've still got.

Jon's full-on running, he's probably trying to get to Natalie first. Garrett just spent half the hover ride filling us in on the things Central can do with evanescent. If it's true then there's no purpose in getting Natalie back, if she's been under evanescent she won't give a shit about him or us.

The hospital doors open and I lose my balance falling forward. Don catches me, hoisting me to my feet again. Kara's at the elevator, her finger jams repeatedly into the button.

"Forget it!" She shouts turning towards the stairs.

"I can't take them." I say to Don as Jon, Garrett and Victor follow behind Kara, all of them take two steps at a time.

Don props me against the closest wall, jabbing the button again. Finally it pings and he pulls me inside the elevator. The music seems outta place, it's slow and peaceful. Totally opposite from the chaos we're dealing with.

The elevator rides straight toward the top and I'm relieved when Don pulls me outta that musical nightmare.

"We need to get to the very top, that means stairs." He says throwing my arm across his shoulders.

I can tell Don's had a hard life of factory work. The way his hands and face crease and his muscles sit tight like cords strung out between his bones. Years of hard work show his strength as he lifts and carries me up the stairs.

"I can do it." I say but he doesn't stop.

"The faster we get there the sooner we can start finding Nessa." He huffs as he moves up the zigzagging staircase.

"Here." He exhales dropping me to my feet.

I push the escape door open as the team starts unloading from the hover.

"Where are the doctors?" Jake screams as they unload Brian from a stretcher.

"I'll get them!" Don shouts across the landing pad.

Right as Don opens the door to leave, Kara and the others come barreling through.

"Brian!" She screams sprinting to the stretcher.

I move closer, it's like I need to be there. It feels sorta like I'm responsible for this mess.

"Kara?" Brian's voice is weak, but it's loud enough for us to hear.

"I'm here." She grabs his bloody hand, squeezing it tight.

"Am I dead?" He asks.

"No, you're alive. We've got you now." Kara answers kissing the back of his hand.

"I missed you." He says between gasping breaths.

"Don't talk, I'm here now."

For a blink she forgets about his injuries, she lets herself be a civilian reunited with the love of her life, not the emergency room physician she is.

That doesn't last long though 'cuz just then Brian's hand goes limp. One second it's squeezing hers and the next it's loose.

"Go get the doctors!" Kara shrieks checking for a pulse.

"Don's getting them," I try calming her.

Brian's hand drops out of hers and the civilian moment is gone. She's thrown into medical mode as she pushes pressure onto his bleeding wound.

"Did you start a transfusion?" She asks.

"Didn't have the bag, it was left inside Central." Gavin answers.

"Damn it!" she yells pushing the stretcher towards the door.

Don meets Brian and Kara with a team of doctors and nurses following behind him.

"Don't leave me Brian, not like this." Kara cries with tears falling down her face. "Don't let him die!" She screams as a nurse grabs her.

Good-luck with that I think as Kara twists and kicks to get free. The nurse holding her doesn't stand a chance. Kara doesn't look back as the nurse hits the ground.

"Kara hold on!" Clint snaps grabbing her wrist.

She whips around to face Clint, her free hand pounds his chest. She looks weak and broken standing there wailing against him.

"Brian's back Kara, at least he's got a chance." Clint wraps her in his arms.

For a blink I'm almost touched to see that side of Clint but that gets forgotten as soon as he lets her go. Right then I remember what he did to Nessa. I know he fooled her into this mission by keeping Garrett a secret from us all.

Jon holds Kara as she cries. The medical team took Brian away. I imagine him getting prepped for surgery like I did nights ago.

"I'm sorry," Clint says looking at me.

I don't give him the chance to keep going. My fist lands hard against his face. He had to expect some sorta retaliation.

"What the hell?" He spits blood to the tarmac.

"I know everything!" I say pointing to Garrett as he hangs near the ledge, "And the mission… you didn't think I'd see what happened?"

"You saw?" Clint asks standing straight.

"Outta everything I just said that's what you ask? You're unreal. Yeah I saw, we all saw." I wave my hand including the others. "We saw the whole thing and I saw Nessa in that room. You were gonna kill her."

"I knew Natalie wouldn't let it come to that." He lies.

"But you would've, right?"

"If they didn't unhook her from that thing, absolutely. It was my only chance at saving her and it would have worked if I'd had more time."

"What about Garrett? You kept him from Nessa 'cuz you're a greedy bastard. Isn't that right? Now she's stuck over there. "

"That wasn't supposed to happen." Clint answers back.

Clint raises his hands. They stay raised, not in a surrendering posture, more like a 'don't come close or I'll hit you' posture.

There's a raspy voice that breaks behind Clint, "I'll help you get her back." She says.

I jerk my head to the open door where Liv stands. She hops outta the hover landing with her rifle bouncing.

"She was our responsibility, we didn't get her back like we'd promised but there's always plan B."

"What exactly does plan B involve?" Liam slides from the hover with his hurt arm holding Natasha's wrists.

"Here you go Jake," he says pushing Natasha towards him.

"Natasha it's me," Jake brushes her matted hair back. She recoils like a beat-down dog.

Jon looks to Jake, "We'll get her help, she's probably got psychological issues she's going to have to work through." Jon says trying to fix the hurt on Jake's face.

I suppose he was hoping for a warm reception that Natasha's weak mental state might never give. Liam reaches inside the hover guiding Dustin out.

Dustin looks around disbelieving. I suppose after six years inside those cells he never thought he'd see another day out here.

"Where's Natalie?" Jon asks pacing the base of the hover.

"She's in there." Liv says brushing her lip off. "A bit lively that one." She smiles with blood pooling at the corner of her lip.

"We had to restrain her, she was pretty wild." Gavin says hoisting Jon into the hover. "She may have some cuts and bruises but she deserved it, she clocked Liv pretty good. You know Liv, you don't get away with that without consequences."

Jon hollers as he steps onto the hover, "Natalie!" He shouts as he looks for her.

"She's over here," Gavin answers leading him to Natalie.

Garrett steps towards our group, I suppose he's a bit conflicted about this whole thing. If I was him I'd be fit to kill someone. I mean, these are the people that took him from the Inner, held him in a cell and beat him for information. To top it off they took him captive so his girlfriend would risk her life to save him. Now that I run it through my head I'm kinda surprised he hasn't gone ballistic yet.

"Who is she?" He asks looking at Natasha bundled in the brown blanket Jake wrapped her in.

I can't get a read on Garrett. There are a million other things I would have done instead of asking who the crazy looking blonde was.

"My sister, Natasha." Jake answers before doing a double-take. "You're the one from the video." He says, his mouth hangs wide. "We didn't rescue you, how'd you get here?" Jake asks looking around.

"You didn't get properly introduced yet, huh?" I say staring at Clint. "See while you were powering off the hover I was letting Clint know that we found out about Garrett. We learned Clint's been holdin' him captive for days now."

Jake looks at Clint, hoping he'll deny the whole thing.

"Tell me you didn't know it was him?" Jake asks.

I answer for Clint, "He knew. He also knew if he told Nessa she woulda stayed and without her he wouldn't get your people back. I wanna say his real motivation for keepin' Garrett under wraps was the money he'll get for returning Natasha and the others safe and sound."

Jake's face screws up as he stares at Clint, I figure this is the first time he's gotten to know the 'real' Clint.

"Is this true?" He finally asks.

"I didn't know we'd have to leave Nessa behind. Just like I didn't know Ink would go down like that. We *all* risked our lives in there. You *hired* us to do a job and that's what we did!" Clint looks to Jon and Jake, "You knew the extractions were all that mattered. You didn't care about casualties until we had them."

"I can't take this anymore." Kara rubs her swollen eyes, "Let go of me, I need to be with Brian." She shakes her arm away from Jon's grip.

"We'll go back for her." Liv says again stepping close to me.

I've never been scared of a woman till now. Maybe it's 'cuz I just watched her take down Borg after Borg, or maybe it's just the vibe she gives. All I know is when she talks, I listen.

"I'm going too." Don steps to my side propping my crutch under me.

"Me too." Garrett says taking his eyes off Natasha.

"An old man and two gimps." Liv looks to Liam, "Better start coming up with plan 'C' and 'D' Ruse." She laughs hopping onto the hover.

"When do we leave?" I ask.

"Can I interrupt?" Zane says peaking from behind the door. "Oh, hi Victor…" he says dropping his eyes to the ground.

It's like he's a kid caught in the act of stealing some stupid thing. Zane pauses, more uncomfortable than usual now that he's seen his brother.

"Are you going to interrupt or not?" Liv asks slapping him.

"I will." Victor announces, cutting Zane off.

He walks towards Clint and Zane, his eyes burn into both of 'em.

"Where's Myra?" He asks.

"What happened to Myra?" Zane swallows hard.

"We saw *and* heard the mission, I hacked into the system. Clint threatened you, he said he'd hurt *her*."

"Victor you scared me." Zane says holding his chest. "*Her*…my lab, not Myra!"

"What?" Victor spits.

"Clint's guy Hank is at the lab. He was going to destroy my files if I didn't follow through. Myra's with her mom, she's safe." Zane says sliding off the hover.

Victor drops his head, shaking it side to side.

"Right?" Zane second guesses as he turns to Clint for reassurance.

"Yes, she's safe and so is your basement of junk." Clint answers.

Zane looks hurt but he starts again, "When we were inside I was doing more than just surveillance. I was pulling information on evanescent too."

"What the heck are you talking about?" Liv groans looking behind her.

"Evanescent. It's a complex matrix Central designed to export a subject's cortical memories into an algorithm. It uploads into a Central database to extract threats. After what I saw tonight it seems Central can import data into the subject's brain as well."

"Holy shit Frames, slow down and speak normal. No fancy mumbo jumbo bullshit." Liv shoots off to Zane.

Zane hesitates trying to collect his thoughts, "That chair they had Nessa tied to." Liv nods, "That probe they stuck in her head connects to her brain. They draw out her memories, ones she's conscious of and ones that haven't happened yet."

Liv interrupts, "Future ones, because she's a Prem you mean?"

"Yes, precisely. With Prems they can extract memories of the future. They can see things that have yet to come."

"Shit." Gavin answers.

"They pull those memories and scan for threats, past or present. Once they've done that they can upload their own memories in their place. Essentially they can turn Nessa into whatever they design."

Victor nods confirming it. "It's true, Garrett was a regulator when he was in Central. He confirmed all of that on our way over here. Where are you going with this Zane?" Victor asks from beside me.

"I was able to get into Central's system and pull some blueprints for evanescent. Not all of them, but if you give me a day I think I can get a replica prepared. We might be able to bring Natalie back and see what she knows."

"Excuse me?" Jon's voice snaps as he hops off the hover. Gavin's behind him holding Natalie's cuffs.

"It might be the only way to get her back." Zane says looking at Natalie as she thrashes like a fish outta water.

"You think I'm going to let you trial your chop-shop experiment on my wife?"

"It's the only way." Zane says pushing his glasses to his face.

"Absolutely not, you better find a different way." Jon stands defiantly.

I talk without thinking. Not that thinking woulda made a difference since I'd have done this no matter what.

"I'll do it." I volunteer pushing my hand up.

"I don't think that's wise." Don says staring at me.

"I'm a Prem, we'll find out if it works and if it's safe. Do ya agree with that?" I look at Jon, "Will you let Zane use it on Natalie if I don't come out with my brain scrambled?"

Natalie's in the background bucking, trying to yell over the gag I assume Gavin or Liv put on her.

Jon hesitates, "You can do it *after* you prove it's safe."

"You can do this?" I ask Zane.

"I'll need help," he looks at the ground but we all know he's talking to Victor.

"I'll do it." Victor answers.

"You've got one day to figure it out. We don't know how long we've got till Nessa's gone for good." I answer.

Zane and Victor nod to each other then hit the tarmac walking towards the door. Those two might be my only shot at getting Nessa back.

"What are we doing with her?" Liv asks Clint and Jon as she jerks her head towards Natalie.

Clint answers, "She's your wife, what do you want?"

I suppose Jon's spent six years imagining a reunion much different than this. There's an ache in my gut wondering if I might get the same reunion when we rescue Nessa.

"She's not the woman I married." Jon steps close to Natalie as Gavin holds her steady. "She's got to be in there." Jon's hand rests on Natalie's jawline for a blink before she thrashes it off.

"This better work." Jon looks at me, both of us knowing it's our only shot of getting the people we love back.

"Can you keep her at the hole?" Jon asks Clint.

"Sure." Liv smiles answering for Clint.

"Enough!" Clint barks snapping at Liv. "Yes, she can stay with us, I'll look after her."

Garrett's voice skips, "Like you looked after me?"

"You were a different story." Clint answers.

"Was I? I was more innocent than she is but that didn't stop you from torturing me." Garrett steps to Clint, his chest puffs out, "If we didn't need your team to get Nessa back I'd finish you right here."

Gavin, Liam and Liv step in front of Clint. No matter their differences it's clear where their loyalty lies.

"You'll have a hell of a time getting through us first." Liam answers crossing his arms.

"I'm not worried about that." Garrett steps closer.

"Enough!" Jon shouts.

Don tugs Garrett backwards.

"I think it's best if we all step away for a while. We'll meet tomorrow once Zane and Victor have evanescent up." Jon says.

Jake's arms wrap around Natasha's shaking shoulders, "I'm flying her home, I'll get her to our parents' house. They will get her the help she needs."

We all look at his pitiful sister, the way she rocks back and forth inside her blanket makes me think of a troubled child that's lost inside a warped head.

"I'll be back tomorrow to take you to Central." Jake adds.

"Take care of your sister, we'll let you know when we need you." Jon nods as he turns away from the group.

Garrett keeps his eyes locked with Clint's as he backs towards the door. Don and I take up the rear, him helping me stay on my beaten leg.

"You sure you want to do this?" Don asks as we ride the elevator together.

"You have another way?"

Don shakes his head, "No."

"Then yes, I'm sure I want to do it." I answer as the elevator lands on the first floor.

Chapter 21: Nessa

"Help me!" My screams sound clear in my head but I can't get the words out.

I'm trapped inside my body, darkness surrounds me. Am I having a vision? I calm my mind and focus. It can't be a vision, I don't feel my body tingling like it does during those times.

I hear someone near me, their breathing and strained cough tells me they're in trouble. There's more life coming, boots pound the ground in a sprint.

"In the cells! Call for backup." A voice shouts.

My brain's fuzzy but through the haze I remember I'm inside Central. It's like I'm looking at everything through a fogged window, but through the mist I find memories of the mission. Me landing in the tree, Ink and Ruse handing me over to the regulators and Natalie.

As soon as her twisted face breaks my foggy brain my body tenses in pain. I remember her torture and then everything went black. Something aches behind my head and that's when I remember the chair. They did something to me, that's why I'm somewhat disoriented, and why I can't remember anything after her torture.

"Give me a hand! We've got a live one." A man's voice echoes just outside the room.

Smoke and ash settle on my skin. That's when I remember the explosion. There was the torture then blackness just before the explosion sounded. I remember hearing Clint struggle to take Natalie. They're gone and I'm stuck to the chair inside Central.

Clint got what he came for, I'm as good as dead now. My eyes struggle to open and I fight and push them up. Black ash floats from the blown-up roof, it spirals down like dark snow. I cough as it lands in my throat.

"Live bodies inside!" A regulator shouts hearing my cough.

I try looking but my head's still locked in the halo. My brain beats inside my skull, it pulls into focus only to fall back into a blur. I hope whatever Natalie did isn't forever. Maybe with time my brain will heal.

Time, it suddenly occurs to me, is something I won't be privileged to. There was a reason she'd driven that probe into my head. She was searching for something and Clint interrupted.

Regulators enter the room and I know this isn't the last time I'll see this chair or probe. The first chance they get they'll hook me back up. This time I wonder if my brain will fall into total darkness. Instead of clouded, maybe it will be empty and blank.

"Holy shit, they came from above." The first regulator says staring at the crumbled roof.

"Help." The half-buried regulator whose breathing I've been hearing manages to whisper from beside me.

"Hurry up and get in here!" The regulator standing at the door shouts, drawing more bodies into the room.

They pay no attention to me, they think I'm dead no doubt. They work like a team, probably desperate to save as many comrades as possible. I imagine they'd consider any life a win at this point. I can't know how many people Clint's team took out, I imagine it was substantial.

"We're going to get you out of this." One says to his downed mate.

"Did we get them?" The pinned regulator asks between panting breaths.

"Not alive. We got one though, some foreigner covered in tattoos. We're running intel, we'll get an ID."

My stomach sinks as I see Ink inside my mind. He's hazy but still there, first catching me under the tree, then him dragging me into Central. He was one of the good guys, I trusted him.

"She's one of them." The downed regulator exhales as they lift another piece of rubble off his broken legs.

"Who is she?" The one asks pressing the pads of his fingers to my wrist. "There's a pulse." He says.

"Vanessa Hollins." The regulator answers as his brothers lift him to his feet.

"You're shitting me? This is Vanessa Hollins?" He doesn't pause long. "What are you two looking at? Get these damn cuffs off her. We've got to get her to a medic."

They follow his orders, each of them pulling off the cuffs that lock me down. I keep my eyes closed, somehow it helps disconnect me from this whole thing. It's like if I don't see it then maybe it's all a dream.

"We need her alive or she's no use to us."

"Use to us?" The regulator to my left questions.

"We need to put her through evanescent. She's the one we've been waiting for."

My head rolls backwards as they carry me out of the room. I let my hazy brain take over and drift into unconsciousness. Blissful darkness falls and I welcome that compared to the alternatives Central could make me suffer through.

Cold wetness hits my face, enough to snap me back to my present predicament. Hands pull at my clothes, dark soot covers the hideous pink and white combination Kara dressed me in.

"We'll need to stabilize her, enough for extraction at least." A familiar voice sounds beside me.

I've heard him before, if it wasn't for my brain fog I'd be able to place him right off. My mind strains to grab hold of his voice and the pitches that his throaty words carry.

"We need to bring her saturation levels up, give me a hundred percent oxygen." He directs and that's when I remember him. It's Dr. Glidden; the one that sunk me into my simulation during the leap test over a year ago.

The mask snaps across my face, I inhale the clean air. It pushes through my nostrils down my ash-covered airways. My breaths quicken as I drag air in as fast as my body allows. Without thinking my eyes roll open and I'm fully awake inside Dr. Glidden's clinic.

"We've got her back. Vitals are strong." Dr. Glidden says to his nurse standing at the foot of my bed.

Two regulators stand guard at the door, their guns half-raised out of their heightened sense of alert. I should tell them to relax, I doubt anyone will be coming for me so soon.

Tyler will come, knowing that scares me more than anything else. He'll risk his life for mine and that thought sickens me. If I could talk to him now I'd beg him to stay. There's no way out of this place for me. Coming here will just mean his death.

"How much of the extraction did she complete?" Dr. Glidden asks one of the guarding regulators.

"Our team's looking into that. What's inside her is of utmost importance, I know that. The foreigners took Natalie but she fought to keep Hollins here. Natalie knew more than anyone how important Miss Hollins is to Central."

"I think it's time we began the extraction again. Who knows how long we've got before they come back to get her." Dr. Glidden leans over staring into my eyes.

More than anything I wish I could stare coldly back but I can't, not with the sadness pushing to the surface. My eyes pool with tears that trickle down my face, brushing against my temples and losing their way in my auburn hair.

"Bring her to the eastern corridor. I'll stay and make sure she's stable."

Dr. Glidden smiles gently like he thinks it's a comfort. It's not comforting knowing that I've got little time left in this world with my mind intact.

Chapter 22: Ty

"Nessa's back," I moan doubling over, as my connection to Nessa gets stronger. Maybe now that she's in danger it's revved up a notch.

"What are you talking about?" Garrett asks staring at my pale, drawn-out face.

"I feel Nessa again." I say.

"Did I ever stand a chance against you?" Garrett crosses his arms staring at me.

"It's not a competition." I try hiding my smugness, somehow it makes me sound even more arrogant.

"It's not going to matter if we don't get evanescent up and operating." Zane reminds us as he tightens the last bolt.

There's something unsettling about Zane and Victor being in charge of construction. They look clumsy with the tools that will soon be used to drive a probe into my brain. I imagine it getting stuck halfway and those two tinkering around trying to figure out which bolt they forgot to screw down.

Zane hands his ratchet to Victor, "It's time," he says dabbing beads of sweat onto the back of his hand.

"You're positive?" Kara asks from the corner.

I didn't expect her to be here, not after what I did to her last night. But Kara's too good to stay away. Brian got out of surgery this morning and while she was torn, she still came to make sure I got through this thing alive.

"Who you asking?" I say to Kara.

"Both of you I suppose."

"I'm ready." I answer looking to the two masterminds for their response.

If Zane and Victor didn't look at each other in that '*I don't wanna jinx it*' way I'd have a lot more confidence going into this thing.

"Are you sure?" Kara asks pointing her question to Zane.

"As sure as we're ever going to be." He cringes saying it.

I imagine he's waiting for some snarky quip like what Liv doles out.

"Let's do this." I say, taking Zane's answer as his cue to begin.

I hoist myself into the chair, it sinks towards the ground, groaning as it goes. Metal grinds metal echoing a horrible screech.

"You sure about this?" I ask. I'm scared to move on this rickety thing now.

"It'll be fine." Victor says, answering for Zane who's turned sheet-white.

I lay back, waiting for the chair to give out from under me. She holds steady, plus there's no more squeaking, which is a bonus. Zane looks like if one more thing goes wrong he's gonna snap.

"There will be pressure as we insert the probe, once we break into the cerebrum you should be pain free." Zane says locking me into the restraints.

I think about Nessa locked to the chair like I am now. My heart bangs inside my chest for her, not for me. It drives hard into my ribs 'cuz I can't imagine doing this like she did, locked in Central surrounded by enemies.

"I can't watch." Emma says from a corner.

She pretty much begged Don to let her come. I didn't expect she'd be able to handle it, I'm surprised she lasted this long.

Don escorts Emma outta the dark room. The musty smell surrounds me. It's from being underground, inside Zane's laboratory which is really a teched-out basement.

"We're ready to start." Zane says from beside me.

I picture the silver probe sitting just under my head, thinking about it sends my heart spiking.

Victor types across his tablet, striking the last key after a blink of hesitation. Whatever he did must have initiated evanescent 'cuz with his last stroke the probe hums to life. The metal prod swirls behind my head, churning my heart and nerves as it coils.

Everything kinda tenses all at once as the blades sink into the back of my head. I picture Nessa laying in the bed next to me like we used to do at Jon's. I see us by our hillside practicing for the mission together. Thinking of her is the only way I'll get through this. She's the anchor that settles my heart, even in this pain.

"We're almost through, you'll be out soon." Victor leans over, getting close to my ear.

I guess he figured my hearing might be shot considering my current predicament. Pretty much on cue I feel the probe push a touch farther and like that, all I see is black.

Chapter 23: Garrett

We freeze as the probe sinks into Tyler's head. I don't think anyone in the room exhales until his eyes close and Zane gives us a thumbs up.

"It's working." Zane sounds surprised.

I imagine Tyler would be upset to hear his tone. I'd be irate if someone hooked me to a creation they weren't confident I'd come to survive. Then again, Tyler and I are pretty different so who knows.

I get that 'kick to the gut' feeling whenever I compare Tyler to me. I've spent over a year working to get back to Nessa and once I found out about her and Tyler, I couldn't help but make comparisons.

Nessa's strong, she wouldn't have been with Tyler just to be with someone. She's too independent to count on anyone unless she wanted to. Up until yesterday I lied to myself, I fooled myself into thinking they weren't as serious as Tyler made it sound.

Everything changed once I found out Nessa was a Prem. Hearing Tyler is a Prem only added insult to injury, and at that moment I knew they had a bigger connection than I'd wanted to believe.

I've been with Nessa since we were six and not once did she mention having visions. I've never kept a secret like that from her and the inside of me wants to break open knowing she kept something so deep from me.

I didn't sleep much last night, there were too many things running through my mind. All of them about Nessa. If I'm honest I was more embarrassed than anything else when Jon and Tyler told me about her visions.

I was supposed to be the one she loved and trusted, but somehow I didn't have the first clue about her biggest secret. After the embarrassment faded I was left sour and pissed. Didn't she trust me? What'd I ever do to deserve secrets like that? By the time the sun was rising I'd resolved myself to being broken and regretful for all the times we were together and I didn't know her truths.

Did she think I wouldn't believe her? Or maybe she thought she was a freak or that I'd leave. No matter what, one day I want her to know she was wrong. I need to tell her that I'd have stayed no matter what.

Tyler lays perfectly still and I can't help but imagine he's gone for good. It's sick and twisted because I don't actually want him dead, but the part of me that believes Nessa and I are meant for each other sees Tyler as an obstacle that I must overcome.

At some point he's probably looked at me in the same light. I know Nessa couldn't have forgotten me easily, there had to be points when Tyler didn't get what he wanted because of her feelings for me. During those times it would be natural that he'd wished I never existed. I tell myself this to try and feel better about picturing him dead.

Don clatters down the stairs, Emma must be tucked away somewhere in Zane's strange house. Maybe she's with Myra, Zane's daughter. I saw her on the way in, she was about Emma's age.

His house is strange because of how neat and orderly everything is. The way he requested we take off our shoes and position them along the wall was so meticulous, just like his home. It looks almost un-lived in, like everything upstairs was positioned at perfect angles.

This basement is another story though. The wires and monitors flash and hang from almost every free inch of space, all of them jumbled and intertwined with each other.

Don makes it to the bottom of the stairs and rounds into the light. These last few days have aged him. The bags and rings that sit beneath his eyes have puffed into pockets of sadness and fatigue. The emotional stress of having to balance protecting Emma while watching Nessa suffer in Central has been crushing.

"Is he alright?" Don asks, rounding into the room.

"So far." Kara says letting go of Tyler's wrist. "His pulse is strong and all his vitals are holding steady."

Don looks to Zane, I have a feeling Don was more concerned with the mental aspects, not Tyler's heart rate.

"It's working." Zane says.

"How much longer?" Jon asks glancing at his watch.

I imagine he's anxious to transform Natalie back.

I was up late last night, I sat in Jon's loft staring into the skyline wondering if this could work. Tyler couldn't sleep either, around two o'clock he made his way into the sitting room too.

It was awkwardly silent at first, neither of us wanting to talk to the other. He was the first to break.

"Why'd you ask 'bout Natasha?" He asked.

I paused, taking a minute to connect Natasha to the blonde haired woman Clint's crew had rescued.

"I'd seen her before." I finally answered. "I had access to the cells when I was in Central."

He stared, waiting for me to keep talking. "The guy who showed me didn't know why the prisoners were there. The cells are supposed to have the worst kinds of criminals. I never thought Central would have innocent people locked in there." I clarified sensing Tyler was judging me wrongfully.

"They let you in because you were a Borg?" He asked stepping towards the bay window.

"Borg is a pretty offensive name." I said sliding my feet to the floor.

"Why else would I say it?"

"Yeah, I get it." I stared at him. "You hate me but let's be honest, it's not just because I was a regulator." Tyler cocked his head, his look was almost condescending. "You hate me because of her. You hate me because she loved me first and you couldn't make her stay."

"Maybe." Tyler answered sitting across from me. His arms folded across his ribs. "Maybe I don't like ya because you think you've still got a chance with her."

"You don't think I've got a chance?" I answered leaning forward.

Tyler's laugh made me want to punch him in the throat.

"Time will tell. Once we've got her back we'll let her decide." He said.

"Can she make that decision? Don't you control her mind or some shit like that?" I asked looking out the window.

"It doesn't work like that, I feel her emotions and nothing more. I can't control her and wouldn't try if I could. You oughta know Nessa's too stubborn to let anyone control her."

That was the only thing Tyler and I agreed on. I thought about all the things that made Nessa the person she is. It scares me that Central could wipe her mind of every memory she's ever had. Zane and Victor seem to think they can recover whatever is lost but maybe they're wrong.

Victor interrupts my mental lapse, "We've extracted his terminal memory. We're working backwards." Victor says, stopping Jon from the frantic pacing he's been doing for the last twenty minutes.

"We'll power evanescent down to see if the extraction worked." Zane says typing furiously into his tablet.

We all stand frozen, each of our minds probably playing its own scenario of what comes next. Zane hits the final key and the metal probe backs out of Tyler's head. My stomach clenches, the idea of what just happened inside his brain doesn't sit well with me.

We're all on edge watching Kara grasp Tyler's limp wrist. Her fingers fumble around trying to find signs of life. Now that the possibility of his death seems so likely I regret wishing it earlier. Enemy or not, the idea of him dying like this doesn't seem right.

"He's still alive." She finally says, her shoulders relaxing a hair.

She lowers his wrist back to the cuff as his eyes lift open. His head jerks inside the halo.

"Where the hell am I?" He asks with his hands thrashing inside the restraints.

"Tyler it's okay." Kara answers, resting her hand on his arm.

"Get me outta these things. Where's Nessa?" He asks still thrashing.

"What's the last thing you remember?" Victor asks from beside him.

"Who the hell are you?" Tyler demands, his eyes wide with fear.

"Sorry, I'm Victor."

"He's my brother, it's me Zane."

"Get me outta this chair." Tyler barks shaking his limbs wildly.

"You're safe but we can't let you up yet." Kara coos, her hand gently strokes his shoulder as she tries calming his rattled nerves.

"We will take those cuffs off after you answer some questions." Victor adds.

Tyler's chest puffs up and down, "Where's Nessa?" No one answers but he keeps firing questions. "Was I caught? Did the mission fail?" Tyler asks frantically.

Zane answers, "You succeeded, but we don't have much time. Nessa is in danger, if you answer our questions we might be able to save her." Zane sounds authoritative for the first time ever. "What were you doing before you woke up?"

"Nessa and I were practicing our hand to hand. Hand-to-hand combat." He clarifies noticing Kara looks confused. "We have a week before the mission. What day is it?" Tyler asks confused.

"What else do you remember? Think deep, take yourself through your memories." Zane presses.

"She just landed a punch. We were supposed to be shadow boxin' but she got carried away and accidently struck a blow. She about took me to my knees but I managed to stay up." Tyler closes his eyes trying to pull the memories out. "I see her staring at me, her eyes are big and blue. She didn't mean to hit me like that. I tried pretending she'd broken my nose but I couldn't keep the lie goin' for long."

Tyler's eyes bounce back and forth under his lids, Kara holds onto his wrist keeping track of his pulse. Jon and the others wait patiently as he tries remembering.

"I broke out laughing and Nessa shoved me to my heels. We were both laughing and that's when we kissed." Tyler's smile lifts the corner of his mouth and I want to walk straight over and punch him. "That's the last of it. It ends with that kiss." Tyler says opening his eyes.

"You're sure there's nothing past that point?" Zane presses.

Tyler pauses, closing his eyes again. "Nope, it's blank." He finally answers.

"His vitals?" Victor asks Kara.

"Strong and stable." She answers still checking his pulse.

"Let's get him back under." Zane says looking at Victor.

Victor nods and they both start typing madly into their tablets.

"What's goin' on?" Tyler asks, panic in his voice.

No one answers even though Kara and Jon look at each other as if telling the other to talk first. Neither of them do, I don't blame them either, it's too much to explain to a person that's hopefully going to be enlightened in a matter of minutes.

"Hey!" Tyler yells as the probe starts spiraling towards the back of his head.

As soon as it passes his eyes fall shut and we're left in silence. Kara's eyes are wide as she stares at Jon. Don's in the corner, rocking side to side in one of Zane's rolling stools.

"We're reopening the memories from the last month. It'll be done soon." Zane says breaking the awkward silence that's fallen.

Don stops his swiveling chair to focus on Jon, "You're still planning on hooking Natalie into this?" He asks.

Jon hesitates which makes me think he's second guessing himself. "If it works, yes." He stops his pacing to look at Don. "It's my only chance at getting her back."

I don't feel sorry for Jon, at least he's got Natalie and a chance at her being whole again. As of right now Nessa's under the watch of Central. She could be strapped to a chair like Tyler is now, her brain turning to mush as they draw out her memories.

There's a glass and metal clock that sits along the western wall of the basement. We all stare at the clock watching the seconds turn into minutes as Tyler's memory gets restored.

Zane's tablet beeps, sending Don out of his seat.

"Time to bring him back." Zane says glancing around the room to each of us.

For a second my jealous head hopes Victor and Zane might have permanently erased the part of Tyler that was attached to Nessa. I shake my head knowing that's a cheap way out.

"He should be coming to." Victor says as the probe draws away from his head. We hold still, exhaling after Tyler opens his eyes again.

"It worked." Tyler says, his grin pulls his mouth wide.

"Prove it." Zane says leaning towards Tyler.

"I was confused when ya woke me. You wouldn't tell me where Nessa was. I thought I was on the hillside, she'd just hit me." Tyler says proving his memory is still intact.

"In reality?" Zane asks.

"She's in Central and I'm stuck in your dingy basement with a musty odor settlin' around me. I'd appreciate it if you'd let me outta these things." Tyler answers tightening his extremities against the restraints.

"Right, sorry." Zane says undoing the straps.

Tyler pushes himself into sitting, his legs fall to the side of the chair. "You gonna let her do it?" Tyler asks Jon.

Jon pauses before he nods. We all relax hoping that whatever's locked inside Natalie's mind will give us clues to getting Nessa back.

"I'll get her." Jon says turning to find Natalie.

Chapter 24: Ty

Kara wraps a bandage around my head. I'm surprised I
didn't bleed more. It's sorta amazing how my mind forgets what
the pain felt like, even though it was only minutes ago.

"Don't touch." Kara says slapping my hand as I reach for
my neck.

"Sorry, just wanted to feel what went on." I say dropping
my hand.

"That's a good way to tear the stitches." She packs up her
medical bag, peeling off her gloves.

"I woudn't wanna ruin your fancy work." I say joking.

"I'm not happy with you Ty. Things might never go back to normal." She lifts her black leather bag from the chair.

"I get it, I'm sorry. I'm not proud of what I did but I thought it was the only way." I push the gauze up higher on my forehead.

"Maybe with time I'll forgive you." She says as Jon comes stumbling from upstairs.

"Natalie stop fighting!" He yells trying to help her down the steps.

"Let go of me!" She screams, leaning backwards into him as she thrashes.

She looks like a child throwing a tantrum, it's almost funny watching a grown woman going berserk.

Don grabs ahold of one of her arms, "Let me help," he says tugging Natalie towards the chair.

Once she sees the chair she throws herself into full throttle crazy.

"No! NO!" She bucks, managing to push Don to the floor.

He's embarrassed which is why I don't offer to help him up.

"Come on," I grit taking over Don's role of dragging her.

"This is for your own good." Jon says with his eyes rimmed with tears.

"Please don't do this to me. Please, I'm begging you." She stares into Jon's eyes, pulling at his weak heart.

Kara touches Jon's shoulder, "It's the only way." She reminds him. "She's not your wife and won't be again unless we do this. They ruined the *real* Natalie, we've got to get her back."

"Don't listen to her," Natalie snarls looking at Kara.

Zane clears his throat, "We've got to try and unlock what's inside her. There's a chance we can pull the key to getting Nessa out alive."

"Please don't fight." Jon says tipping Natalie back into the chair.

She doesn't listen. It takes four of us to hold her down while Victor secures the restraints. The way she spits and shakes reminds me of the exorcism movie I'd watched when I was recovering in the burn unit months ago.

"Secure the halo and we'll start." Zane says nodding to Victor.

The metal ring clamps down and we step away from the chair. I think of the movie and how the girl levitated, hovering above the bed. I imagine Natalie doing that, I think she's crazy enough and pumped full of enough evil that it could happen.

Zane and Victor get to work, fingers flying across their tablets as Natalie shakes in place. The probe inches towards her neck. I can't believe that was me just minutes ago, it looks barbaric.

Her shaking stops once the probe sinks in. It lines up with the scar from Central's own probe. I wonder if there's an expiration date on memories.

Maybe if you hide memories for so long they can't be brought back. If that's the case, Jon will waste away. Everything that drives him has been about getting Natalie back. Beads of sweat form on his forehead as he paces, a ball of nerves. The rest of us stare at Jon wondering if we should escort him out.

"What?" He says wiping his forehead.

"Ya alright?" I ask staring at him.

"Are you? Because I'm fine, nervous but fine." He answers.

Don and I share a look, a *'this guy looks crazy'* look. We both turn our backs to Jon, his bouncing is too distracting.

"We're extracting memories." Zane says fixed on his tablet. "We'll need to go all the way back, it's the only way to ensure we haven't missed anything." Zane looks to Jon.

"How long will that take?" Jon asks, obviously put off that this process might go on for a long time.

"Hard to say, depends on how many memories they implanted in her. We have to pull out a lifetime of her real memories and possibly a lifetime of fabricated Central ones too."

"That could take days." Jon cusses turning on his heels.

"More like a day, maybe two." Victor answers, forcing Jon to wheel back around.

I cut Jon off, I don't care about him or Natalie, just Nessa.

"I don't have a day or two to wait. We gotta start gettin' Nessa now."

My tone says I'm serious about this.

"I'll go with you." Don chimes from the corner. "Ty's right, we need to go before it's too late."

"I'm going too." Garrett belts from across the room.

His puffed chest is his way of telling me not to argue. I'm not intimidated by him. I woulda wanted him there anyway. He used to be a regulator, that kinda past might help us get to Nessa.

"Good, it's settled then." I say nodding to Don and Garrett.

Victor talks without lifting his head, "I should have your information from evanescent summarized within an hour, two at most."

"You only did a month, right?" I ask thinking if there was anything significant that coulda made itself inside my brain in a month. "I only ask 'cuz I doubt you'll pull anything interesting from these last thirty days."

"You're a Prem, what's inside your brain could make all the difference in the world. You might never even know it. It'd be careless if I didn't look for premonitions."

I wait to talk, trying to decide if I believe it's even possible I've got future predictions just floating around. I'm pretty sure this evanescent-Prem connection is a theory, not a fact.

"Jake's supposed to be at Clint's any blink now. Liv and the others will be waitin' for us. I'm not about to miss this chance so that you can play around with that computer thing."

Jon steps closer to Natalie, brave enough to touch her now that she's knocked out.

"We can contact the team through Jake's broadcast feature. If we learn anything we'll communicate it with you." Jon says resting his hand on Natalie's arm.

"Sounds good." I holler over my shoulder as I take my crutches and head for the stairs.

"You're doing that all wrong." Garrett says stopping me on the second step.

My face screws up, "Excuse me?" I ask trying to hop onto the third step.

"I was on crutches after I left the Inner. The regulators gave me a little 'welcome to Central' ass-kicking after the banquet."

He's the last person I want advice from, I hop up the third step and manage to almost face plant onto the fourth.

"Shit!" I yell teetering on my heels. Don braces my back, stopping me from falling.

"What's the trick?" I finally ask rolling my eyes.

"May I?" Garrett asks.

I'm not sure why he asked since he was prying the crutches outta my hand before I even nodded yes.

I hate to admit it but he was right. He flies up Zane's steps, holding one foot up to prove I don't need it. I try to listen even though everything he says makes me boil. I finally cut him off mid-sentence, snatching the crutches back.

"Thanks." I manage saying as I bounce up the stairs faster than before.

I don't like hating him but I can't help it. It feels immature to fight over a girl, but here we are doing it anyway. I try exercising patience when I'm around Garrett but as soon as he opens his mouth I wish he'd shut up.

I think it's because I still see Nessa crumbled on stage screaming for him as the regulators took him away. My heart hurt hearing his name come outta her mouth. I know there was a time Nessa loved him and part of me is scared she could fall for him again.

"Liam's supposed to meet us. He should be here in a blink." I say as Don, Garrett and I stand outside of Zane's small yellow house.

"Which one's Liam?" Don asks, fidgeting with his shirt cuffs.

He's not used to tailored shirts like the one Jon loaned him.

"Red-headed guy." I say watchin' him mess around with the buttons.

"That's him." I say pointing down the street to the orange hover that's approaching.

Don turns to Emma, she's standing in Zane's screened doorway.

"They will watch over you while I'm gone." He says blowing Emma a kiss.

The screen door squeaks as Emma pushes it open. "Be safe papa, I love you." She says climbing down the stairs.

"I love you too. Don't worry Emma, you'll be safe. We'll bring Nessa back." He says squeezing her tight.

"Load up!" Liam shouts slapping the roof of his hover.

"I'll see you soon." Don says kissing Emma's forehead.

Don cranks his head around to make sure Emma's made her way back into Zane's place. Once the screen door closes he takes a massive exhale. It makes me feel sorry for the guy.

"You don't have to do this." I say.

"I do. I failed Nessa once, I won't do it again."

"What were you supposed to do? You didn't know Central had lied to you." Garrett says from behind me.

Obviously they've shared some sort of conversation about this before. I find it hard not to hold the past against Don. I was part of the lie that convinced the Inner to believe Nessa and I were scouts, but I wouldn't have bought it if I were him.

If that was my daughter on that telecast saying she was leaving after the way things went down with Garrett the night before, I'd have known something was up. You better believe I'd have fought to make sure my daughter was safe.

Maybe Don's way of righting that wrong is by going with us now. He doesn't look like the type of guy that takes risks regularly. His pale face looks nearly transparent, the color draining the closer we get to Clint's.

"This looks familiar." Garrett says from the back.

"Should, we're going to the hole. Isn't that where Clint was keeping ya?" I ask looking at him and Liam.

Now Garrett's face is draining like Don's. Both of them terrified of the things they're about to face.

"Don't worry, we're not going to hurt you." Liam says.

"Forgive me if I don't trust you. The last time I was under your care I was bound and beaten." Garrett shifts uncomfortably in his seat.

Liam ignores him and looks at me instead. "You're not in the best condition, you really think it's wise to go?" Liam asks.

"Are you talking to me?" I ask stunned.

"No, the other guy with bullet wounds and crutches." Liam shakes his head, "Yes you, who else?"

I'd be stupid if that thought hadn't crossed my mind. Of course I recognize my condition is less than ideal. It doesn't matter to me, I've got to do something to get her back.

"I'm not about to stay here while you have all the fun." I swallow knowing that what's about to happen is far from fun. "Plus you've got your own bumps." I nod to his arm.

"That's nothing, I'll patch it up later." Liam smiles.

Don chimes from the back, "Liam has a point Ty. You're not really fit for walking much less fighting."

"I'll tell ya what, if I hold you back just go on without me. I'll take care of myself."

"I'm not going to leave you there." Liam says turning a corner.

Garrett speaks without missing a beat, "Did you tell Nessa that too?"

Liam shakes his head, the frustration is pretty clear. I've got a feeling that if Garrett keeps pushing his buttons Liam might snap.

"Nessa knew what the risks were." Liam answers back.

"She didn't know Clint had me though. If she did she wouldn't have gone."

"I'm not so sure about that, it wasn't all about you Garrett. She didn't want Central bombing here either." Liam grits his teeth in the rearview mirror.

I'm sick of listening to them, "Enough!" I yell. "Does it matter *why* she went? We can worry about settling scores once we've got her back."

"Settle a score with us?" Liam laughs turning the hover into the hole.

"Maybe I won't have to. We get Nessa back alive and I'll forget this whole thing happened." My face is stone cold.

Liam doesn't press me, I think he sorta sees that without her I'm a man that's got nothing left to lose.

"What is this place?" Don's legs creep outta the hover, landing on broken glass.

"It's Clint's training facility. Nessa and I came here before our mission, he calls it the hole. Clint taught us how to fight and stay alive."

My crutches grind on the broken glass that litters the parking lot. This place looks like a dump but it's got its own touch of nostalgia with me. I step towards the doors, looking down at the blood stained sidewalk where I fell yesterday. A brutal reminder of how fast things can change. In a blink Nessa was in front of me and then she was pulling away on a suicide mission to Central.

Garrett mutters behind me, "This is where Clint and his people were holding me hostage."

It's a good thing Liam took off in front, if he'd heard one more mention of that from Garrett I think he woulda flipped.

"They'll take care of Emma right?" Don says striding next to me.

The human part of me wants to say 'yes' straight off. It's the nice thing to say since it would put a hurting man's mind at ease. I walk forward wondering what the chances are that Emma is safe here.

"The one thing I know is that nothing is guaranteed in this world." I hobble forward, catching Don's confused look. "I don't know if she'll be safe. I think they will look after her but nothing is for sure."

Garrett reaches for Don, "You can stay with Emma, Tyler and I understand. We'll bring Nessa back."

"Can you call me Ty, I keep thinking my mom's in the room whenever you say Tyler."

Garrett's eyes shoot daggers but at last he nods.

The grimy brick walls of the hole look dingier than when Nessa and I were here. I imagine that with every passing day this place is gonna age and slowly crumble. I don't see Clint or his team being the ones to decorate or repair this shoddy spot.

"Here it is." I say pulling the door open.

The boxing ring and benches line the room, the broken lockers gleam against the flickering lights.

Clint's sitting on the first bench, his feet rest apart as his shoulders hold straight. He's solid and looks frightening sitting there.

"We're going to have some serious hurdles to overcome." He says rising.

"Like?" I ask, wobbling on my crutches.

He nods to my unsteady steps, "That for starters."

"I'll be fine, if you think I'm holding ya back, ditch me."

"Can you keep up?" Clint asks looking at Don from head to toe.

It's an honest question since Don looks aged beyond his years.

"I carried him up the stairs yesterday." Don nods to me but Clint doesn't budge. "I'll be fine, you've got my permission to leave me too."

Don nods to me, confident that he won't be the one left behind.

"Don't think we won't." Clint barks turning on us.

That's a whole lot different than Liam, at least he said he'd stay. We follow behind Clint, walking through the winding halls into his briefing room.

"This will be quick." Clint says taking his seat.

Jake, Liv, Gavin and Liam sit around the steel table looking us up and down as we enter. We fall into the empty chairs and wait for Clint to talk.

"It's safe to assume Central's going to be using evanescent to clear Nessa's brain. For whatever reason they want what she's got, they will do just about anything to get it. I don't think they'll keep her alive once they're done, not unless what they find shows her death as a disadvantage."

Clint stops for a blink, my mind races. At first I thought Central was extreme for threatening war on an entire nation over one girl but once Zane told us about evanescent I started to see why.

Clint's right, Central must know that somewhere inside Nessa's mind there's a key that only she can unlock. That's why Natalie wouldn't let Clint kill Nessa, she must have known it too. Once Central gets what they need she's disposable to them.

I wonder how far back this whole thing goes. Did some Prem see Natalie years ago? Maybe that's why Central kept her and the team. Maybe Natalie's time in evanescent was what started Central's push for Nessa. Who knows, maybe none of it is true and my head's getting the best of me?

Clint starts again, "You got Natasha taken care of?" He asks Jake.

"Yes, she's with our parents. They'll get her treatment."

"Good. I assume you're still willing to fly?" Clint asks Jake.

"Wouldn't miss it, if it wasn't for Nessa we wouldn't have Natasha back. I owe her."

"You still on board?" Clint directs his sharp eyes to Liv, Gavin and Liam.

"Yes Sir." Liam answers proudly.

Liv nods her head, "Prem was good. Jake's right, we owe it to her. Plus I want to kill those regulator bastards."

Liv's the type of person that would kill for sport but I know her want for vengeance comes from a hurting place.

I don't even know her but I can tell she guards her heart fiercely. She's also someone that's had her heart crushed. I'm thinking Ink was special to her. He was more than just a member of the killing squad Clint's assembled. His death sparked her need for revenge and I'm scared for any regulator that gets in her path.

Clint nods. "I don't expect Zane to have much intel from Natalie for a while so we'll be going in blind." Clint doesn't sugar coat the truth. "Liv, Liam, Gavin and I will be the initial drive team."

"What about me?" I ask noticing my name wasn't included.

Clint looks at my leg, "You can't enter in your condition, it could compromise everything. I don't think it's wise you go at all but I've got a feeling you wouldn't be alright with that."

"And me?" Garrett asks.

"You'll be with Ty, he knows how to use a gun if you get in a pinch out there."

"You know I was a regulator right? I know how to use guns *and* I know my way around Central better than any of you."

Clint sweeps his eyes to Garrett, "I know who you are and what you know. We're going to need you with Ty in case things go south, we don't want just one armed man out there."

"How am I helping?" Don asks trying to get a grasp on his role.

"You'll be a decoy if we need one. Chances are we will." Clint looks at me, "We'll leave some RPG's with you, when we need a distraction you'll use them."

"There's no way you'll let me go with you?" Garrett asks Clint.

"Not a chance." Clint says ending the conversation.

"Stop freaking out, we'll get her." Liv says piercing us with her cold eyes.

"Central will be expecting something so we'll have to exert extreme caution. It's safe to assume Central's going to increase their radar field so we can't parachute close to the Capital."

"You parachuted in?" Garrett asks shocked.

"Dropped them at 13,000 feet." Jake answers.

"Nessa did that?" Garrett can't believe it.

"She's done a lot of things you'd be surprised about." I blurt.

Liv snaps, "We get it, you both want the same girl. It's not the first time a piece of tail has got in the way of a mission, but not on my watch." Liv points her finger at both of us, turning her hand into an imaginary gun. "Either put your issues aside or I'll get rid of you." She waves the imaginary gun back and forth towards our heads.

"Got it." Garrett answers as her gun holds in the direction of his dome.

Liv shifts her finger to my head, waiting for my answer.

"Got it." I say ready to end this threat.

Liam speaks from across the table, "If you think she's bluffing you're wrong. She'll drop you without flinching if she thinks it's best for the mission."

"I believe her." I say remembering Liv's hologram clearing rooms full of regulators the other night.

Don looks to Garrett and me, "Now that we've cleared that up?" It sounds like he's asking a question.

We both nod.

"We'll have to parachute far out from Central's radars. Jake will be able to see where they are but he expects Central to extend them to twenty miles outside the city limits." Clint directs.

"Try thirty-five." Garrett chides from his side of the table.

We stare at him, Don's the only one that doesn't give him a dirty look.

"Maybe being a regulator won't be such a bad thing after all." Garrett says eyeing Clint.

"Fine, Jake will most likely be dropping us thirty-five miles outside the city. We'll still parachute in." Clint stares at Garrett. "Did your regulator training cover that?"

"I was a pilot, I know how to parachute and I could probably teach you a thing or two."

If Liv could kill with a look Garrett would be dead. He stays calm and focuses straight ahead.

"In that case you'll be jumping with Ty."

"Excuse me?" I ask Clint, hoping I heard wrong.

"Remember…" Liv says pointing her imaginary gun at my head. "You two play nice now."

Clint cuts her off, "Garrett seems to think he could teach us all a lesson so I'm going to let him go tandem with you, might bring you two closer." Clint grins. "Don, you'll be jumping with me."

"How are we penetrating the AO?" Liam asks moving the briefing forward.

"Hover-choppers. Jake will make the drop just before we jump. He'll also be dropping those RPG's. Once we recover those we'll high tail it to the AO."

I'd seen some commercials for hover-choppers at Jon's, but I've never actually seen one directly. Jon told me they were modeled after motorcycles but that didn't help me get a picture either.

"Two riders to each chopper." Clint continues. "Don will stay with me, Garrett with Liam, Liv you're with Ty." Of course I'm stuck with the most mentally unstable person this side of the divide. "Gavin will ride solo."

"We'll take the woods toward the city. Once we're within the ground radars range we'll split up. The initial drive team will go through the hole Jake left inside the cells. You three will be outside the Capital waiting as a decoy."

"Once we fire this RPG, then what?" I ask picturing shooting off a rocket just to get pounced on by Borgs in a matter of minutes.

"You'll run." Clint answers and I know that means we'll try to escape but we won't make it.

No parta me wants to die but if that's the only way to rescue Nessa then that's what we'll have to do.

"Keep the hover-choppers in close range, you can push them to the decoy point if needed."

Don looks at me and Garrett, "Do either of you know how to fly one of those things?" He asks

Both Garrett and I shake our heads no. Having choppers isn't comforting when you don't have a clue how to use 'em.

"I suggest you watch your driver then." Clint snaps. "None of you *have* to go. Decide now if you're staying or not, I can't have you wasting valuable time."

None of us back out.

"How will we be extracted?" Gavin asks swaying calmly in his chair.

"Once we make the call, Jake will come in close for the pick up. We'll have three resistance fighters with him. They'll be dropping bombs to help distract Central from Jake. Once we've recovered the team the resistance fighters will break away and we'll try to outrun Central's crafts."

"That won't be easy, not unless you disable the CC's tower command." Garrett says from across the table. "Pilot patroller, remember?"

"Can you do that?" Liv asks before Clint has a chance to talk.

"It won't be easy but I can get into the CC, I'll need help though."

"How much time?" Clint asks.

Garrett sits while his head adds and subtracts all the variables that go into this equation.

"Ten minutes from arrival to departure. I'll need a set of guns to protect me on the way in and out. We'll need someone like Zane or Victor. They can be on this side of the wall. I just need them to hack into the CC when we get there. The system's flawed, they only use one program to control the entire center. If that went down all their crafts would be grounded."

"To disable it?" Clint asks knowing it sounds too good to be true.

"It's underground and guarded by five regulators at all times. Once we take them out the hack will break us into the control center and it's as simple as cutting some wires. That will buy us enough time to get to Nessa."

"This one is on you." Clint says staring at Garrett.

It's pretty clear that Clint's not used to taking directions from anyone. The way his eye twitches shows his annoyance.

"Sounds like we've got a decent plan. I'm on board." I say trying to build camaraderie.

Instead Don and Garrett sit somber while Liv, Gavin and Liam look eager to start the killing. Clint's eyes meet with mine, I can tell he doesn't trust Garrett's plan.

Clint snaps back to his leader position, "Questions?" He asks.

"Only a million but none that you can answer." Don says dropping his eyes.

I've been overwhelmed before but not the way Don is now. Don looks worried and pained at the same time.

"We're going to get her back." I say looking straight at him.

I give him my word 'cuz out here that's all I've got, but I mean it.

Chapter 25: Nessa

The chair wheels down the expansive halls, regulators and researchers surround me. I find it hard to believe they need so many escorts. Every one of my extremities is restrained, I couldn't move even if I tried.

Dr. Glidden walks level to my head, I see the side of his face as I am wheeled farther into the Capitol. The back of my head feels raw which isn't surprising considering the probe they just took out.

I shudder thinking about going through the process again. At least Natalie's gone, hopefully that means the pre-probe process won't be filled with torture. She must be with Jon and the others right now. I hope Ty is torturing her.

As we move along, I wonder which room Garrett's in, maybe he's feet away but I'd never know. My lips peel apart as I try calling for him.

"Garrett," I say weakly, getting louder with each attempt. Finally I shout, "Garrett!"

Dr. Glidden stares down at me, his eyes warning me but I don't listen.

"Garrett! It's me Nessa." I scream as the chair glides down the hall.

"Let's take her to the boys' room." Dr. Glidden directs to the regulator in the lead.

"Sir?" He asks.

"Take her to Garrett, let her see him." Dr. Glidden says.

My heart skips. When he sees me he'll know I tried saving him, I need him to know that.

"You are supposed to release him. That's what the broadcast said." I mutter.

"That's what Natalie said, but she appears to be missing. I'll tell you what… we'll honor that promise once she comes back." Dr. Glidden smirks.

In other words, Garrett's as good as dead. Jon and his team won't let Natalie come back, and even if she did, Central wouldn't let Garrett live. I should have known this would happen.

The lead regulator steers the pack to the right, my chair bangs into the wall. Nobody apologies, as they don't look at me as human.

Dr. Glidden turns to me, "You can see Garrett and what we've done with him. After that we'll wipe your memory and start clean. By this time tomorrow you may be dead, or taking Natalie's position if that's what we want."

We turn down another hall before the regulators stop. We must be at the place Garrett's being held. Maybe there's some way Zane is getting my sonar signal still. Maybe he'll be able to find Garrett and rescue him. Thinking of Garrett being saved makes it easier to accept that I won't be.

"Show her in." Dr. Glidden says as my escort's wheel my chair into a dark room.

"Where is he?" I ask trying to see in the dark. "Garrett!" I yell with my voice echoing back.

"Light's on." Dr. Glidden directs.

There's a second where my hands tremble as I wonder what I'm about to see. The overhead lights flutter on one at a time, working their way from the back towards the front.

"Garrett!" I scream looking at him tied to the chair.

"He can't hear you." Dr. Glidden says whispering in my ear.

Garrett's head rolls side to side, I see him sitting alone in the sterile room, he's still tied to the same chair. There's a large glass window separating our two rooms. It must be one-way glass since his brown eyes look right at me without reaction.

"Let him go!" I scream thrashing.

"You were willing to die for him?" Dr. Glidden asks pointing at Garrett's limp body.

"Yes." I say staring into his brown eyes.

There's a part of me that will always hold Garrett close to my heart. Seeing him now reminds me that we are bonded for eternity in some way. Maybe everyone has an eternal connection to their first love, or maybe it's something only Garrett and I share.

"We'll see about that." Dr. Glidden grins. "Let's deliver a message," he says to the regulator closest to him.

I can't turn my head to see the man leave, but I hear his steps march to the room across from me. He swings the door open with his gun raised. It points at Garrett's head as he marches behind him.

Dr. Glidden nods to the regulator next to me, "Let's make things interesting." He says.

The regulator smiles, radioing across to his comrade. "Roulette," he says.

I watch the regulator empty his revolver of all but one bullet. He closes it, spinning the chamber around.

"Do you like games Miss Hollins?' Dr. Glidden asks. "I bet you do. How about we play a game." He walks around to the other side of me. "You answer my questions, or not. If not then Ben over there is going to spin his barrel, point his gun at Mr. Blaine and pull the trigger."

"Don't do this!" I scream as the regulator spins the chamber again.

"Focus." Dr. Glidden says squeezing my chin. "Who did you come here with?" He asks staring deep into my eyes.

"Foreigners, there were eight of us." I answer desperate to keep Garrett alive.

"Good Miss Hollins. Who was in charge of your group?" He asks brushing my cheek.

His first question was simple enough, it didn't put Clint and his team at risk. I hesitate not knowing how to answer his second.

"I never met the leader. They were soldiers, they took orders from someone they'd never met."

"Lie." Dr. Glidden says banging the glass behind him.

The regulator presses his gun against Garrett's head and pulls the trigger. My gut squeezes as the gun clicks. Garrett's safe.

"Once again, who was the leader?" He asks as the regulator spins the chamber again.

I hesitate and Dr. Glidden reaches to bang the glass again.

"Wait!" I scream, stopping him. "His name was Clint. I don't know anything else about him. I was hiding with some foreigners, they didn't know who I was. That's when Clint and his team took me. They'd seen the news and I guess wanted to be the ones to surrender me. I don't know why."

It's a lie but I've got to protect Jon and his organization.

Dr. Glidden paces, deciding if he'll believe my story.

"How did they know where you and Natalie were? How did they find the cells?" He asks leaning in front of me.

"I don't know." I answer.

He bangs the glass again as the regulator aims his gun. He pulls the trigger and my heart clenches tight. Another empty shot clicks.

"Lucky, lucky, lucky." Dr. Glidden says pacing again. "No more games, no more lies." He says nodding to the regulator beside me.

He radios to his comrade and my throat squeezes as I watch the regulator across from me re-load all the bullets.

"No more chances Miss. Hollins." Dr. Glidden says. "How did they know your location?"

He reaches for the window ready to pound his fist, only this time it will mean Garrett dies.

"Stop! I'll tell you!" I scream. "I've got a second implant, it's a sonar that was feeding the layout to our team."

Dr. Glidden smiles, "Good girl." He bangs his fist against the glass.

"No! I told you!" I scream as the regulator pulls the trigger one last time.

Garrett lifts his eyes and looks at me, just like he did on the broadcast. The regulator wraps his finger around the trigger and my entire body collapses inwards. This is my breaking point, after this I'll never be the same.

The gun fires and just like that Garrett's head snaps down. In an instant he's gone. He was my friend and my first love and now he's dead, lifeless and empty.

"You bastard!" I yell, spitting at Dr. Glidden. "Garrett!" I scream trying to tear from my restraints.

"Not to worry Miss Hollins." Dr. Glidden says rubbing the top of my head. He turns to the regulator nearest the door, "Reboot." He says, his hand still stroking the top of my head.

The lights power down as the building groans. The regulator thrusts another switch and the lights come back to life.

The sterile room's empty now. No chair, desk, or Garrett. Just unforgiving white walls.

"What the…" I say looking for signs of Garrett.

"We always get what we want Miss Hollins, which is why you and your foreigners will never win."

There's a flicker in the room across from me as a shadowy image of the chair and Garrett flash. On the third flicker they stay lit up and clear. Right in front of me is Garrett again, alive and beaten as he slumps in the chair.

"It wasn't hard creating the hologram of Mr. Blaine, I've got to admit it does look rather convincing." Dr. Glidden leans over my shoulder. "Convincing enough to sacrifice myself and my team for…that I can't say." Dr. Glidden says.

"You don't have him?" I ask confused as I watch Garrett across the room.

"It was a bluff Miss Hollins, one that paid off rather favorably."

If I'd known he was safe I would have stayed with Ty. There would still be the chance of Central attacking the foreigners but the Republic must have ways to prevent that. There are so many things I would have done differently if I'd known Garrett wasn't here.

Dr. Glidden and his pack of regulators wheel me out of the room and down the hall. I begin questioning why I'm so important to them. All this trouble just for me?

My chair turns around a corner as I try reasoning why they need me. It has to have something to do with that probe they pushed in my head.

"Miss Hollins it's been a pleasure escorting you, now it's time to put you to good use." Dr. Glidden says stopping my chair beneath the fluorescent overhead lights.

"What are you going to do?" I ask swallowing hard.

"No need in telling you, you will forget everything soon enough." Dr. Glidden nods to one of the regulators beside my chair.

The probe spirals from behind me and my chest pounds in time to the grinding. They are going to wipe me off this map. I'll be a lifeless body without family to send me off properly. No last words as Central takes my body, silence just like there was for mama.

My beating heart wails as I hope Clint and his team will burst through the door to save me. I picture them swooping down right before the probe sinks in.

The grinding metal closes in and I know what's about to happen. Just as I close my eyes the probe pushes into my head and I'm left without Clint or his team. Instead I'm left with Dr. Glidden breathing next to me as I sink into darkness that I might never come back from.

Chapter 26: Ty

Everything's blank again and I know they've got her back in evanescent. I push outta my seat and shove my fists against the metal tabletop.

"They are putting her back under. We need to leave now!" I say slowly lifting my head to look at Clint.

Garrett stands, folding his arms across his waist. He and I will sort our Nessa issues out later, right now we're in this together.

We all stare at Clint, all of us ready to risk our necks to get Nessa back. Clint looks at us, each of us wearing our own emotions. There's Don who looks terrified, either for himself or for his daughter. Liam looks straight ahead, once he's committed himself to something you can tell he won't back down. Liv stares at Clint, her index finger taps her hip. She's got the look of revenge in her eyes. She wants into Central to finish what Marcus couldn't. Jake looks ahead, his eyes softer; his motivation comes from a place of gratitude not revenge.

I look over to Garrett and I imagine my eyes looking the exact way his do now. He's on his feet ready to fight for the girl he loves. If it wasn't over the same girl I'm fighting for, I might almost think it's sweet.

All of us stare at Clint until he finally exhales and rises up.

"What are we standing around here for?" Clint asks, catching us off guard.

He's not the joking type so none of us know how to respond.

"Let's go!" Clint yells pounding the table.

All of us jump, we weren't expecting that, even though we should've; it was definitely a more Clint-appropriate response. We file outta the room with Clint leading us. I hobble behind the pack, losing ground even though we haven't left the hole yet.

"Keep up tripod" Liv yells over her shoulder.

Liam laughs looking back at me struggling with my one crutch. I left the second one in the room. I think I'm faster without it. I don't bother defending myself, I've got a feeling the harder I resist the harder Liv will push me.

Clint's just unlocking the steel door that must be some sort of safe. Normal doors don't have turn-knob combinations and metal bars you need to spin to get inside, that's how I know this isn't a normal room.

He pushes it open and the bright lights flick on. Liv, Gavin and Liam hop around the room, jumping on their toes and beating their knuckles together. Don helps me inside, their excitement makes sense.

"This is all yours?" Garrett asks in awe.

He reaches for one of the hundreds of guns that hangs inside Clint's armory. His hand almost touches the black stock but Clint gets to him first, slapping his fingers away.

"Don't touch." He says narrowing his eyes at Garrett.

"Yes sir." Garrett answers putting his arms behind him.

There was a blink when the regulator in Garrett came out. I saw his understanding that Clint was his leader and needed respect, even if it's for this mission only.

"Liv get silencers for everyone, Liam and Gavin assemble a D-day pack." Clint directs keeping his eyes on Garrett.

"D-day pack?" Don asks.

"None of your concern. Suffice it to say it holds enough bombs and weapons to take down three capitols if we wanted." Clint answers.

Liam and Liv race around the room laying equipment into a neat line. It sits across the table that cuts the room in half. Each of them pack their weapons into individual duffle bags.

"I assume you don't know how to shoot." Clint asks Don.

"No I don't." Don answers with wide eyes.

"Today's not the day to learn." Clint answers shaking his head.

He pulls one of the small guns outta the drawer behind him. He hands it to Don who holds it like a dead fish.

"What am I supposed to do?" Don answers pointing it towards Clint.

"Not that way!" Clint answers pushing the barrel aside. "You point it at things you want dead, you still need me so no pointing yet."

Don nods as Garrett and I divide our attention between Clint's lesson and the racket Liv and Liam are making as they clear the shelves.

"You point it at what you want to shoot, press this and pull the trigger." Clint says. "Don't forget to press this, without it the gun's on safety and won't shoot."

"That's it?" Don asks.

"Hell no that's not it, but I already told you today's not the day to learn." Clint rips the gun outta Don's hands and tucks it inside a holster. "You only use this if it's the last resort, because that's what it would have to be, the last resort."

"Okay, I've got it." Don says with his hands shaking as he fastens the holster around his waist.

"Okay boss, we've got everything packed." Liv chimes from across the table.

"Get your suit and load up!" Clint yells pointing across the room at a collection of canvas jump suits that hang from a wall.

We each grab a heavy suit, it's pulled down by the weight of the harness and parachute attached to the back. I take two steps with my suit slung across my back when I realize I can't handle it, not with my bullet wounds throbbing like they are.

"I've got this." Liam says pulling my suit from me.

He hauls outta the room carrying two suits and two monstrous bags of weapons. He makes it look easy, even with his bum arm that's dripping blood.

"Keep up tripod." Liv says walking in front of me. "Liam's not gonna be out there to carry your weight in Central."

"I've already told him you can leave me there." I say between gritted teeth.

Liv spins, "That's exactly what we'll do, so I suggest you man up and get moving. We've all been hit before, you either find it inside to dig deep and push on or you die."

There's nothing I can say to that, she's harsh but she's telling the truth. I stagger forward, pushing myself to keep up.

Clint steps outta the hole with us marching behind him. Garrett's been beat up pretty bad, I've been shot twice, Liam and Clint both took shots in their arms. At least there's Don, Gavin and Liv, the only ones that seem somewhat whole.

Our team may be wounded but I sorta think it's those wounds that are gonna push us harder. I'll use my pain to dig deep and get Nessa back.

Clint's the first to step onto Jake's hover. We all file in after him, I take the longest. I feel Liv lookin' at me, I don't bother to turn towards her, I'm the weakest link and she's probably thinking of ways to terminate me.

"Same drill as yesterday." Clint looks at Liv and Liam.

"Except Ink's not here." Liv says looking down.

"You need to turn that pain into rage Bull's eye." Clint says. "Use it to get Nessa out."

Liv nods, scrunching her face.

Liam sits next to her. He just finished dumping some sorta powder into his bullet wound. He hums to himself as he wraps his arm in a tight band of gauze.

"For the rest of you," Clint says looking at Garrett, Don and me, "you'll be suiting up in those, and your partner will secure your harness."

My gut flops thinking about Garrett helping me suit up. He stares straight ahead, his dark brown eyes are empty of emotion.

"Suit up!" Clint shouts sending us all scrambling.

My crutch keeps sliding across the base of the hover as I try holding to the strap above my head. Garrett gets his suit on fast but doesn't try helping me. I can't pull it over my back without help. Don finally steps up.

"If you two love Nessa like you say, then put your issues aside and help each other. It's the only way we'll get her back," he scolds. He pulls my jumpsuit over my shoulders zipping it tight.

"Harnesses!" Clint yells as he and his team jump into the complicated system.

Garrett's a little off balance, I imagine dehydration and malnutrition are to blame for that. Even so, he gets his harness on and steps to me.

I swallow my pride and let Garrett help, I keep tellin' myself that Don's right and we need to bury this feud, even if it's temporary.

"You sure you know how to do this?" I ask Garrett as he pulls the last strap tight.

Don stands across from us as Clint secures his last strap too. I don't think I've given Don the credit he outta get. He's got more reasons than most to back down, Emma's with the foreigners, he coulda stayed and we wouldn't have thought twice but here he is. He holds the loop above his head and sways.

Maybe he is where Nessa gets her courage from. I can almost picture her standing there holding the same strap with her head held high, just like his.

"I'm shutting down communications with the outside!" Clint barks ready to flick the switch.

"Clint!" Jake yells from the cockpit, stopping him before he can.

"What's going on?" Clint mutters stepping towards Jake.

"Zane just patched through, he says he needs to talk to Ty and Garrett." Jake answers.

"No way, we don't have time." Clint barks.

There's a pause as Jake delivers Clint's message. Clint turns to flick his radio off again.

"Zane said it can't wait." Jake hollers back.

"Shit!" Clint yells directing Garrett and me to the cockpit.

We both stare at each other, confused as to what the meaning behind this is. This better be worth it, every blink we're out here is one that Nessa's in Central.

"What's goin' on?" I ask ducking into the cockpit.

"Put these on." Jake says handing Garrett and I headsets.

"Hello?" I say into static.

"Ty?" I hear Zane answer.

"Yea, it's me. What the heck's going on?" I ask.

"There's something you should know…" He says leaving us waiting.

"Yay?" I ask as the headset blurs.

"Evanescent *did* get something from your head." Zane says.

"Okay…"

"You both listening?" Zane asks.

"I'm here." Garrett answers, we both look at each other.

"It was something that hasn't happened yet, I wanted you to see it." Zane pauses. "Ask Jake to start the broadcast feature."

Garrett turns to Jake, "Broadcast feature?" He says.

Jake scrunches his face confused, Garrett shrugs his shoulders in reply.

"Yeah, here." Jake says digging around in the compartment beside him.

He flicks on a bulky tablet. It flashes green then black.

"Okay, it's on." I say.

"Just watch." Zane answers with his voice shaking.

The video flashes on, the background is hazy and I can't tell where it's from. Smoke sorta rolls through and that's when I start to see Nessa, Garrett and me all running.

Even in evanescent the scene flashes like it does during my sight. Through the flashing I see a red laser holding steady on Garrett's chest. He's on his knees now, hands held in surrender. He's ready to take the bullet that will kill him. There's another flash as Nessa jumps in the way, sacrificing herself for him.

Garrett looks pale as she drops to the smoky ground, blood spills from her head. Her glassy blue eyes close for the last time ever.

Garrett starts to talk but the broadcast resets. It's the same smoky background except this time I'm the one to die, the red dot hovers over my chest. Nessa's the one to jump in the way. She crumbles again, dying to save me.

The broadcast keeps cycling the same scenes over and over.

"What's it mean?" I ask.

"Think of it as a prediction, a warning of what's to come." Zane says.

Garrett's voice shakes, "You mean Nessa's going to die?" He asks.

"It can be changed." I say, "I saw her die in that fire but I stopped it, maybe we could stop this."

Zane interrupts, "What I just showed you was what Central calls a terminal scene." He says. "It's the last scene you had inside your brain, that's because it's the *last* thing that happens to one of you."

"So either Nessa dies for me or she dies for him?" I ask with my gut churning.

"It could be the end of *any* of your time." Zane answers.

"You mean one of us could die to save the other, and maybe her?" Garrett asks.

"If our understanding of terminal scenes is correct, then yes." Zane answers. "The only way Nessa gets out alive is if one of you dies for the other."

Garrett and I look at each other as a yellow light flashes inside the hover. Clint hollers from behind us.

"Prepare to jump!"

Zane's signal cuts out and we're left knowing that one of us has to die, there's no way around it. There's a resignation between us that when the time comes, one of us will die to save Nessa.